SAY YOU NEED ME

CARRIE LOMAX

Arhea —

Wishing you many hours of happy reading!

— Carrie Lomax

© 2018 Carrie Lomax.

All rights reserved. No part of this book may be reproduced or used in any manner without the express written permission of the publisher except for the use of brief quotations in a book review.

This book or parts thereof may not be reproduced in any form, stored in any retrieval system, or transmitted in any form by any means—electronic, mechanical, photocopy, recording, or otherwise—without prior written permission of the author, except as provided by United States of America copyright law. For permissions contact: info@carrielomax.com.

This is a work of fiction. Names, characters, businesses, places, events and incidents are either the products of the author's imagination or used in a fictitious manner. Any resemblance to actual persons, living or dead, or actual events is purely coincidental.

Cover by Velvet Madrid.

ISBN: 978-1-7321531-3-4

※ Created with Vellum

For Christine & Nichole
I wish you both a happy ending

SAY YOU NEED ME

Carrie Lomax

Also in this series:
Say You'll Stay

1

Janelle Carlisle's phone beeped, waking her long enough to squint up at the bright, warm Florida sun. Even in March, she could sunbathe by the apartment complex pool. With one hand, she pushed up her cheap sunglasses to read the message.

Happy Birthday! Crystal's in town. We're taking you out.

It's not until tomorrow.

Crystal was more her roommate, Rachel's, friend. Janelle had taken over Crystal's room when she'd gone to law school.

Besides her ambivalence to both her birthday and toward Crystal, Janelle had only the sixteen dollars she'd earned in tips from her second job at the coffee shop to last her until Friday, when her paycheck hit. Drinks were out of budget, birthday be damned. She relaxed onto the chair. Her phone made another noise. Janelle sighed and dragged herself up.

Nobody goes out on Sundays. Are you really going to mark turning twenty-five by staying home to watch *The Bachelorette* for the millionth time?

A second, impatient beep. **Seriously, what's the appeal?**

The fantasy of having hot, successful men compete for a woman's attention. *Duh.* Was it so strange to enjoy the idea of sitting in the power seat for a while? Of having a little romance?

It wasn't as if she hadn't seen every episode of every season, at least twice.

Only if you're buying. My car's done for, she texted back.

Thursday, the Volkswagen rust bucket almost as old as she was had developed a sickening clanking sound, then ground to a halt two blocks from home. Friday she'd cadged a ride to work, and this morning Janelle had swallowed hard at the bad news: she needed a new set of wheels, STAT.

Come to think of it, Janelle could really use a birthday drink or two. Even if it was charity.

If you MENTION money this evening I will personally pour a drink over your head. Come out with us. Make out with some random guy just because you're single and you can, FFS. Pick you up in an hour?

Well, okay then. Time to get off the chair and into makeup and actual clothes. Janelle lay there for another ten minutes trying to summon the energy.

Tomorrow was her twenty-fifth birthday. Only another fifty more to get through, before she could legit give up trying to get somewhere in life and die in peace.

Although they were friends, Crystal was not one of Janelle's favorite people. Her confidence bugged Janelle for reasons she didn't like to articulate.

"How's law school?" Rachel asked as the waitress delivered their margaritas.

"Great. I love the professors, and the students are really dedicated. I'm planning to go into public service."

"Careful you don't wind up like me," Janelle's tone came out waspish where she meant to be flippant. She gripped the slippery stem of the margarita glass hard enough to snap it. Catching herself, she eased off. *Quit with the jealousy.*

Crystal didn't bring out the best in Janelle. Law school was the inevitable place for someone like Crystal, who made a habit of asking annoyingly incisive questions. She was the kind of person who skated right past barriers, then gave them a good kick just to watch them topple over.

"In what way?" Crystal turned wide brown eyes toward her. She'd dyed her hair blonde, though a half-inch of dark roots showed through. Curvy, smart, and adventurous, Crystal had been notorious for sleeping around in college. She'd had a lot of friends but not many close ones. Rachel was one of the few.

"Mired in debt." Janelle sucked the dregs of her margarita through her straw. Her life had peaked in college. She'd had a great boyfriend named Ben, and she'd been confident her psychology degree would get her a decent-paying job after school—though she was vague on what it might be.

Then her parents had run out of tuition money and offered her the option of moving home for three years to finish school. In love with Ben, she'd opted to move off-campus and pick up another job, instead. Her grades had suffered, and she'd ended up taking out too many loans.

In three years since graduating she'd chipped away almost a third of her debt, but the payments still took almost half her monthly income. Rent was another third, leaving her with a few hundred dollars to cover utilities, gas, food, and incidentals. Forget getting ahead. Janelle was barely hanging on.

"Want another?" Rachel asked, indicating her empty glass.

"Sure. It's not as if I'm not driving," Janelle deadpanned.

"Why aren't you driving?" Crystal asked, her thin, red-painted lips wrapped around a straw.

"Car broke down. The White Knight finally gave up the ghost." Janelle slurped the last of her margarita before the waitress could whisk it away.

"The gleaming steed lays down its life." Rachel clutched her heart, giggled, and reached across the table to dip a chip in salsa.

"The only thing gleaming on that car was the bumper I had replaced," Janelle said ruefully.

"You should get a sugar daddy. I have one." Crystal continued sucking her neon green drink, brown eyes bouncing between Janelle and Rachel, assessing their response.

The astonished laughter burst out of Janelle in a hot rush. "Funny, Crystal."

"You have a what?" Aghast, Rachel nearly knocked over her new drink.

"A sugar daddy. An older man who pays some of my law school bills and housing expenses in exchange for sex." A knowing, worldly smile played over Crystal's lips. "Georgetown's expensive."

The sentence hung there, a bomb gone off in the middle of their margaritas.

"You're a prostitute," Janelle said flatly.

"No. I have an arrangement. Sort of like a mistress in the nineteenth century."

Rachel's mouth hung open. Janelle snorted dismissively. "Lucky you. Those arrangements always worked out so well. It's all fun and games until things go south and you're stuck with an illegitimate kid and no way to get a job."

Undeterred, Crystal kept smiling. "I'll have a job, and a good one. The modern miracle of birth control almost guarantees I won't get pregnant. It's not the Victorian era. It's not prostitution. It's a mutually beneficial system that allows bright young women like myself to exploit rich older men for their money."

"It's sex for money," Janelle replied flatly. "Call a spade a spade."

"I'm not a prostitute," Crystal insisted. "It's more akin to having a rich boyfriend who pays for everything with a specific agreement up front. Like a prenup. The arrangement only lasts for as long as both parties want it to. It's one-hundred-percent about consent."

"It's exploitative." Janelle's fingers were relaxed around the stem of her glass. This was simple, easy. Sex for money was bad. How clear-cut could it get?

"Don't be so judgmental, Janie. It's a fair exchange between equals. Didn't your sister have a rich boyfriend in New York?"

More to the point: How had Crystal known?

Rachel's gaze dropped guiltily to her lap. Janelle shot her a glare. They'd be discussing her loose lips later.

"Yeah, Alyssa had a boyfriend. They broke up right before she and Marc got together." As in, literally the evening before. That hadn't gone over so well. Janelle liked to think she'd had a hand in helping them work it out in the end, even though she'd been cheering for Alyssa's ex at the time.

"How is what I'm doing any different from your sister dating a rich guy?" Crystal demanded, calmly placing her crossed forearms on the table.

"I need another margarita if we're going to continue this conversation," Rachel interjected, summoning the waiter.

"It's…she…Alyssa loved Zach, for a while. What about you, Crystal? Are you in love with your sugar daddy?"

"No. But I am faithful to him." Crystal smiled. "It's monogamous, at least on my part."

"On his part?"

She shrugged. "It's not part of the deal. He's married."

"Okay, this is too gross, Crystal. I can't believe you'd do that." Rachel looked sick, but she quickly drained the third huge margarita anyway. "It's wrong."

"Why not? I didn't make his wife any promises. If he wants to cheat, that's his business." She leaned against the vinyl booth.

"Rachel, eat some more chips. Let's get another round of appetizers." Janelle tried to flag a passing waiter, and failed.

"I'm going to head out in a few minutes." Crystal pulled out her phone, the latest Apple model.

"How's the sex?" Janelle blurted.

"Not bad, honestly," Crystal barely glanced up. "You should consider it, Janelle. You could find a really good protector with that rack of yours."

Eww. *Eww.*

No.

"Send me the info. I'm curious." Only curious. She'd never do something so morally compromised. Rachel's eyelids were hovering half-open, and a stab of worry hit Janelle. "Maybe we should skip the appetizers and head home."

"Sure," Rachel slurred. "Or shots."

Crystal reached over and moved a strand of hair over Rachel's shoulder. "No shots for you, Rach. You never could drink worth a damn. I've got the bill. I'll charge it to Barry's credit card."

"Thanks, Crys." Janelle suddenly remembered why she liked Crystal enough to be casual friends. She could be very generous. Although, apparently, someone else was paying. A stranger she'd never met. One who cheated on his wife. It was hard to summon much outrage about a couple of birthday margaritas in the grand scheme of things, but it left a queasy feeling in the pit of her stomach that had nothing to do with tequila.

Janelle focused on helping Rachel out of the booth. Her part in the Crystal/Barry/Barry's wife mess was incidental. They all abandoned the table, Crystal and Janelle on either side of Rachel, supporting their drunk friend.

"I don't think she's going to make it home," Janelle said worriedly.

"Are you okay to drive?" Crystal asked.

"Not really, no." Never a big drinker, two margaritas were the upper limit of Janelle's tolerance, and she'd had three. "We'll get a car service and come pick her car up in the morning."

"Okay. Be safe. I'll go let the restaurant know she's leaving it overnight." Crystal unwound herself from Rachel, who lurched against a lamp post.

Then she gave Janelle a warm, if awkward, hug. "Happy birthday."

"Thanks, Crys."

"Oh, hey, I meant to tell you. I heard Ben's getting married."

It was as though Crystal had raked claws across her face. "My Ben?"

"He hasn't been yours in a few years, right?"

Now Janelle knew how birds and mice felt when cats toyed with them. Her body felt disengaged, almost paralyzed. She swallowed. Janelle ought to be happy to know someone she'd cared about—still cared about—was in love. If she were truly a good person, she wouldn't feel the hot sting of jealousy. But she did. "No. He hasn't. Who's the lucky girl?"

Crystal shrugged, nonchalant about the bomb she'd dropped. "Some Texas blonde. You know the type. Big hair. Blue eyes."

"Thanks for drinks," Janelle replied tightly, suddenly hating every blonde-haired woman in the Lone Star State with a raw, unreasonable passion. The driver pulled up, sparing her from further humiliation. Janelle tugged the seat belt over her friend's petite body and clicked it into place.

"Oh, Janie, I meant to tell you earlier. I got distracted by Crystal's sugar buddy news." Rachel slumped against her shoulder, a fine sweat breaking out over her pale forehead. Her skin practically glowed, she avoided the sun carefully.

"Sugar daddy," Janelle corrected automatically. "Can you believe she'd do something like that?"

"Crystal? Yeah, I can. Listen. I forgot to tell you. I'm moving out."

The car swerved. Janelle's stomach heaved as though she might vomit half-digested margarita all over the upholstery. "When?"

"At the end of the month. Caleb wants me to move in with him. He says he wants to get engaged, and so do I. It doesn't make sense for me to renew the lease. Do you think you can find someone to take it over?"

For the past two years, Rachel had been the sole lease holder on their apartment. Janelle paid her cash for her share of the rent and utilities. Her friends' lives were progressing normally. Jobs. Careers. Starting families. She was flailing in quicksand, and now they were all leaving her behind.

"I'll try." Janelle pushed her friend upright. On Friday, she'd received a check from her sister, Alyssa, with a note: *Hang in there. More to come. Enjoy your birthday.*

If she'd saved it, she might've had enough for a deposit on a new apartment. Or a down payment on a car. Instead, Janelle's heart had swelled up like a desiccated sponge dropped into a bucket of gratitude, and in a fit of determination she'd sent the entire amount directly to her student loan servicer this morning. If Rachel had told her sooner, she'd have planned differently.

Given a do-over, Janelle would've done a whole lot of things differently. Trying to be responsible had gotten her nothing but too much debt, a dead-end job, a broken-down car, and no way to rent an apartment of her own. She was slipping backward. If she didn't stop the fall, her entire future would be buried under an avalanche of debt and regrets.

Something in her life had to change. It had to change now. Today. Tonight. Maybe Crystal's unexpected visit was a sign.

After she hauled her roommate upstairs, dumped Rachel into her bed, and set a glass of water and two painkillers on the nightstand beside it, Janelle checked her email.

Crystal had sent her a link. Janelle clicked it. She was twenty-five years old—almost—and broke as fuck, with no hope of escape unless she took a big risk. A huge risk.

The screen popped up. Janelle shook her head and closed it. *No way. I deserve better than some gross, old guy cheating on his wife.*

Yet maybe Crystal was right. Being good wasn't getting her anywhere. Maybe it was time to try being bad. What better day to commit to a big change than on her birthday?

2

He shouldn't be here.

The red carpet and gold chandelier recalled another world, another lifetime. One that beckoned with the thrum of muted excitement, even now. He could go back. If he wanted to. Poker was mostly math and patience. But he wasn't that person anymore. Six years ago, everything had changed here in the banquet hall of the Astoria Casino Hotel. His life had crashed down from the high only this palace of chance could give.

He was here to pay his respects. To remind himself why he needed to stick to his chosen course. He had find out whether his old life still had any power over him.

It did.

Trent Mason ran one hand over the back of a red velvet chair. The soft fabric slipped beneath his palm like a lover's back.

Six years ago, he'd lost millions. Professional poker was a game of probability, not money. It didn't matter whether you were up or down at any given moment until you bet wrong and lost. Everything he'd built had been vaporized in a flash of inattention and bad luck. A few weeks before, everything else that mattered had been vaporized, too. He'd been twenty-three, and left with nothing.

Trent walked around the first floor, though he knew that if security caught him on the premises he'd be arrested on the spot. He was counting on the six intervening years to have wrought personnel changes and faded memories. He wasn't here to make trouble. Only to pay tribute. In a few minutes, he'd move on.

Indignant-woman noises punctuated his reminiscence. Garbled words, spoken in a low hiss, then louder, reached his ears. Security guards appeared from shadows and swarmed toward the elegant lobby.

"Let go of me! I need my things. You can't just toss me out with —*oof*." A flash of long leg, obscured high at the thigh by a flash of jade green appeared at the center of a cluster of security guards.

Time for him to go. Damsels in distress were usually up to no good in this town. He knew from crushing experience. Whatever heart he'd had left had been smashed, stomped, and blown to pieces when Penelope betrayed him.

Bad Penny. A name he'd rather forget. One imprinted indelibly on his soul.

Penelope, whom he'd met in this very casino. She'd been far away from this luxury, or faux luxury, when she'd nearly died. It might've been a kinder fate than the heroin that had eaten her from the inside out.

At least he'd escaped. He was sworn off rescuing Vegas damsels, for life.

"Can I at least get my stuff?" The angry woman pulled futilely against the burly guards. Her gold high heels threatened to rip holes in the carpeting.

She didn't stand a chance. Trent relived the helpless feeling for a moment. Then he took one last look at the elegant light fixture and the glittery gold lights and plush red velvet of the Astoria, tossed his suit jacket over his shoulder, and headed for the door.

Sunglasses topped the bridge of his nose even before he made it to the first set of darkly tinted automatic doors, but he ducked his head as the security guards returned into the building. Just in case.

They passed him without a second glance.

"Send someone upstairs and get her boyfriend to pack her bag. I'll take it out to her if she's still there."

She was. The skimpy strapless dress looked cheap and trashy in the broad light of day. Her bare shoulders shook. Crying, probably.

No tan lines.

The expanse of smooth, evenly tanned skin between the bright fabric and the thick dark hair between her shoulder blades *would* be the first thing he noticed. The sight made his cock perk up.

Down, boy.

Trent glanced at his watch. Quarter to noon. The conference sessions that had broken fifteen minutes ago wouldn't resume for more than an hour yet. He ought to find out where the attendees were clustering for lunch and try to make some business contacts. It was the only reason he'd come back to this town. Otherwise, he was content to never set foot in Las Vegas again for as long as he lived.

She wobbled a few steps away, then stopped as though unsure where to go. Trent sighed. He could at least let her know she'd get her belongings back if she hung around. "You all right?"

The girl stiffened as though he'd smacked her. A loud sniff. Then she raked back her mane of dark hair and rubbed beneath her eyes, a gesture that turned the dark smudges of mascara into huge circles. Like Elizabeth Taylor as Cleopatra, minus the poise.

"Fine." She glanced over her shoulder as though trying to figure out the best way to run if he attacked her in the middle of the street at high noon. The sun was at its zenith in the sky, the air hot and unforgiving.

Then Cleopatra turned to face him directly. It was as if the sun had fallen out of the sky and landed on him.

Holy tits, Batman.

Trent choked. The tiny scrap of a dress clung to the two biggest, perkiest breasts he'd ever seen defying gravity *sans* bra. The distinct shape of nipples dead in the center of each globe strongly suggested he bend down and suck them until they pulled into hard, tight buds.

The rest of the woman read his mind, and was less than enthusiastic about the direction of his thoughts. Her raccoon-rimmed eyes flared wide with outrage.

He jerked his attention away. It'd been years since he'd been near a woman, and he wasn't about to break his celibate streak with this one. If she was a woman and not a confused teenager. She looked very young.

"Here." He held out the suit jacket he was carrying over his shoulder. "I overheard the security guys saying they'd bring your things out if you stick around."

She sniffed and reached for the jacket. Then, she turned away to push her arms into the sleeves so he couldn't get a second look at her.

Trent turned away, too, trying to erase the image of Cleopatra's rack from his memory.

"Thank you."

He spoke over his shoulder, not trusting himself to keep his eyes where they belonged. "You're welcome. I'm staying at the hotel across the street. When you get things sorted out here, you can leave it at the front desk."

"What's your name? So I know what to tell the clerk."

Right, she didn't care to know the name of the guy who'd shown a little kindness. He didn't want to know hers, either. Trent knew she'd caught him checking her out, but he hadn't been a complete asshole about it, and she probably got that reaction all the time. Understandable if she wasn't in the mood for a pickup line, but he hadn't offered one.

"Mason."

"First or last?"

"Both." The less Cleopatra knew about him, the better. The less anyone knew about him, the better. "Here's the guards. Good luck with everything."

"You too. Thanks again."

Clearly, she was a nice girl. Well-bred, probably had two married parents and a nice suburban upbringing. Like he'd had once. Before they'd died, and he'd gone off the rails with grief and teenage hormones. He was old enough now to know better than to get dragged into whatever trouble she was in.

Trent was here for business, and it was time he got back to it. He waited at the curb for the traffic to clear. The Las Vegas strip was always busy, but if you caught the lights right you could make it across the street without walking to the corner. He'd hit them dead wrong, so he was still standing there, eyeballing cars, when Cleopatra's outraged voice rang out.

"Son of a fucking *bitch!*"

Whew. The girl could cuss. Trent chuckled. It was almost funny to hear the string of foul language come from a cute chick. Maybe she wasn't as young as she looked. Whoever she was, she reminded him of Penny, only with a worse attitude.

"Goddamned bastard *stole* it. Wait. Come back—my wallet's missing. My driver's license, my debit card, my phone. They're all gone. How the hell will I get home? Wait!"

Trent turned to see the guards manhandling her away from the Astoria's front door. One of two refrigerator-box-sized men grabbed her by the collar of his favorite suit jacket and dragged her back to the little pile of items on the sidewalk. He winced and hoped it hadn't torn.

"Stop touching me, you oaf!" Cleopatra fought the good fight, but it was hopelessly one-sided and she was losing.

There was a tearing sound, and then the giant shoved her away. Trent closed the distance in two strides to steady her. Cleopatra gaped up at him with fierce green eyes that stole his breath.

"You won't win," he told her. "Do you want to file a police report about your wallet?"

She pulled away hard, out of his grasp. "No."

"Why not?"

"I can't."

Oh, shit. Now he for sure didn't want to know what she was into. "Is there someone you can call?"

"No. I have to figure this out on my own." Her hands shook as she bent and rummaged through her scant belongings, searching desperately for something that didn't appear to be there.

Pride. Trent recognized it, and pitied her for it. If she was into drugs, or prostitution, or any variation of those problems, he couldn't help her. He couldn't go down that road again.

Cleopatra stuffed a jumble of soft fabric back into the small duffel bag and slung it over her shoulder as she stood up. She heaved a great sigh. It would've done wonderful things to her breasts if they hadn't been obscured by his ruined jacket. It covered more of her body than her dress did.

But he was trying not to think about that.

"You've been very kind, Mason. I hate to ask this. May I borrow your hotel room for a few minutes to clean up and change clothes? I'll get out of your hair right afterward. Promise."

Clean up, as in wash the makeup off her face.

Change clothes, as in get naked before putting on something less slutty. Or not. She could hang out naked and a certain part of his anatomy wouldn't mind a bit.

He'd bet his left testicle Cleo shined up like a new penny.

Bad Penny. Bad memories. A good reminder, though, of why he had to get Cleopatra Trouble Tits out of his life immediately.

"Sure." Well. His dick had won control of his mouth, and his brain was left flashing silent red warning signs.

You'd have wanted someone to be kind to Penny if she was in a bad situation.

Yeah, and she'd have made them regret it.

History might not repeat itself, but as the saying went, it often rhymed.

How the ever-loving hell had she gotten herself into this mess?

Janelle hunched her shoulders down inside the too-large suit jacket. It smelled of Mason, which was strangely comforting given she'd met him barely ten minutes ago. The warm, faintly spicy scent and the breadth of the jacket's shoulders were the ghost hug she desperately needed to get through this humiliating shit show.

Unlike Crystal, she hadn't gotten a Barry for a sugar daddy.

On the last night she'd had her own internet access in her own apartment, Janelle had submitted a brief and thoroughly halfhearted application to the website Crystal had sent. The application fee was fifty bucks, but it was refunded if they didn't accept you. There was no risk, and she was desperate enough to try it.

Janelle's money had bounced back to her bank account a few days later.

Rejected.

We look for sugar babies of your age who are either enrolled in graduate school or pursuing non-remunerative employment (i.e., internship). Your credit report is an additional source of concern. Babies with poor credit have been known to attempt blackmail or other illegal extortion of their Daddies.

Of course. Her entire life could be reduced to a three-digit summary: not trustworthy.

But...her age? She'd just turned twenty-five, and she was *too old*?

Rage of a kind she'd never experienced had blinded her for the last few hours of unpacking at her parents' house. It wasn't that she wanted to screw some guy having a midlife crisis for money; it was the principle.

This should've been the nail in the coffin of her sugar baby experience, but pride had intervened. She was not too old, and she was going to prove it. In a fit of fury, she'd gone online and filled out applications at two other, less reputable-looking websites. One rejected her.

The other called a week later.

"I see you have some boundaries. No married men," the woman on the phone noted. "No bondage, no threesomes, no more than two encounters a month, no anal sex, no rough play, no...is there anything you *are* willing to do?"

"Oral sex," she offered begrudgingly. "If I have to."

Janelle liked giving head, but the concept of doing it for a stranger was too weird to be more than abstraction.

"Role play?" the agent countered.

"I cannot imagine adults getting off by playing dress up. No."

"You're limiting your prospects," the woman replied crankily.

Yeah, well, Janelle was used to not having a lot of options.

"Is there anything else you're willing to do?"

"Travel," Janelle said immediately. "But the, uh, daddy has to pay for all expenses."

Thus, she'd been matched with exactly one prospect. She'd spoken with Kyle, aka Rich Jerk (aka her new sugar daddy) on the phone twice, and bought a plane ticket to Las Vegas at his request. He'd promised to pay her back when they met. Janelle had scheduled a Friday and a Monday off from work and flown into McCarran International Thursday evening, ahead of Rich Jerk's arrival. Since then, not one thing had gone according to plan.

Now she was trotting after a tall, broad-shouldered, extremely good-looking man with only one name, while looking like she'd fallen off the back of a paddy wagon full of hookers.

"Mace," a male voice rang out. Her protector turned. Janelle kept walking as though she didn't know him, eyes glued to the hideous hotel carpet. She turned the corner and waited out of sight.

A minute later, "Mace" Mason appeared. She inhaled and finally took a good look at the man who'd gone above and beyond to help her. He had to top six feet, and Janelle was certain his muscles had muscles. Thick biceps stretched the fabric of his dress shirt. "Please don't tell me my rescuer's nicknamed for pepper spray."

Her reluctant protector's mouth quirked up at the corners. She'd made him laugh, or at least, almost smile. This was the first good look she'd gotten at his eyes since he'd whipped his sunglasses off on entering the building. They were dead sexy, deep blue and fringed with lashes that would've made any girl abandon mascara for life if she'd been lucky enough to own them.

"No, for a blunt weapon from the Middle Ages," he shot back.

"Too bad it's not the spice." Janelle inhaled, and all it did was send a hit of pheromones straight to her brain. He stared at her a long moment. Yeah, dumb comment. Her mind was busy plotting how to get her wallet and phone back so she could get on the first plane back to Florida. It had nothing to do with the weird drugged sensation that came with being near Mysterious Mace Mason, hottie and, apparently, decent human being.

The world could use a few more of those.

She'd have to meet him looking like this, too. It was too much to ask fate to show any hint of mercy.

Janelle followed him into the smallest hotel room she'd ever seen. Instead of the usual double queen beds, there was only one. Shoved against the far wall was a two-seater couch, next to a chair and a table that could be used as a desk. Facing the bed, there was a clunky dresser topped with a large television. In other words, it was a normal hotel room except for the size.

Small hotel room. Muscular, attractive man. What could go wrong?

"I'll just be a minute." She pushed the bathroom door open, hung Mason's jacket on the back of the door, and upended her sloppily packed bag. Then she ripped off the skimpy dress she'd packed to make an impression, never once imagining it would be seen outside the confines of a hotel room, and stuffed it down to the very bottom of the bag. The gold heels almost chipped the tile wall, she kicked them off so hard.

Janelle cringed at the sight that greeted her in the harsh light over the mirror. The toiletries by the sink were still wrapped. Janelle tore the paper off a small bar of soap and rubbed her hands in the water, then scrubbed her face until it was clean of makeup. Afterwards, she tugged on a bra, t-shirt and leggings and finally stuffed everything back into her bag and squared her shoulders.

The least she could do was try to mend Mason's torn jacket.

"Feel better?" he asked as she emerged.

Janelle nodded, hardly able to look at him. "I think I can fix this."

Mason plucked the fine wool from her hands. "Right now, you have bigger problems. I'm going out for a sandwich. Want one?"

"I don't have any money. It was in my wallet." She was always broke, but she'd never been penniless until now.

"It's a sandwich. Don't worry about it." He'd rolled up his sleeves so his sinewy forearms showed. His hair was short on the sides, a little longer on the top, like someone in the military who'd recently been discharged and hadn't quite adapted to civilian life yet.

"Why are you being nice to me?" Janelle pulled at the hem of her shirt. It was a V-neck and clingy, not her usual style, but all the clothes she'd brought were revealing. By her standards, anyway.

"Good question. Maybe I should throw you out of here, like those bouncers did."

Mason took one step closer, and for a second she thought he'd do it. Her heart flapped like a pigeon desperate to take flight, but all he did was reach for her shoulder bag and drop it onto the couch.

"I'm leaving my phone here, unlocked. If there's anyone you can call for help, do it while I'm not here to listen. I'm here for a conference, and I can't babysit you."

"I'm self-sufficient."

Mason raised an eyebrow. Janelle ducked her head. His skepticism was warranted.

"Go to your conference, I'll figure something out. Promise. I'm not a mooch." The instant Mace departed, Janelle reached for the phone. She sucked in a hard breath and dialed her own mobile phone number.

A familiar male voice answered. "Janelle?"

She shivered as the air conditioning chilled the sudden sweat that broke out over her neck. "Kyle."

"If you want your wallet and phone back, get back here and get naked. Now."

"I'm not doing that."

A beat of silence. "I'll ruin you."

Janelle's teeth caught her lower lip. The words were punch in the gut. "I'll report you."

He laughed. "For what? Rape? Assault? You consented. In writing."

"For being an asshole," she seethed, knowing full well she'd have a hard time convincing anyone she'd resisted, and he'd insisted, even after she'd emphatically told him no.

Kyle laughed, that rat bastard. "There's no statute against hurting your feelings. But prostitution is definitely illegal. So is breach of contract. I can sue you."

"I didn't—"

"Oh yes you did. If you want to go crawling back to your pathetic life in Florida without anyone knowing what you've done, you'll come back to this hotel room and get on all fours. Naked. You'll pretend to enjoy everything I do to you or everyone in your contacts is going to get a copy of the little video I made this morning. Check your email."

Call terminated. Janelle's mouth hung open, a tangle of retorts about revenge porn being illegal dying unspoken. Even if it was, he could say she'd consented and what then? She set the phone down carefully. Her stomach heaved as a fine cold sweat covered her forehead. She'd never wanted a stiff drink so badly in her life.

The door clicked open. "I hope ham and cheese is okay. You're not vegetarian or anything...Did something happen?"

Janelle felt her head move as though she were a puppet dancing on a string. "No. I called my phone. It's fine. I'll get it back."

Eventually. Right before she was arrested for Kyle's murder, just long enough to make her one phone call to a lawyer. Crystal was in law school, maybe she'd handle it pro bono. Janelle figured Crys owed her a favor for her role in this debacle.

Janelle unwrapped the sandwich on the table and stared at it until Mason's voice called her back to the present.

"You have parents who can help?"

"And tell them how I ended up here? No way." She picked up the sandwich and took a bite without tasting it.

Mason's appetite was in fine form. He tucked into his sandwich and licked a bit of dressing off his thumb. "How bad is it?"

"The mess I'm in? Pretty bad."

"Drugs?"

Did she look that strung out? "No!"

Drugs were one problem she didn't have. Though she'd sure looked like a potential addict in the excuse for a dress with makeup running down her face. Janelle shifted uncomfortably and examined her sandwich.

Mason, on the other hand, perked up considerably. "Sex?"

"How'd you guess?" The return of her habitual sarcasm was unbelievably welcome. She bit into the sandwich. "Was it the outfit?"

Mason's mouth ticked up at the corners. "Money?"

"The root of all evil." Janelle rubbed her forehead. Now that her anger had leached out, fear, failure, and loneliness had stolen her appetite.

"What's your name?"

"Jan-" *Hey, wait a minute.* "Janie."

He crumpled the paper of his sandwich and waited a beat. "No last name?"

"You gave me one name, I'll give you one name. If you want to know more, spill."

Mason stood up and tossed the ball of sandwich paper into the trash can by the desk. "You're cheeky for someone in a fix."

"You like it, though." *Whoa.* Where had that come from? This was no time to get flirty.

He chuckled but admitted nothing. Instead, he stood up and pulled out a wooden door on the dresser. Inside was a dorm-sized refrigerator. Mason removed two airplane bottles of gin and a pint-sized bottle of tonic.

"No limes. You want a gin and tonic anyway?"

Mysterious Mace Mason was her guardian angel. She must've done something right in her life if he was offering her the drink she needed. "Yes, please."

"Are you twenty-one?" he asked skeptically.

Oh, for fuck's sake. She was too decrepit to sleep with a dirty old man but appeared too young to drink? "I'm twenty-five."

"You look younger." He cracked open the bottles and mixed the contents into matching hotel glasses. "A lot younger."

"Especially without makeup." She took the glass and downed half of it in a single gulp.

"You looked like a baby raccoon with all that shit on your face. I thought you were sixteen."

"Nope. Completely of age. Next milestone is running for President, and then AARP discounts here I come."

The sound of Mace Mason's startled laughter was a balm to her pride. The gin and tonic was the perfect temporary antidote to threatening Rich Jerks and hot, untouchable guardian angels. The booze went straight to her head and took every pleasure synapse of her brain hostage.

She had a problem to solve. Except that instead of thinking through how to get her wallet and phone back from Rich Jerk, all she could think about was Mace Mason's broad shoulders and narrow waist. "How old are you, Mace?"

"Thirty."

"Cheers." Janelle held up her glass. He tapped hers, looking straight into her eyes as he did. Everything inside her went hot and soft. But attraction wasn't going to get her a pass.

"What happened this morning, Janie?"

3

Janie's expression turned as sour as a lemon. "Why should I tell you?"

Exasperating woman. For a minute there, she'd gone relaxed and flirty. Now she'd flipped like a switch back to wary and defensive.

At least it wasn't drugs. Sex, well, he could be broad-minded about whatever she was into. He had exactly zero moral standing to judge anyone on that point. Money, though, the jury was still out.

Trent glanced at his watch. "I'm leaving in fifteen minutes for the afternoon half of my conference. If you want to stay here and figure out how to straighten things out, I need to know that it's not going to boomerang back on me. What kind of trouble are you in?"

"Big trouble," she said softly through pink lips.

"How big?" Trent wished they were talking about sex. This conversation could play out so many dirty ways. His rational brain was holding the door against lusty ideas like a doomed character about to get eaten in a zombie flick.

Without makeup, Janie's fine bone structure was clearly visible. Large green eyes rimmed by dark lashes, a manicured sweep of dark eyebrow, the straight slope of her nose above the perfect philtrum that led to plump, pink lips. Below, a stubbornly pointed chin that spoke volumes about her frankly shitty attitude.

In addition to that face, Janie was blessed with a long, elegant neck, and he'd not forgotten the one instinctive glimpse he'd stolen of her incredible breasts. He was only male, after all.

And it had been a long time.

Janie, if that was her real name, licked her lips and dropped her gaze to the floor. "I came here to meet a man. For sex."

"Turning tricks?"

"No!" Her eyes searched his, pleading and outraged. "He was supposed to be my…my arrangement."

"An arranged encounter," he repeated, half understanding and half perplexed. His cock was certainly enjoying the diversion of talking about sex with an actual woman after a years-long, self-imposed drought. Her t-shirt dipped at the center, showing a couple inches of bra-trapped cleavage. Trent didn't look lower than her neck, unless you counted a furtive check of her legs. Encased in thin cotton, they were toned and slender. She was slim everywhere, except for the chest.

"I was supposed to be his sugar baby," she blurted, high cheekbones flushed red.

Oh. That's what the kids were calling it these days. "He was older, I take it?"

"Much. And he's an asshole. I arrived last night, but I was out when he checked into the hotel this morning. He left a note to wear the sexiest thing I'd brought and be ready around noon. You saw how I was dressed. I tried, but I couldn't go through with it. He threw me out of the room."

"That's it?" Mason sat back on the bed. "You almost screwed some old guy for money but didn't?"

"I couldn't!" she almost screamed, tears welling in those green depths.

"Why not?"

"Because…" She downed the rest of her gin and tonic. "Because I've only been with one person before."

One partner at the age of twenty-five. By his low standards she was practically a virgin. "I assume that was true going into the situation?"

Janie hung her head. "Yes."

"What changed?"

She shrugged. "Up to that point, it hadn't felt...real. He told me to do a strip tease and tried to stick his dick in my mouth, and I told him I couldn't do it. I wanted to go home. He tried to pin me to the bed, but I fought him off. He called security, which I guess is where you pick up the story."

Janie raked her hand through her dark hair. It was a soft, rich cloud glinting with reddish highlights. Probably dyed.

"Now he has my cell phone and wallet, and he's threatening to send some video to everyone on my contact list." The words came out in a whispered confessional rush. "He says he emailed it to me."

Internet security. Sex tapes. Those were things he could help her with. As long as she wasn't into drugs, he could help her without dredging up memories that could send him spiraling downward in this most dangerous of all cities. "Was he paying you?"

If Janie blushed any harder she'd turn into a tomato. "Not directly. He'd offered a stipend. A thousand dollars a month for two weekend encounters."

Trent sighed. This girl was a babe in the woods if she thought it was a fair deal. She was stacked, attractive and clearly educated. "You'd have gotten more working at a crappy escort service."

"Plus travel expenses," she replied indignantly.

As if that made any difference. Trent downed his drink and set the glass on the table. Between a beautiful woman crashing his hotel room and him standing in the hot sun for a sandwich, his shirt was sweat-damp and wrinkled. He'd have to change unless he wanted to chase off any prospective business contacts with BO. Pushing off the bed, he went to the closet and slid the door open.

"You can stay here for a few hours. Make some calls. Get your ID replaced. Call your parents to get money for your own room. I'll be back around five." He unbuttoned his shirt, aware of her watching him.

Cute little Janie who'd only slept with one person. Person, not man. Maybe she was a lesbian?

Judging from the way her eyes were riveted on the mirror before him, not a chance.

The placket opened gradually. Her eyes widened. How long had it been since any woman had watched wide-eyed as he undressed? He'd lost count. Trent knew he should stop now, before innocent little Janie's eyeballs popped out and stood on stalks. Instead, he unbuckled his trousers to pull out the hem of his shirt.

Janie's mouth went slack. She swallowed, and he bit back a smile. Totally innocent. How the hell had a chick like her gotten mixed up in quasi-prostitution?

The world could be an incredibly shitty place. Trent tossed the shirt onto the floor of the closet with the small pile of dirty laundry growing there. Then, he pulled up the undershirt he wore and chucked that too. He balled it in his hands and looked over his shoulder.

"Enjoying the show?"

Janelle coughed and grabbed her drink. "Sorry."

Trent tossed the wadded undershirt onto the heap and went to the bathroom. He couldn't exactly tug one off with her out there listening, but he wanted to.

"Your tattoo's interesting." Janie declared the instant he came out of the bathroom. "I apologize for staring."

She sounded properly contrite, which was disappointing. Trent supposed nice girls from the suburbs didn't see a lot of half-naked ex-Army guys with giant tattoos spread across their backs. He'd enjoyed her momentary interest for what it was—momentary—and didn't want her feeling bad about checking him out. After all, he'd done the same to her, and he didn't feel remotely bad about it.

"It's the story of Icarus, isn't it?" The ice cubes clinked against the glass as she took a long, fortifying sip.

Yeah, she was educated.

"No. It's my story." He pulled a fresh undershirt over his head and a new shirt out of the closet before conceding, "There's a few similarities."

"For a minute there, I thought you had actual wings."

Like he was some sort of angel. Which given where he'd found her, maybe he was. Her crappy luck if she believed for one minute he was any kind of savior. Dressed, Trent ventured over to the table she sat behind and picked up the hotel stationery and pen. "Here's the guest password to use my computer."

She accepted it with small, lovely hands. Trent took Janie by her stubborn chin and tilted her face up. "I am an expert in cyber security. If you attempt to do anything other than check your email, I'll know. I will nail you to the fucking wall if you attempt to hack into any other system. Understand?"

Wide-eyed, she nodded. He let go, but the sensation of her soft skin under his fingertips stayed with him.

THE VIDEO WAS BAD. She'd been out of the room when he'd arrived, and Kyle had clearly planted a camera in her absence. That required a coldness of calculation that implied he'd done this kind of thing before.

Everything she'd done up to the point he'd dropped his pants and tried to shove his semi-hard dick in her mouth was caught on tape. It was grainy, but there was sound and there was no point pretending it wasn't her, there willingly at least up to that point.

Mason seemed like a nice enough guy, provided she didn't attempt to hack into his computer—which she wouldn't know how to do even if she wanted to—so she helped herself to another drink from the mini bar. Vodka cranberry this time since the gin was gone. He'd understand. Janelle jotted an IOU on the hotel-branded notepad.

Then she used the hotel phone to call the agency hotline. She wasn't going to let Kyle get away with this. If he was doing it to her, he'd probably done it to someone else, and he'd probably to it again. *Solidarity, ladies.*

"Your contract doesn't specify no filming, and oral sex was something you agreed to perform," the woman on the other end replied unhelpfully.

"I didn't sign any image rights release forms. I read the paperwork before signing it," Janelle seethed. She was fucking literate, after all. *That is beside the point. The point is that Kyle stole your personal property and is threatening you. Focus.*

It wasn't easy after she'd consumed the gin and tonic and half of the vodka cranberry, but she voiced her complaint anyway. "Revenge porn is illegal."

She wished she'd been quick enough to point that out she she'd been on the phone with Kyle. Stupid.

"We don't get involved in personal disputes," the woman on the other end of the line replied. "I recommend you call the police."

So much for female solidarity. "He is threatening to send an illegally obtained video to my friends and family to force me to have sex with him."

"You *agreed* to have sex with him."

"Well, that was before I met him, and now I want my goddamn wallet back so I can get home!"

"I am not a law enforcement agent. I have no authority to assist you. I can call him, that's it."

"You could throw him out of the program. I doubt this is the first time Kyle's done something like this."

Click. Janelle gave the phone a dirty look. *She* was dirty. She was such a pathetic failure; she couldn't even succeed at screwing an old guy for cash. She sucked at being good. She sucked at being bad. She was a waste of a human being. *Ugh.*

Janelle needed to wash the thoughts away as badly as she needed to rinse off the lingering creepiness of Kyle's hands on her body. A faint bruise marked her left wrist. Another bloomed over each bicep, though they were probably from the guards. She took a quick shower, since Mace was out of the picture for a bit, and she didn't want to impose later. Then, she put her clothes back on and braided her hair while considering her next move.

A next move that definitely shouldn't involve sleeping in his bed, but it did. The sheets smelled of bleach, clean but impersonal. She rolled out of bed, plucked Trent's undershirt from the pile, and sniffed it.

It was, hands down, the weirdest impulse she'd ever given in to. Nevertheless, she rolled it into a ball and hugged the wad of cotton like a teddy bear while she rested, unable to fall asleep for fear Mason would return and find her cuddling his dirty laundry. The spicy, deodorant-scented bundle made her feel safe, and a little bit stronger. Janelle needed the comfort, and she wasn't going to overthink it.

After a while she got up, returned the shirt to the pile, and made the bed. She turned on the TV and pulled out her toiletries. While the TV ran in the background, she removed the chipped nail polish from her toes and fingers. Then she applied a new coat of pale pink instead of dark red. One day she'd be able to afford salon mani-pedis.

Along with a new car.

Fake it 'till you make it.

She was never going to make it. She was going to die here of boredom in this weirdly small hotel room, and all alone. Janelle shoved her misery away and booted up the computer to research her options.

4

Midway through the afternoon in a fascinating but highly technical panel discussion of two-factor security weaknesses, Trent realized he'd been sitting there for forty-five minutes without absorbing a thing. He hadn't paid two grand for the privilege of sitting in a stale conference room in the middle of the desert for four days to rescue green-eyed sirens with other resources to fall back on, like caring parents.

Business contacts were the only reason he was here.

A sharp elbow in the ribs brought his attention back to the present.

"Captain," he replied, sitting up straight and nodding.

The dark-skinned woman to his left smiled slyly. "Daydreaming, Sergeant?"

"No ma'am."

Old habits died hard. He'd served for three years in Afghanistan under Captain Olivia Davidson, the last two working cyber communications for military intelligence's field operations. Now they were both on the outside and partners...of a sort. She'd been out for eighteen months now, and she'd built up her own company by going after government contracts with a ruthless strategy honed on the battlefield.

Trent had declined to re-enlist. He'd thought he was ready to get back to normal life, by which he meant an approximation of Olivia's life before it had cracked against the rocky shoals of divorce. Married. Children. But once he'd severed from the military and gone on reserve duty, he'd drifted for a few weeks before deciding to follow Olivia's path.

Within a few weeks, Trent knew he didn't have the same talent for managing people and growing a business. She'd helped him win a few government contracts and generally get off the ground. She'd been the one to recommend this conference as a potential source of contacts.

He'd followed her like a duckling waddling after its mother. Olivia was not his mother, but she was his mentor. The very last thing he should be doing was mooning over the dark-haired nymph hiding in his hotel room when he ought to be making the most of this opportunity. Yet his body kept flushing with heat at the memory of Janie watching him undress.

"May I confide, Captain?" he asked.

"Let's get a coffee. This speaker's been droning on so long I can't even remember his point." She stood up and made her way past a full row of scowling men who didn't like being interrupted by a woman, especially a black one. Olivia never let that shit get to her, though.

Outwardly.

They found a pair of comfortably overstuffed chairs in the lounge area and availed themselves of free, terrible coffee. Considering the deprivation they'd endured on the base, neither complained.

"What's on your mind, soldier?"

Trent gave her the thumbnail sketch of his predicament. He imagined most people would've laughed at his problem—most men didn't think a pretty girl taking refuge in your room would qualify—but Olivia was a mom through and through. If there was one person in the world who knew him, it was Captain Davidson. She understood why this was a serious challenge for him.

"Well. You can't turn her out into the street," she finally said.

There went that plan. "Can I hand her off to you?"

"No you cannot, soldier. I'm already sharing a room to keep expenses down, and there's no space for a third. Why don't you give her the other bed for a night?"

Because there is no other bed. Though the names and décor of hotels changed, Trent knew most of the Las Vegas venues from his days as a professional poker player. He'd thought he was being smart by choosing the awkward line of smaller rooms to save a few bucks and, more importantly, give him some breathing room between long days of socializing. He hadn't counted on Janie.

"Who are you rooming with?" he asked, sidestepping Olivia's question.

"My twin," Olivia deadpanned. It was an inside joke. People frequently mistook her for her roommate, another black woman, though they looked nothing alike.

Trent winced. "You still get that shit?"

Olivia snorted. "You might be the only white guy here who can tell us apart. So, what are you going to do about the gate crasher?"

"I have no idea. She has no money. I can't keep feeding her all weekend."

Olivia grinned widely, her teeth a little gapped in the front. "Lucky for you, I'm not attending tonight's dinner. I have other plans."

"Oh yeah?"

"Gotta get back on the dating train sometime. I'll drop by your room with my dinner ticket later."

"Thanks."

That took care tonight. Maybe Janie would be gone when he got back. Trent ignored a little stab of disappointment at the thought.

IF SHE EXPLAINED the situation rationally instead of retreating into sarcasm, Mason would let her stay. Probably.

Maybe.

She hoped.

The door opened softly and her pulse leapt. "You're still here. I was hoping you wouldn't be."

Janelle swallowed. "Me, too. As I have yet to invent teleportation, I'm still stranded. I'd have left a thank-you note, though. So long, thanks for the sandwich, have a nice life. And for the drink. And for the second one I made after you left. There's an IOU on the table."

Mason sat on the edge of the bed, since she was curled up on the small couch. Loveseat. She could hardly even think the word. His knees splayed open and he leaned back on one hand. Her attraction had sharped to a knife's edge. She cleared her throat and continued.

"I called the agency. They talked to the sugar daddy. He says he doesn't have my wallet, and the agency told me there was nothing they could do for me. Without ID, I can't check into a hotel room even if my parents agreed to rent one for me."

"Your parents wouldn't help you?"

"They would if I told them about this situation, but frankly, I'm too embarrassed to do that if there's any other way to fix this mess. My plane ticket isn't until Monday. I can probably talk my way past security at the airport, but I'd rather not have to."

Mace rubbed his forehead. "How did a girl like you get into this mess?"

"A girl like me?" What the hell did he mean?

"Pretty. Smart. Capable."

Right now, Janelle felt like none of those things. "Student loans. I missed a few payments early on and my credit's trashed and my debt load's high."

"How about getting a job?" Mace demanded.

"I have two, thanks for asking." Ah, sarcasm was not her friend here.

Mason made a face. "Sorry. If you're employed, why are you so broke?"

"My loans take up a huge chunk of my monthly income. It makes managing the loans damn near impossible. I've paid a lot of it down since I graduated, but my credit's still in the gutter. I've had job offers rescinded because of it. My boyfriend moved to Texas and broke up with me shortly after. Now he's getting married to someone else." Janelle gritted her teeth hard enough to almost crack her molars just to keep her chin from wobbling.

"He was the one partner I take it?"

"How'd you guess?" Janelle watched Mason slowly collapse backward on the bed and for one embarrassed moment she wondered what he'd say if she told him she was ready for partner number two. He lay back with such controlled motion that even if she hadn't already checked him out with all the subtlety of a bride picking out housewares for her wedding registry, she'd have known his abdomen was solid muscle.

Mason clapped both large hands over his eyes and rubbed them. "What is it you need?"

Not sitting here ogling a guy who wasn't her type at all. She liked nice men. Not too big, not too tall, a little earnest, kind and funny. Guys who'd remember your birthday, your mom's birthday, and your anniversary without fail. Like Ben, her ex.

Mason was none of those things, except kind. Though her presence was wearing on him, and his patience seemed ready to snap. "I need a place to stay for a night or two until I figure out how to get my wallet back from the Rich Jerk."

Mason made a crack between his fingers and peered out. "Rich Jerk?"

"That's what I call him."

"There's a simpler term. They're called johns."

If he'd smacked her across the face it would've hurt less. "You know what? I think I'll take my chances with the police. There's probably a women's shelter I can check into somewhere around here." Janelle snatched up her bag from the floor beside her and headed for the door.

Only to nearly ram into his chest as Mason rose and blocked her path. Janelle stumbled back two steps and peered up at him.

"What does the Rich Jerk want?" he demanded in a low growl.

"What do you think he wants? A belated Christmas card?" *Mayday, mayday. Do not burn this bridge. It's the only one you have.*

Mason watched her. "What's your full name, Janie?"

"If I tell you, will you let me stay?"

He sighed. She had the feeling that he'd been doing that a lot since meeting her this morning.

"I promise I'll sleep on the couch," she offered, cajoling.

"No one can sleep on that couch. It's tiny. We'll figure something out. But first you have to tell me your full name."

"Do I get to know yours?"

"Janie," he growled. Irrationally, it made her smile.

"Janelle Carlisle from Verona Harbor, Florida." She stuck out her hand. "And you are?"

"Trent Mason."

"Pleased to meet you, Trent." His hand engulfed hers and pumped it once. When he let go, a tingly aftershock made its way up her arm and reverberated throughout her body. Trent wasn't her type. But she wasn't blind, either. He was all kinds of gorgeous.

Just not her kind.

Really.

Even if he was, the chance that he was single was nonexistent. She'd already checked for a wedding band. Nothing. That didn't mean he didn't have a girlfriend, though. A girlfriend who wouldn't take too kindly to a strange woman crashing in his hotel room, no matter what the circumstances. "Are you seeing anyone?"

He jerked around, blue eyes startled. "What?"

Ask without sounding like you're trying to get in his pants. "I don't want to get you in trouble with a girlfriend, if you have one. I'll understand if I can't stay."

Trent Mason shook his head. "No girlfriend. I got out of the Army about eight months ago. Listen. Before you decide you want to crash here, take a few minutes on the computer and do a background check."

He reached over to the computer and raised the lid. "Go on. I'll wait."

By the time Janelle recovered from her total shock that some lucky girl hadn't snapped him up, Trent had returned to lounging against the headboard. Earlier, she'd noticed a dog-eared copy of *The Iliad* on the nightstand. He picked it up and thumbed to the center.

She dropped her bag and sat in the chair, fingers perched over the keyboard. Typed his name into the search bar. It popped up instantly.

"You have a Wikipedia entry?" she asked, bewildered.

Trent nodded once, without looking up.

Janelle clicked the link. The entry included a picture that looked an awful lot like a younger version of the man on the bed. "It says Trent Mason was the youngest top-ranked poker player eight years ago."

Another silent nod.

"Left the game circuit after losing…" *Jesus.* "After losing millions of dollars in a high-stakes game of top-tier poker champions. World Series of Poker?"

Nod.

Her money problems seemed puny in comparison. Janelle kept reading. "Dated adult film star Penelope Roberts, who performed under the name Bad Penny."

Terse acknowledgment from the vicinity of the headboard.

"After an arrest for drug possession, spent time at the Glen Harbor Rehabilitation facility in Colorado for a rumored cocaine addiction."

Holy shit. Her guardian angel was a drug addict and gambler into dating porn actresses. How could this get any worse?

"Mason appeared in a sex tape with Ms. Roberts…" Oh. *That* was how it got worse. Her fingers were as sturdy as Jell-O, hardly capable of scrolling down the page. "After a year of legal disputes, the film was formally released and distributed. Mason subsequently joined the Army and served in Afghanistan."

"Two tours," Trent added without glancing up from his book.

"And now you're here for a cybersecurity conference?"

"I'd rather you didn't update the entry with that information. There's a reason I only use my last name. The point of this exercise is that if you want to click your heels and go home, Dorothy, your best bet is calling your parents and telling them everything. It won't help your case if they find out you're shacking up with Trent Mason."

Janelle couldn't look at him, that six feet of sexy brawn sprawled out over the bed she'd napped in a couple of hours ago. Desperate for anything that would make this better, she clicked on the next link.

The video began playing immediately. *Maybe it wouldn't be so bad…*

Her eyes widened. Her cheeks flamed. Her entire body throbbed as though she'd swallowed a bucket of jalapeños. Raw.

Trent Mason was *hung.*

Also, she'd never realized a woman's body could bend like that.

The video went on and on and on, the sounds of two people going at it like a pair of enthusiastic, horny rhinos echoing in the small room. He hadn't had the tattoo across his back then, although there was one on his hip right below one well-defined oblique. Young Mason's body wasn't as bulky, though he'd been built even then. The Army must've chiseled away any remaining fat.

When Janelle looked up, Mason's expression was contorted with emotion. Pain. Pleasure. Sadness. It struck her that he might not feel as casual about the video as he let on.

She fumbled with the keyboard until the video stopped. "I don't know why anyone would be into that…that dirty stuff. I don't understand the appeal."

When Janelle looked up again, his eyes were locked on her. Hot emotion seethed in those dark depths, but his voice was even and cool when he spoke.

"Heard Penny say a lot of things, not one of them a complaint."

Fair enough. Janelle swallowed and clicked the window closed. The blonde woman had been pretty into everything he'd been doing to her. Then again, she was a porn actress. They had different standards, or something. Bad Penny done a fair number of pulse-revving porny things to Mason, too.

"You actually enjoyed doing it?" She was trying to play it cool, but she had no idea what the social protocol was here. Everything she said came out as an insult, when she was equal parts mortified and dying of curiosity.

"Didn't hear me complaining either, did you?"

His phone beeped, and he rolled over on the bed as he gave her a very good look at his taut behind. Along with an excuse not to respond.

"Nice little girl from the 'burbs, educated, good family. I bet missionary sex once a week was all there was to it." He shot the words over his shoulder, casually insulting.

The barb hit home. "Some of us are happy to be with the person we care about and don't need to go looking for distractions. I like it sweet and gentle. Besides, at least I didn't wind up in a porn video on the internet."

You may well end up in a porn video on the internet.

"It's a sex tape. There's a difference. It's meant for personal enjoyment, not public consumption," Trent shot back lazily.

"Either way. It's sick." She picked up her bag. She'd made a mistake, but he'd done the same thing and more, on purpose. If he was going to be a dick, he didn't get the benefit of the doubt. Teasing her about her sex life was just mean. No, she'd never had anything like what he'd done in that video, and it made Janelle uncomfortable. How many bad decisions did she have to make before she learned her lesson? Mason wasn't the nice guy he'd seemed.

"Where are you going?" Mason demanded. Trent. A name like a curse, hard in the mouth, easy to spit when angry, like she was now. Trent.

"I'll take my chances with the cops," she declared, desperate to get away from her second hotel room catastrophe of the day. This time, he didn't try to stop her.

Instead, he went to the computer and opened the window she'd used to view her own unwitting sex tape. He hit play.

Janelle got the message loud and clear. *Don't you dare look down on me.* "Turn it off."

The sound stopped immediately.

"I know exactly how badly a leaked sex tape can screw up your life, Janie. Going to the cops won't protect you, and it'll invite all kinds of questions about how he came into possession of it. I don't think you want their noses up in your business. With a little time, I can help you neutralize the threat. Everything goes back to the way it was before. You can go back to wherever you're from—"

"Florida."

"Right. You go back to Florida, get on your feet, keep digging out of your student loan debt, and move on with your life. Put this whole thing behind you."

He closed the computer. A knock at the door startled Janelle so badly that her shoulder bag slid down her arm and snagged on her elbow.

"Your choice." Then he moved to answer it.

5

"Everything okay, Sergeant?" Olivia asked when he cracked the door but didn't fully open it.

"Yes. Come in, Captain." Reliving the memories of that video and Janelle's subsequent cool dismissal had jackhammered Mason's nerves into pieces.

Olivia's bright yellow dress, blue enameled jewelry, and blue shoes set off her bronze skin. She wore her hair longer now, in thick, manicured ringlets that spilled to her shoulders. It was still weird to see his former commanding officer in anything but fatigues or business suits.

She held out a green ticket. "Dinner is served."

"Thanks, Olivia. I appreciate your bailing us out."

"Is this the stray you picked up?" she asked, her eyes darting to Janelle.

"Janie, yeah."

His uninvited, unwanted guest shot him an irritated glare and stepped forward to offer her hand. "Pleased to meet you. Thank you for feeding me. Mason is helping me while I try to get my wallet and phone back. As soon as I do, I'll be on my way."

Olivia's dark eyes darted between the two of them. "Mhm. Well. I hope you brought business casual attire for the next few days."

Janelle's shoulders went even more rigid than they'd been a moment before. Despite his annoyance, Trent almost reached over to rub away the stress. He'd pushed her hard. Maybe too hard.

"I hadn't packed for that kind of trip," Janie responded after a moment.

Olivia shook her head, a small movement that spoke volumes about her opinion of the situation. "I brought an extra jacket if you need to borrow it. It'll be a little big in the shoulders. I still have Army arms."

"Thank you."

"I'd want someone to help my daughter if she were in trouble. Stick with Mace. He's good people, no matter what anyone tells you. Including himself."

"Reassuring to know. Thanks again for dinner. And the jacket."

Trent closed the door on Olivia's bright back, leaving him alone with Janelle a semi-erect dick which had nothing to do with the unexpected trip down memory lane.

He hadn't been with a woman in years, and not only because he hadn't had much opportunity. They'd been the wrong kind of opportunities, that's all. Women who'd seen the stupid video he never would have made if he hadn't been high out of his fucking mind and believed, not unreasonably, that he was up for anything at any time.

Too bad. He wasn't up for casual sex anymore. Yet eight months in civilian life had taught him the gulf between his past and his present was most sensitive at its deepest point—sex and relationships. Janelle might as well have taken a stick and poked him right where it hurt the most. Not that he'd ever let her see it. Janelle was a nice girl with a ruthless streak. Who knew what she'd poke into next?

He was such a sucker. He'd given her exactly what she wanted, and now he was going to spend the rest of this conference chasing down some asshole for a two-minute sex tape instead of making the contacts he needed to get his business off the ground.

Why hadn't he let her go to the police?

Because you like your dirty pleasure shot with a chaser of pain, dumbass.

Nothing had changed since Penny. Because of her, he might never find his way back to what he'd been: a mathematically-inclined kid with a film studies professor mother and an English professor father, his entire life ahead of him—until it had all gone to shit in the space of a few months. Not that he'd done himself any favors along the way. All Trent had done was dig the hole deeper.

SHE'D OFFENDED HIM DEEPLY. It was written in the stiff line of his shoulders, in the way the sensuous curve of his mouth had gone flat and hard.

Janelle didn't know what to say. Should she try to make things better, or keep him at arms' length? What if he tried to do...those things in the video?

What if he didn't?

She wished Trent would say something, anything. He remained sulkily silent, so she offered a tentative, "Olivia seems nice."

Trent only nodded.

"It was really decent of her to give me her dinner ticket. And the jacket too. I only have a cardigan with me."

He jerked his head toward the bathroom door. "Better get dressed. You can write her a thank you note later."

The door slammed behind her a little harder than she meant it to. Janelle added insult by turning the bolt. Then she flipped on the fan to cover any noise.

Only then did she exhale.

She stripped out of her clothes for the second time that day.

That video.

Would he do those things to her, if she asked nicely?

You don't want him to. You have boundaries, and those don't include dirty sex. Look how she'd reacted when Kyle the Rich Jerk had tried some of those moves. She'd been terrified.

Janelle hooked her thumbs into her panties and pulled them down. She had one other pair of regular panties with her. Most of what she'd brought was risqué. Well, her version of it. Trent would probably laugh at the sweet balconet bra and matching thong she was hooking herself into.

Trent's opinion of your underwear does not matter and never will.

This had been the most confusing day of her life. Worse than the day Ben had dumped her. Worse than losing her car, her apartment, and her fantasy of getting back together with Ben all in a few hours.

When you meet the right person, you know.

Really? she demanded of the little voice. *That is such crap. Trent Mason is a gambling drug addict who likes porn stars. You have higher standards, woman.*

She'd known Ben was the one for her from the instant they'd met in freshman psych, and now he was marrying someone else. Maybe Trent wasn't Mr. Right, but he could be Mr. Right Now. A long-delayed rebound to help her finally get over Ben, while she figured out a solution to this pickle.

A solid rap at the door. Janelle fumbled the mascara wand she was using on her short, dark lashes. "You coming out? Dinner starts in ten minutes."

What the hell was wrong with her? Fantasizing about getting it on with the one person with any capacity to help her was the same foolish thinking that had gotten her into this mess. She didn't need another opportunity to screw this up. "Be right out."

Janelle emerged from the bathroom wearing a tiny black dress that dipped in the front as if putting her mouthwatering breasts on a platter. Almost as soon as Trent had registered the fact of how stacked she was for a second time, she stuck her arms into the pink suit jacket Olivia had left and buttoned herself away from view.

Trent took his turn in the bathroom with resignation. The next few days were going to be impossible. He had to find a way not to touch her. Easier said than done when his dick interpreted every word that came out of her sassy mouth as an invitation. She was alone and clinging to him like a life raft. Taking advantage of her made him an asshole, not a hero.

She stood before the dresser mirror waiting for him in her too-large jacket, too-short dress, black open-toe sandals and hair curling from her braid. "I think I should use an alias. A fake identity, just in case we run into the Rich Jerk."

"You could be my secretary," Trent offered, opening the door.

Janelle side-eyed him. "Can you be more cliché? How about Business Operations Manager?"

Despite his foul mood, Trent stifled a laugh. Good thing she wasn't really on his payroll, or he'd be over budget on salary already. "Sure. It's your fantasy. Name your title."

She shot him an annoyed look. "You would call it a fantasy. It's self-protection. What if the Rich Jerk is at this dinner? He could be here for the same conference."

It was possible. Unlikely, but possible. There were dozens of conferences in Las Vegas every week. Weren't there?

"What should I call you?" he asked as he followed her into the elevator, taking the opportunity to check out the curve of her ass above the short hem of her skirt. What was she wearing under there? Anything? His inquiring mind wanted to know.

"Rachel."

"Okay, Rach."

"I said Rachel. No nicknames. Rachel....uh, Stone." Janelle flicked her hair over the shoulder of the pink blazer. It nipped in at the waist and she'd rolled up the sleeves to display the striped silk lining. She'd be noticeable among a lot of tech geeks, government flunkies and sales reps. There were a few women in the mix but usually not more than a handful. He'd never seen one as attractive, either.

In the lobby, they passed a miniature drug store with a rack of reading glasses.

"Hold up." Trent picked out a pink frame with minimally magnifying lenses. Ten bucks. Well, he was in this deep. What was another few dollars?

He held them out. "Try them."

"Fake glasses?" Janelle cocked her head at him, a hint of a smile playing over her lips.

Trent's abs tightened against the blow to his solar plexus. He reached over and slipped the ear pieces into place under the fine threads of her hair. Like the first time he'd touched her, the physical contact sent a spark flying along the fuse of his nerves straight toward the bundled dynamite of his long-restrained libido.

Fuck, he wished he'd ponied up for the bigger hotel room. Not having to share had seemed ideal, until it turned out he was sharing after all. He'd checked at the desk, but they were booked up. There was no hope of changing rooms. At least he'd been able to pick up an extra key card for her.

"Very you, Rachel," he deadpanned as he paid for them at the kiosk.

"She's my roommate, so I know I'll respond." Janelle discarded the paper tag and propped them onto the bridge of her nose.

"Thought you lived with your parents?"

"Right. Rachel gave up the lease to move in with her boyfriend. I tried to take it over, but the landlord wouldn't rent to me because of my credit. I had to move home a few weeks ago." Janelle shrugged with feigned nonchalance. Relying on her parents clearly bugged the shit out of her. "I'm pretty sure they don't want me crashing at their house indefinitely."

"So what's your exit plan?" he asked.

"You're looking at it. This was it." Her expression was so crestfallen, Trent didn't have the heart to tease her about it.

He changed the subject. "So how much do you know about IT security?"

"Nothing, other than I can't access a lot of websites from work because they have everything locked down," she replied without hesitation.

"Then this is going to be an exceptionally boring two hours. But at least you'll be fed." Trent led Janelle/Rachel down a hallway marked with a sign that bore the conference's logo and title. It was filled with suits. Men in navy, gray or black suits, some with pinstripes, some with checks, some wearing power ties, others wearing no ties. An occasional woman dotted the landscape. While a good chunk of the men came from varying ethnic backgrounds, all the women were either Asian or Caucasian.

No wonder Olivia hadn't wanted to attend. After dealing with being the only black woman in the room all day, no one could blame her for wanting to take a break. He didn't see Olivia's roommate, either.

Janelle stood out for her pink jacket and matching pink glasses. If Trent hadn't been glued to her side, he had no doubt that she'd be deluged by a sea of testosterone-fueled inappropriate attention.

"Do we get to keep these?" Janelle whispered, holding up an inexpensive USB charger, notepad and flashlight on a keychain. She'd leaned close to whisper her question, and the faint scent of her glossy dark hair made him momentarily light-headed.

"First conference?" he asked.

"Yes." Janelle turned the plastic-wrapped giveaways over in her fingers.

"You can keep them."

She brightened and stuck them in her pocket. Olivia's pocket. The jacket barely buttoned over her breasts. Trent swallowed at the sight of her lovely flesh snuggled between pink wool.

He wasn't the only one who'd noticed, either.

The man sitting to Janelle's left began chatting amiably. "Russel Solomon. What's your connection to the IT world, Rachel?"

"I'm the Business Operations Manager for Mason." Janelle elbowed him sharply in the ribs.

"Mason Technology Security." He stuck out his hand.

"Specialty?" Solomon's curtness was accompanied by a New York accent.

"Custom-designed, secure cloud systems. Malware, ransomware, cloud data security with expertise in terrorist threats. Recently ex-Army. We're still in startup mode."

"Me too. Launching a high-value mergers and acquisitions team in the spring. We're too small for the big vendors to take an interest in, but our security needs are too complex for the lower-tier vendors. We'll issue an RFP soon to potential contacts. Ms. Stone, do you have a card?"

Panic flashed behind the cheap lenses. "I left them in my hotel room. Mace, did you bring yours?"

What's an RFP? she whispered. Trent's mouth tried to smile at the excellent save, but he didn't let it. Trent leaned over until his mouth was an inch from her ear, he soft floral scent of her shampoo teasing his nose. "It stands for request for proposal. It's the start of a formal bid process."

He passed a small rectangle of card stock across Janelle's shoulders. Hell, if anything came of it, he could thank Janelle for making the contact. He wasn't any good at these events. Too reserved, too anxious someone might recognize him from that damned video Penny had released. TMS had been slower in getting off the ground than he'd have liked. There was a very distinct possibility he'd latched onto the project of saving Janelle from herself simply to avoid going out of his comfort zone and talking to people.

Janelle had no such inhibitions. By the time the keynote speaker took the stage, she'd gotten the entire table talking. Even Trent joined in. Adding a woman to the mix broke the ice, especially since she had a seemingly endless reservoir of curious questions that a bunch of men might not have bothered to ask. Or maybe it was just Janelle. Rachel. Whoever she was, she was chatty.

The keynote's comments on the global threat of ransomware to companies and governments were right in Trent's wheelhouse. He should've been rapt. Instead, he kept glancing at Janelle, who was properly riveted. She'd pushed the glasses up on top of her head, unaware that the top button of Olivia's jacket had given up the ghost.

Don't look, asshole.

He had the perfect vantage. It was impossible not to sneak a peek.

Perfect, plump mounds snuggled a two-inch V of cleavage. Saliva flooded his mouth, and it had nothing to do with the mediocre conference food.

Which was still a sight better than MREs.

Two-factor security. Global hack attacks. C'mon, man, get your mind back on track.

Bankruptcy if you don't find a way to expand your business beyond a few government subcontracts.

It did the trick. There was nothing like being responsible for five people's livelihoods to bring focus. He needed to land some clients that Olivia hadn't tossed him as a handout. Right now, he was tapping the inheritance he'd received from his parents' deaths to cover shortfalls, long held in trust by his aunt. It was a lot of money, but if he kept burning cash at this rate, he'd run through it in no time. Considering he'd lost millions at twenty-three, Trent couldn't let the business fail and lose everything all over again.

He was here to prove himself, not ogle his unexpected roommate.

Who dropped her forearm over the back of his chair for a few minutes as she turned to watch the speaker. Lilliputian darts of awareness prickled along Trent's shoulders. If either of them moved half an inch, they'd be touching. Touching through layers of wool and cotton, sure, but making physical contact.

She removed her arm from the back of his chair, and the moment passed. The speaker droned on through dinner before handing the podium for another speech. Trent heard none of it. When it was over, hundreds of people thronged the cash bar or headed for the exit, depending on their preferences.

Janelle-as-Rachel continued chatting with the older man she'd been seated next to, Solomon. He seemed annoyingly interested in Trent's fictional Business Operations Manager, quizzing her about the business while she ad-libbed her way through the conversation. It was impressive, in a way. He only hoped she wasn't spinning too many lines about MTS he'd have to explain away if the RFP came through.

He was busy watching her talk, so Trent knew something was off the moment her body stilled. Janelle reminded him of a mouse sensing a cat, a prey animal on high alert and ready to run. Slowly she lowered the glasses to the bridge of her nose and turned to face him.

Hiding. Janelle was hiding.

Janelle's attention was fixated across the room. Trent tried to follow it, but all he saw was a cluster of older men in dark sports coats or suits. Indistinguishable, paunchy, and middling to a one. Mid-level executive types.

She leaned close to speak low in his ear. "Short man, glasses, gray at the temples. It's him. The…" Janelle swallowed. "The man I came here to meet."

"The john."

The delicate point of her chin dipped. "Whatever you want to call him."

Trent's gut tightened with regret at his choice of words. She'd gone up to the door and knocked, but she hadn't gone inside the house. Until this minute, he hadn't believed the guy posed any real threat.

It hit him like an IED under a truck, how dangerous it was, what she'd done. He'd focused on the sex, and treated the situation as a joke. It wasn't. Meeting a stranger in a distant city, alone, could get a woman killed. Janelle had every reason to be scared. His fingers tightened around her elbow. "Let's go."

Wordlessly, Janelle dropped her napkin on her plate.

"Can you change your appearance? Put your hair up or something?" Trent demanded.

She kept her eyes focused on the hideous carpeting and produced a rubber band, quickly tucking her long, dark hair into a sleek bun. It added five years to her appearance.

"Stand up straight," he ordered, military training kicking in.

Janelle's shoulders went rigidly square. Instantly she looked taller. Older, bigger and all-business. Her john wouldn't recognize her in the few steps they needed to make to get out of the conference room. There were hundreds of people milling about.

But not many women.

He'd never considered the scrutiny that came with being the only one of your kind in a room. He'd observed people's reactions to Olivia, but until recently, she'd been the one in authority. Only in the civilian world was he beginning to understand the under-appreciated value of being able to fade into the background, one among many. Unless someone knew about the video, he didn't stand out for anything but his height. Trent couldn't imagine how exhausting it must be, when there was no passing unseen.

Janelle's hand clamped over his forearm, her nails digging through the wool, and sent his body into high alert. "He's walking toward us."

Trent gestured down a darkened hallway and pushed her against the wall. "He won't see us down there. We'll follow him out."

The tip of Janelle's tongue moistened her lips as she darted into the shadows. At the end of the hallway was a cart with folding chairs. People streamed by. Trent leaned against the wall, blocking her from view. Janelle peered over his shoulder. "Kiss me."

"What? No. Why?" Hot desire sluiced through his body as if a pipe had burst. This was a terrible idea. He needed every barrier he could get between them. Now.

Janelle's green eyes searched his. "It works in the movies."

Why couldn't she have chosen another example? Trent's mind barreled back in time to when his mom had made the family watch classic movies together, a gut punch that left him disoriented. "You don't have to do this."

Janelle gave him a funny little smile. "I know."

6

On tiptoe, she tried to close the gap between her lips and his. He couldn't react, frozen between protest and acquiescence. Eventually, instincts kicked in and Trent bent to close the remaining distance.

He tasted her lipstick first, a little waxy. Janelle didn't open her mouth. Trent inhaled the faint perfume of her hair, the warmth of her skin, and desire lunged hard against the leash of his self-control.

Sweet.

He didn't want to be sweet. He wanted to do all the things he'd done in that horrible video she'd watched, and make her love every second of it.

Janelle wanted nice. This maddening, slow, sensual tease that left him breathless.

Had he ever been innocent? In high school, maybe, before his entire world had collapsed, and he'd started tearing down the remaining structures of his middle-class, suburban life. Too long ago to remember. All his innocence had long since been wiped away by too much gambling and too many drugs. Whatever had been left had been ruined by Penelope.

Kissing Janelle reminded him of liftoff.

Taking flight meant crashing down. Wings were the province of angels and birds and insects, not men. He'd already learned the lesson. He didn't need to retake the course.

Trent pulled back and sucked in a breath. Slowly, the sounds of conference attendees talking as they shuffled into the main hall filtered into his brain. Sleeping fucking Beauty hadn't been this dazed by a kiss. Trent shifted his weight back, uneasy.

Cute little Janie had woken something buried deep inside him. He didn't know what it was, and he didn't care. He only wanted it to go away.

Her eyes were bright beneath lowered lids. "Again. Your way, this time."

Everything in Trent's body tightened at once. "Dirty."

Janelle nodded once. All blood flow directed itself to one uncomfortable, demanding place, a divining rod pointed at her. Helpless, he leaned back in, wrapped one arm around her waist, and shoved her hard against the ugly hotel wallpaper. Janelle's lips parted in a gasp. He took full advantage, kissing her hard, all the while expecting her to resist.

Instead, she parted her lips. Her tongue slipped over his, and Trent groaned.

She was soft. So, so soft. He dug his fingers into the hair gathered at the base of her skull, tipping her face up for better access. His other hand slid from the curve of her waist to grab a palmful of her ass. Trent ground his hips against hers, letting her feel exactly how badly he wanted her.

She whimpered, a little desperate sound that shredded his remaining self-control, and tilted her hips forward. With a final hard, openmouthed kiss, Trent pushed forcefully away. He adjusted his clothes to hide his raging arousal and peered into the hall. Only a few straggling conference attendees were left.

"Let's go." His voice sounded rough, even to his own ears.

She leaned there against the wall, her magnificent chest rising and falling erratically, her skirt hiked up and lipstick smudged. After a minute, she nodded. Her hands were unsteady as she straightened her skirt and closed the top button of the pink jacket.

Trent wiped away any lipstick that had transferred to his face with the back of his hand and silently cursed himself. Sharing that tiny hotel room for the next couple of days was going to be impossible.

SHE SHOULDN'T HAVE DONE it.

Trent's mouth had crashed down over hers, possessive but gentle, and sent her heart rate into overdrive. It made no sense. She'd lost her virginity to Ben, wanted to marry him. Yet her ex was a pale shadow compared to the neon pleasure that Trent sent cascading through her body.

It had been a terrible idea. Crammed up against the wall, she could neither fight him off or squirm away easily. It should've made her afraid, being pinned against a wall in a deserted public hallway by a near-stranger. But all she'd felt was a lightning surge of excitement.

Bravado leached out of her like color out of a dying coral reef. By the time he jammed the plastic key card into the slot on the room door, her armor was back in place.

Mostly.

"I'll take the couch," Janelle announced, eager to paper over her massive fuckup.

"You'll never fit."

"And you will? Besides, it's your room. I'm the one crashing."

"We could share the bed." Trent offered neutrally.

Janelle gave him her best sardonic smile. "I'm sure that wouldn't be weird at all."

"The offer stands if you change your mind in the middle of the night." Trent yawned and began to unbutton his shirt slowly. Janelle turned her back, but she caught a glimpse of him in the mirror again. He pretended not to notice until he had to unbuckle his belt to pull the hem out of his waistband. She paused midway through arranging sheets on the little sofa. Trent stopped what he was doing until she glanced up and their eyes met briefly in the mirror. She dropped her gaze instantly.

The man had starred in a porn video, but it didn't mean he was interested in screwing some random girl who'd barged in on his conference. How could she keep making so many stupid mistakes?

A toxic knot of self-loathing lodged in her stomach. *Keep your hands and lips to yourself.* Shame wormed its way in, one more bad feeling to add to the mix.

Janelle snatched up her bag and retreated stiffly into the bathroom. She had to say something. Clear the air. But words tumbled through her mind, incoherent and useless.

She pulled on the only pajamas she'd brought. They were new, like several of the items she'd splurged on in a fit of optimism about this doomed venture. The white silk tank top and matching shorts were simultaneously too sexy and too sweet, a whisper-light fabric that left nothing to the imagination. There was no help for it. She exited the bathroom with a standoffish, "Your turn."

So much for clearing the air. Was there anything more to say?

She collapsed onto the makeshift bed couch and clicked on the TV without looking at Trent. Dignity was hard to come by when you'd thrown yourself at a hot guy and had to sit on his couch with your nipples showing through your jammies. Another fail.

She was so sick of failure.

MASTURBATING in the shower took the edge off the frustrating attraction Trent knew he couldn't act on. He had to be better. She was in trouble, and he refused to take advantage. His job was to help her, not fuck her. Besides, she radiated embarrassment. He should find a way to let her know that she didn't need to feel like that.

Clean, he waltzed back out to the bed in nothing but his boxer briefs and a t-shirt. It was more clothing than he usually slept in, and she wasn't any more modest. Janelle didn't look away from the TV. If he hadn't already deflated, her lack of attention would've done the job in a far less pleasant way.

"*The Bachelorette?*" he commented after a minute.

"It's my favorite show, okay?"

"This is trash."

Janelle turned and shot him a green glare that would've slayed a lesser being. "Says the man who starred in a porn video."

She turned back to the TV. Dismissed. Easiest way to win a fight: *no matter what I've done or said, at least I didn't film myself having sex with a porn actress.* Argument over.

Trent tried not to be depressed about it.

The TV went to commercial. Janelle hit mute before turning to him. "I'm sorry. Low blow. I catch a lot of flak for my preferred entertainment."

Trent shifted on the bed. "It's a fantasy. How come you like it so much?"

"You answered your own question. I like it because it's a fantasy. That's the point." Janelle settled back against the couch arm, her feet propped up on the opposite end, a thoughtful expression on her naked features. Warranted or not, it gave Trent the sense he was seeing the true side of her, not the armored version she presented to the world.

He hadn't been around women in a very long time. The Army didn't encourage consorting with the comparatively few women who enlisted, and Afghan women had been strictly off-limits. "What's the fantasy?"

"The show is about men competing for a woman's attention, instead of assuming they have it automatically. It's the fantasy of having a selection of partners, instead of having to settle. I don't expect you to understand this problem."

The show returned, and Janelle unmuted the TV.

Someone had taken Janelle for granted. It had to be the one partner. Trent couldn't decide whether he wanted to punch the guy or thank him. Hurt him for causing Janelle pain, or slap him on the back for breaking her heart and leaving her for someone more deserving to find.

Like you.

Shut up, he told his heart. *You're the least deserving man on the planet.*

Deserving or not, if Janelle gave him another opening, Trent was taking it.

"You're a romantic," he observed.

"Absolutely and unapologetically. I like men who remember my mother's and my sister's birthdays and bring flowers on our anniversaries, even the silly ones nobody cares about but me. There must be a few out there. I only need to find one who loves me back."

That one is not you. Trent wasn't stupid. He understood the substance of what she was saying: the kiss had been an experiment, a novelty. Nothing more. Don't get any ideas. Understanding slashed through him, clean and cold and bloody.

Janelle had poked and prodded—gotten under his skin all day—and the impulse to give back as good as he was getting elbowed out common sense. "You had your one. Your Prince Charming left you, didn't he, princess?"

The television blinked off. "Yes. He did. So, I need to find one more decent man."

Trent snorted dismissively, though her words carried an unexpected sting. "Says the woman who demanded to be kissed dirty."

"Good night, Mace." The lamp winked out.

JERK.

I can't believe he'd say it.

Yes, she could. She hadn't been very nice, either. Janelle lay still with her feet propped up on the end of the couch. Alyssa had once told her elevating that your feet above your heart made you feel calmer. It wasn't working.

Darkness, soupy with tension, pressed down on her body. Mace wasn't asleep. She could hear his breathing, the sheets crinkling every time he moved beneath them.

She shouldn't ask. But questions had been bubbling away in her mind ever since her perfunctory background check. Night gave her cover to voice them.

"If it was a sex tape, why are there credits and a cast listed?"

"They were added later."

"Why?"

A long silence stretched between them. She sensed him shifting a few feet away on the bed. *Answer the damn question, Trent.*

"Penny was the one who wanted to make the tape. We'd been on the skids for a while. I wanted her to quit her job. She insisted it was only work, except when she was with me. Her star was rising, and she didn't want to stop when she was starting to make real money, but I told her I wouldn't share her anymore. We got back together because she'd promised to get out of acting."

Janelle nodded. He couldn't have seen her, but he must've sensed her movement.

"A week later, that video was everywhere. Not because anyone gave a shit that she was in it. Because I was. The youngest top-ranked pro poker player in history."

Janelle gasped. What a betrayal. And she'd played the video, or part of it, out loud. She'd forced him to relive an incredibly painful experience. Her very soul writhed at her thoughtlessness. *Another fuck-up.*

Nothing she did was ever right. The earth should open up and swallow her before she bungled anything else.

"I hired a lawyer and fought tooth and nail to get it taken down," Trent continued after a long minute. "Spent a fortune on legal fees. Every time we got it taken down with a cease-and-desist letter, it would pop back up somewhere else. I tried appealing to US copyright law to prove I owned the video. I can tell you our legal system hasn't evolved to cope with 21st century technology."

"That still doesn't explain why there's credits." Janelle sat up, legs curled beneath her under the blanket.

"I'm getting to it. Are you always this impatient?"

"I like to get to the point." She had to know, though she knew Trent owed her no explanation.

"Penny leaked the tape because she needed money for drugs. She'd sold it to fund her new heroin habit. She wasn't getting out of the adult business willingly. She'd been blacklisted for intravenous drug use."

Oh. My. God.

"I kept trying to pull her out of that world. She was determined to drag me in deeper. That was the breaking point. Penny spiraled out of control fast after we broke up. She overdosed a few weeks later."

"Is she dead?" Janelle whispered, afraid to know the answer.

Another weighty silence. "No. It would've been kinder."

Janelle was hyperaware of his stillness.

"Penny suffered extensive brain damage from oxygen deprivation. She can walk, but her memory's gone. She'll never hold a job. She can't live alone. She needs help with everything—cooking, bathing, paying bills. Hell, she can barely get up a flight of stairs on her own. That kind of care is expensive, and she'll need it for the rest of her life. Someday the royalties from her acting career will dry up. I tried to win the money to pay for it at poker, but I was off my game, and I lost everything I had. All of it, except what was in the trust I couldn't touch. So, I agreed to license the video on the condition if all revenues went into a trust for her."

The information smacked Janelle like a boxer's glove. "I'm sorry. I'm so, so sorry, Trent."

He was a damn hero. Her nose felt thick and her cheeks were hot. Janelle raised one hand. Her lashes were damp. And she'd been downright unkind to him this evening, feeling prickly with embarrassment and wounded pride.

"Get some rest," he replied.

Though she couldn't see him, the bedclothes shuffled as Trent turned away.

Breathing hurt. Her lungs were being crushed. Janelle sipped air until the tightness in her chest eased. It didn't matter that she'd met him barely twelve hours ago. She was halfway in love with Trent Mason.

When you meet the right person, you know.

She believed it. She always had. Trent was right to call her a romantic. As stupid, hopeless, and pointless as it was. She'd already blown her chance at a happy ending, and she no longer deserved love, success, or anything else good in life.

7

Trent kicked hard against the tangle of cloth imprisoning his legs. He rolled over, nearly fell out of bed and staggered to the bathroom. The door opened as his hand connected with the handle. Light stabbed him in the eyeballs. A female gasp.

Janelle.

Hotel.

Shit.

Pieces of dreams kaleidoscoped through his mind. Sex dreams. All. Damn. Night.

Trent didn't need to look down to know he had a raging case of morning wood. One glance at Janie's shocked face and he followed the direction of her attention down to his extremely naked, erect cock.

Weird. He hadn't gone to bed naked.

"Sorry," he muttered, belatedly moving his hands to cover his genitals. Now that he was wide awake, a vague memory of tossing his restrictive boxer briefs across the room came back. Sure enough, they'd landed on the lamp and knocked the shade sideways.

"Nothing I haven't seen before," Janelle replied coolly. Then she yanked on the hotel room door and let it slam closed behind her.

Where's she going? He was too late to form the question out loud.

Trent took care of his bathroom business, retrieved his underwear from its perch on the light fixture and pulled on running clothes. For the next hour, he tried to outrun, out-lift, and otherwise exhaust his mortification and pent-up frustration.

What she'd said bothered him. It shouldn't. By this point, millions of strangers had seen his erect dick online. If he had any shame, he sure hadn't demonstrated it with Penny. But it had been years since then, painful years of discipline and self-regulation, and Trent couldn't help feeling he'd earned a modicum of privacy.

It wasn't as though he could do anything about the video, though. He'd signed his rights away long ago, against his lawyer's advice.

Sure, he'd done it to support his disabled, drug-addicted adult film actress ex-girlfriend, but, regardless of his reasons, it was a lot of baggage to cart around. The few times he'd tried dating since his discharge from the Army, women had tried to speed past dinner straight to making him dessert. Those experiences had made him paranoid, and he couldn't stop worrying about it.

If he was going to replace memories of Penny with new ones, they had to be better than a mindless fuck with a near-stranger.

There was also the not-small question of whether he *could* fuck sober. Whether it would be too intense—or *worse*, not intense enough. Better not to find out than to resign himself to a lifetime of longing for the sickening combination of cocaine and hardcore sex.

Trent swiped his hand across his face and pushed harder, muscles straining against memories. His eyes stung with sweat.

When he got back, wet with punishing exertion, Janie had showered and dressed, her long hair braided and sleek against her scalp. If she wore makeup, he couldn't tell. She'd pulled on a short black skirt and a form-fitting pink tank top, over which she'd draped a loose cardigan like a shield. She'd tucked her leg under her body to slouch over his computer, but she straightened as soon as he came in.

"I was looking for phone numbers in my email. Everything is in my phone." Her posture radiated humility and discomfort, and she barely looked at him.

"Go ahead and make calls while I clean up." It was for the best. The sooner she called her parents, the sooner Trouble Tits would get out of his life. He stayed in the shower longer than necessary, trying to wash away the way the sting of disappointment. She was pretty and lively and full of attitude, and a large part of him wanted her to stick around. Specifically, the large part in his fist as he tugged one off. Pathetic. Penny would've teased him endlessly, if she'd known what he was reduced to.

Janelle bounced up again when he came out of the bathroom, in wool suit pants and an undershirt. Saturday, the second day of the conference, was the main event. He had a full schedule.

"I made coffee. Do you drink coffee? It's not very good. I work in a coffee shop most mornings, before my job and on weekends. So, I'm opinionated about the quality. But I'm also a raging caffeine addict. I'll drink anything."

"Is that why you were up so early?" Trent pulled out a fresh shirt and started working on the buttons.

"I'm a morning person, generally." She studiously turned her back while he finished dressing. Trent tried not to take it as an insult. He knew she felt bad about kissing him yesterday, and wished she wouldn't. It wasn't as if he'd resisted. At all.

"Me, too," he responded evenly. "I swear I didn't mean to surprise you this morning. I wasn't really awake."

"It's okay."

"Nothing you haven't seen before, right?" Trent tasted bitterness, and it wasn't from the coffee. Which was pretty bad, just as she'd warned.

"I...sleep however you want to, Trent. I'm not a prude. I'm in your space, not the other way around."

If he were in the market for no-strings action, he'd give his left testicle to be in her space. She'd tasted so good, and now he couldn't think about anything but kissing her again, about all the things kissing could lead to. Yet she'd been downright rude in her embarrassment last night, and now she was working awfully hard to pretend nothing had happened.

Which meant...he had no idea what it meant. Did she hate him? Or think he'd pounce on her if she acted normally?

Trent didn't have time to figure out whatever was going through

Janie's restless mind. He had other priorities. A business to launch. Employees. Maintaining Olivia's respect for his professional capabilities. Janie was self-sufficient, so she claimed. Let her work out her own issues. He had more than enough of his own.

"Here's my phone. I'll be back around eleven-thirty. There's a breakfast bar in the lounge until ten. Get your situation sorted out, Janie." Trent's words came out curt.

"I will."

The hurt in her eyes stayed with him all morning. Janelle was made for lighthearted banter and witty retorts, and she took criticism hard. Midway through the second conference session, Olivia poked him to ask if he'd slept all right, her lips mischievous.

"No," Trent replied, and forced his attention back to the speaker. Maybe when he got back to the room, Janie would be gone. The prospect should please him, but it didn't.

"RACH?"

"Hmm? Janelle?"

"Are you sleeping?" Trent would be back soon. Unlike her, real-life Rachel was decidedly not a morning person, but it was mid-afternoon, Florida time.

"It's Saturday," she yawned. "I was napping. With Caleb."

Lovely. She'd interrupted their post-coital, blissed-out haze. Janelle's resolve hardened. "I need your help."

There was a beat of silence, then a rustle, as if Rachel was getting out of bed. "Is everything okay?"

"I'm in Las Vegas and I did something stupid. I lost my wallet. I've canceled my debit card, but I don't have an ID to get on the plane to come home. I have an old driver's license in a box at my parents' house. Can you get it and send it to me?"

"Um. Not exactly. I'm camping this weekend with Caleb."

"Oh. How's it going?"

"Fine, except I have to pee, and the bathroom is like a million miles away." There was more rustling and the sound of a squeaky door opening, then slapping closed.

"Bathroom? It's the woods. Can't you pee on a tree?" she demanded of her former roommate.

Trent chose this moment to walk in. Janelle scrambled to take the phone off speaker.

"It's a campground full of people, Janie, and I'm not dropping trou—"

Janelle finally found the right button before Rachel described what she'd be revealing, and to whom.

"Who are you...? Oh." The corners of Trent's sexy mouth ticked up. The man was devastating when he smiled. He didn't do it often.

"Janelle. Did I hear a *man* in the background?" Rachel gasped.

"Don't sound so shocked. It was just, uh, someone walking by."

Trent smirked and walked by again. Janelle almost missed her friend's question. "I don't believe you for a second, Janelle Carlisle. Why can't you ask your parents to find your ID?"

"Because they don't know I'm here. I told them I was house sitting for a friend in Miami for a few days." *Among other reasons.* Janelle kept her attention riveted on the notepad on the table, her face burning. She pressed one hand against her cheek to cool it.

"This doesn't have anything to do with Crystal's ridiculousness about sugar buddies, does it?"

"Of course not," Janelle replied a little too hastily.

"You'd never do that. You're too…"

"Too what, Rach?"

"Too uptight."

"What's that supposed to mean?" Janelle glared at the phone, then at Trent, who was still smirking.

"I mean, Janelle, you have to get over Ben. You haven't been on a date in like a year. It's as if you gave up. Just sleep with someone and get it over with."

"You do remember what happened last time I went on a date?" Janelle demanded. The horror at having this conversation in front of Trent made her skin prickle.

"You made out in the back of the car. You said it was a great night!" Rachel insisted.

Janelle rolled her eyes at the phone. "The guy texted me a dick pic two days later to show me what I was supposedly missing out on. Believe me, it wasn't much."

"Who're you talking to, babe?" Trent asked over her shoulder, loudly.

"You're totally with a guy!" Rachel shrieked.

"Gotta go. Enjoy camping!" Janelle disconnected the call and surrendered the phone. "If she calls back, don't answer."

He slid the phone into his pocket. "I dunno, you were getting into the good stuff. Maybe I should give your friend a call."

"Don't. You. Dare." He was teasing. At least, she hoped he was teasing. "That wasn't cool, Trent. I'm trying to keep this fiasco quiet."

Trent laughed. "Apart from catching up with your girlfriends, any progress getting home?"

"Until now, I was kicking ass." Janelle read from her notes. "My bank card is being overnighted. It'll arrive at the hotel on Monday morning. The government won't send a replacement ID, so that's a dead end, but I can probably get past airport security with the card on Monday afternoon. Changing it to an earlier flight won't work without the credit card, but at least I can get home. I also called the phone company. Records show it hasn't been used since the Rich Jerk stole it, and I've temporarily disabled service."

Trent cupped her chin in his palm. She resisted the impulse to nuzzle, and let him tip her face up.

"Nice work, Janie."

The approval she read in his expression sent a warm thrill down her midsection. Or it might be the rough warmth of his fingers against her skin, or both. Trent Mason knew how to push every button she possessed, and a few she didn't know she had.

No shit he does. He dated a porn actress.

She was deluding herself. Trent was a genuinely kind person who'd gone out of his way to help a stranger. Above and beyond. She'd kissed him, insulted him, and he still hadn't kicked her out. "Thanks."

"You like Vietnamese food?" he asked, breaking the tension.

"Yeah, sure. Why?"

Trent gave her a rare smile and jerked his head toward the door. "Lunchtime. Everybody's gotta eat."

As if on cue, her stomach growled.

"Okay, thanks. I'm keeping track of everything you've spent. Once my card gets here, I'll pay you back for everything. Including the hotel room."

"You don't have to pay me back for anything, Janie. I haven't spent very much on you. Pay me back by getting out of sex work permanently."

Janelle shuddered. "My one foray was traumatizing enough."

On the street, they walked down the Las Vegas strip for two blocks, then turned down a side street. A few blocks away from the action was a modest strip mall. In the middle was an unassuming storefront boasting authentic fresh Vietnamese.

"This was my old haunt when I was playing pro poker. I'm glad they're hanging on. The food's great."

They slid into opposite sides of a small table. Trent's knee bumped hers. They both retreated.

"Sorry." They spoke simultaneously.

"Jinx." Janelle rested her forearms on the table. She had no idea how to smooth things over. The situation was awkward times infinity. "Do you ever miss it? Playing poker?"

"No." Discussion over.

"Why not?" She couldn't resist prying. Nothing about this man made any sense. He'd saved her ass and acted like it was no big deal. Despite that video—and the accidental exposure—Trent had been an absolute gentleman. He was built enough that she believed he was recently out of the army, but how did that square with his choice of literature and his tattoo? Janelle's curiosity was a living, tentacled creature. It wanted to wrap around Trent and suck the information out of him.

"It's not what it looks like on TV. It's all about statistics. I was always good at math, and after my parents died—"

"Wait. Your parents died? When?" She didn't need tentacles. Trent let details slip whenever he let his guard down.

"My dad when I was a junior in high school, my mom when I was halfway through my senior year. A heart attack and a car accident, respectively."

"Oh, my god." Impulsively, Janelle closed both hands over one of his. The light contact radiated up her arm and echoed through her body. Trent didn't pull away.

"It was a long time ago."

Their food arrived. He squeezed her fingers and let go.

"But how did you get into poker?" Janelle continued. She picked at her noodles with chopsticks.

Trent hesitated. "My Aunt Suzie had financial control over most of my parents' estate. She moved me to New Jersey from Colorado. I hated it. I resented her for selling the house and putting everything into a trust fund, even though she was only following my parents' directives. According to the will, I could use the money for education, but otherwise I couldn't touch it until I turned twenty-five or graduated from college, whichever came first."

Trent fiddled with his water glass, rolling it around the rim, idly making wet circles on the wood table. "But there was one life insurance policy where my mom forgot to change the beneficiary. It listed my dad first, then me. Turns out the beneficiary trumps a will, so Aunt Suzie couldn't take it and stash it with the rest of the estate money. Since my dad was dead, I got a quarter-million-dollar check out of the blue. I'd just turned eighteen. I moved out of my aunt's house, dropped out of high school and studied poker like it was my job."

"But how does that happen? I mean, some of the guys watched it in college, but I didn't realize it was such a huge deal. How'd you get into the professional circuit?"

"I'd been playing online for a while. The game's a weird combination of control and chaos, and it was easier to focus on poker stats than on how fucked up my life was. There was a lifestyle that came with it, once I started winning. Girls. Drugs. I did a lot of incredibly stupid shit." Clearly, he didn't want to talk about himself anymore.

"Is that how you met Penny?" Janelle didn't know why she was pushing. Everything she learned about Trent made him more appealing. If she'd met him in his poker-and-Penny days, she wouldn't have liked him at all. But now, as a man who'd gone through so much and come out the other side? She had no business being fascinated by him.

Yet she was.

"That's a long story, Janie." He brushed her question aside.

Weird to think that they'd known one another for twenty-four hours and they already had a rhythm. She pushed, he gave up to a point, then Trent closed down. Little by little, she'd get his life story out of him. It wasn't like he never pushed her, either.

When you know, you know.

Oh, shut up. Little voices bearing clichés had no place in this misadventure. She didn't know what to call this feeling, but romantic it was not. Janelle wanted to fuck him so badly it made her hands shake and her thighs tingle. There was nothing sweet about it.

8

"Where'd you go this morning?" Trent's curiosity overrode sense. They walked side-by-side down the bustling sidewalk, the early afternoon sun steamy, a temporary truce sealed by inexpensive noodles.

"Swimming."

Trent had no response for several steps, his mind busily concocting a slideshow of Janelle in very skimpy bathing suits.

"I'm usually up early," she continued. "I've worked at the coffee shop since my sophomore year in college. On days when I'm not working, I swim."

"You like it?" *Dumbshit, she just said she did.*

"Any other form of exercise requires multiple sports bras. It's a pain in the chest. Literally." Janelle gestured vaguely to her breasts, over which she'd buttoned her pink cardigan, despite the warm day. "We'll coordinate better tomorrow morning, if you're planning to wake up at the same time."

One form of exercise requires no bra at all. Trent mentally swatted away the unhelpful thought.

"What's on your agenda for this afternoon?" she asked.

Trent inhaled hot desert air and dragged his mind out of the gutter.

"There's a conference panel at one I think I'm going to skip. The session after that starts at one-thirty. How about you?"

"No plans. Maybe walk around the city, but it's too hot to go far."

"You can come with me, if you want to sit through a boring talk on IT procurement and business development," he offered, expecting Janelle to wrinkle her nose and decline.

"What's that?" She peered up at him as if he'd spoken a foreign language.

"Business development? Applying for jobs, only as a corporation."

"Huh. I used to apply for jobs all the time. Sometimes I even got offers," Janelle mused.

"So, why are you still working a job you hate?" he asked, puzzled by her lack of ambition.

Janelle dark eyebrows knit over the cheap frames of her sunglasses. "The offers were contingent on a background check. A few days later, they called back to rescind it because of my credit report. It happened a couple of times, and I stopped trying."

Trent whistled, low. "Cold."

Janelle didn't say anything for a few steps. "It's illegal to do that in some states, but considering I can't even sign a lease, it seemed like too big a risk to look that far away. I sound like I'm making excuses, but I wasn't just throwing myself a pity party. I chose to stay in Florida and work extra hard to pay down my debt. I just didn't quite realize what I was up against."

They stopped at a street corner. Janelle touched his forearm. Trent glanced down, but her eyes were shielded behind black plastic. "I'm sorry about yesterday. I didn't mean to be short with you. It was a long, weird day."

Olivia must've touched him like this a hundred times over the years they'd worked together. He couldn't remember a single instance. But Janelle? Trent felt the burn of her light fingers through the cotton of his dress shirt long after the light changed. "Does your apology include the hallway?"

She laughed, embarrassed. "I got carried away pretending to be Rachel Stone. I'm sorry about that, too."

"Don't be. But Janie, fair warning. If you make another move like that, I can't promise not to take you up on it."

The hotel lobby was dark and almost too cold, prickling his skin. Trent's eyes adjusted to the sudden change in light. He couldn't tell if Janelle had picked up on the subtext: if she made another pass, he'd respond with a guaranteed yes.

"I'm a good girl, Trent. Your virtue is safe with me."

Bummer.

BACK IN THE ROOM, Janelle flopped onto the bed while Trent disappeared into the bathroom. He sure took a lot of showers. Maybe it was his way of getting some privacy, since there was none to be had in the tiny room. Housekeeping hadn't come by to make the bed yet. The scent of his hair clung to the pillow. Janelle nuzzled her cheek against the crisp cotton.

"Tired?" Trent had pulled on jeans, a clean shirt and a blazer.

Janelle sat up. "I didn't sleep well. Too much on my mind."

"I'm leaving for the panel. If you want to come along, I'll wait, but don't take long."

Staying in bed wouldn't help her get her wallet back. She might as well try to learn something while she was here. Besides, the only time she felt safe was with Trent. She wanted to be wherever he was, including boring conference panels.

"I'll be quick," she promised.

Five minutes later, she'd fixed her makeup and buttoned Olivia's jacket over her tank top. With the silly reading glasses, she was back in her Rachel Stone persona. Her legs were freezing from the air conditioning. She should've worn her leggings, though they weren't as professional-looking as the skirt.

"Here," Trent dangled a plastic square on a string. "I photocopied my badge and stuck it in an extra holder. As long as no one looks too closely, you'll be able to get in and out of the conference. It's not like you're here to enjoy the experience. I'm just keeping you out of housekeeping's way."

"Thanks." Janelle tucked the counterfeit conference credentials into her jacket so the corner was visible, then trailed Trent down the hall to the elevator and through the lobby. She held her breath as they passed the entrance to the conference hall. No one stopped them. Her. Trent had every right to be here. She was the imposter. Janelle released a breath and tried to act normal.

Olivia found them outside the sterile conference room. She winked knowingly at the fake credentials. The three of them filed into the seats, Trent's long legs nearly touching the chair in front of him.

Janelle found herself absorbed by the presentation. She scribbled notes on the free notepaper, and jotted down the link to download a copy of the deck later. "This doesn't sound so hard. You said there's jobs for people who do this kind of work?"

"There's a lot of money in business development, if you're good at it. Some companies use consultants to help them get an edge in the pitch or procurement process." Olivia cast her a speculative glance.

Janelle couldn't hide her wistfulness. It was nice to fantasize about being good at something for once, but if business development meant dealing with money, she'd probably get tripped up by her credit problems before she got started.

As if he sensed her thoughts, Trent leaned close. "You already got me one contact. The only viable one so far."

"I'm glad I could help, Mace." An ember of satisfaction flared in her chest, bright and scorching. She'd done something right, for once. She'd helped *him*.

The title of the next session Trent was going to didn't sound like English, so instead Janelle tailed Olivia to one on government procurement for IT contractors instead.

"This is my bread-and-butter," Olivia explained. "Solid, long-term contracts that pay decently and on time. I'm providing for my extended family." She flashed a grin.

"Extended family?"

"I hire veterans, mostly. A lot of them struggle in the civilian workforce. I provide good jobs, and I get to make all the big decisions."

"Does Tr... er...Mace run his business the same way?" Janelle asked.

"Nah, he likes the specialist security work. He keeps his team small, works them hard. It's a riskier path, but that's his style. He has a talent for thinking five steps ahead of anyone else. He struggles with the human connection, and so much of IT and business is about the human element. I'm glad you're here, Rachel. You're good at getting people to talk, and if anyone needs to, it's our man Mason." Olivia winked as she used Janelle's fake name.

Our man. Olivia made her feel like part of a team. She knew exactly what to say to make Janelle feel capable and bold. She drank in the feeling of competence, so different from her usual defeated inertia. Janelle again took notes, intent on learning everything she could. She'd come here looking for a path forward, and, unexpectedly, she might've found one.

When Janelle arrived back at the room, the shower was running again. What the heck was he doing in there? Was he OCD?

The next event was a cocktail mixer. Armed with her new understanding of the field and Olivia's encouragement, Janelle planned to make business contacts like it was her job. She was going hunting for business cards.

Housekeeping had stopped by, so she found all the sheets and blankets and began remaking the couch into a bed. Absorbed in laying out the unruly white cloth, Trent's voice startled the hell out of her.

"Nice view." He smirked, naked but for his boxer briefs.

Janelle whipped around so hard, the ends of her hair smacked her cheek. Her ass had been exposed as she bent to tuck in the bedding, skimpy thong and all. A flush of heat coursed through her as she sat said behind on the couch.

"Likewise." She narrowed her eyes.

"Nothing I haven't seen before," he smirked, sprawling out across the bed to give her a front-row view of his package. It grew longer and stiffer. Janelle felt her eyes widen. Trent had a truly impressive cock. The glimpse she'd had this morning had confirmed the video proof from yesterday. Now she was watching him get hard, just talking to her.

Tongue-tied, Janelle tried to breathe. No oxygen reached her lungs. They burned. All of her burned.

If you make another move like that, I can't promise not to take you up on it.

If she made a move, he'd fuck her. Would it hurt? Trent's cock was huge. She'd give anything to feel like Penny had in that video, which she'd watched the morning Trent had left her alone with his computer. All the way to the end, where Penny had put a strange device up his ass. No wonder he was hung up about that video. He must've taken a ton of flak while he was serving in the military.

It sure looked as if he'd enjoyed it, though.

"I'm a good girl." She swallowed. She'd come here to try on being bad. What was the worst thing that could happen if she asked Trent to sleep with her?

He might split her in two with his massive cock. Definitely not worth the risk.

"So you keep telling me. But you're the one who came to Las Vegas to have sex with a stranger for money." Trent truly didn't seem fazed by her idiot plan. He didn't judge her for it, only pointed out her inconsistency.

"I backed out when I realized it was a terrible idea!" Janelle threw the pillow at him. "Put some clothes on, Trent."

Before she threw herself at him, instead.

He didn't. He caught the pillow, gave it a fluff, and lay back with his hands behind his head. The tattoo on his oblique was clearly visible, a tribal motif that probably didn't mean anything. It was the kind of decoration an eighteen-year-old left to his own devices would think cool. "Hope you're enjoying the view from up there on your high horse."

Her cheeks flamed. Janelle wished she'd brought more t-shirts and khakis so she wouldn't have to sit here in her thong and short skirt staring at her roommate's mouthwatering chest. Her limited wardrobe made his point for him. She'd packed for a weekend in bed, not a business conference. She'd come here to experience casual sex in a context that wouldn't ever get mixed up in her real life, only to discover that being ordered to get on her knees and give her sugar daddy a blowjob was nauseating, not hot.

Janelle shuddered at the memory.

"I can prove I'm a good girl, Trent Mason." Why was she so obsessed with this?

"Yeah? How?" He grinned up skeptically, the sharp lines of his face turning wolfish. She wished she had another pillow to toss at him.

"I didn't like *anything* Rich Jerk tried to do to me. Most of which wasn't dissimilar to what you and Penny did in the video. Which I watched."

That wiped the smugness of his handsome face. Good. *Get your feet back in those high-horse stirrups, Janie.*

"Maybe because he wasn't the right person to try it with," Trent shot back.

Suddenly Janelle was clinging to her high horse's saddle for dear life. If he made the slightest move she knew she'd jump at the chance to try it all—the dirty talk, any position he wanted her in, even putting something in his ass, if he wanted it. The idea made her abdomen clenched, hard. She shifted on the little couch, cursing the short skirt as it rode up high over her thigh. He didn't need to see the wet spot on the crotch of her thong. She wiggled her bottom, looking for relief. The blanket and sheet slid halfway to the floor.

"If you're not comfortable on the couch, you can take the bed tonight. I'll sleep on the floor. I've slept worse places."

"It's your room. You keep the bed." The reason for her discomfort had nothing to do with stiff foam and polyester stain-resistant upholstery. She could lie to him all she wanted, but she'd never fool herself. "We could share, if you promise to stay on your side."

The outline of his dick stirred under his boxer shorts. Not that she'd stolen a glance or three. The man was delicious, and he was putting it all out there for her to enjoy. Janelle could only look on helplessly, clinging to her good girl status even though she was less and less certain what it meant.

Or that she wanted it anymore.

"Probably not a wise idea," he finally responded before picking up his book from the nightstand.

"It would be fine," Janelle declared airily. "We've established I don't like dirty sex. Your innocence is safe, whatever's left of it."

The rest of the blankets slid off the couch and puddled in the gap between the bed as she shifted again, trying to ease the pressure between her legs and still maintain some modesty. She was such a liar. Her body was burning for his touch. She shouldn't be this turned on. All they were doing was talking.

"I can't say the same for yours." He sat up and swung his legs into the gap between the bed and the couch.

Janelle was very aware of Trent's large, nearly naked form two feet away. Her pulse rate picked up like the time she'd accidentally hit the treadmill button for top speed. All she could think about was the sensation of his hands holding her wrists as he'd kissed her in the nicest dirty way possible.

Harder. Longer. Now.

It could only lead to frustration and disappointment. Loss.

More failure.

"Besides, Janie, we haven't established anything, other than the fact that we have enough chemistry to blow up a lab."

Words, only words. Janelle swallowed, but couldn't respond. She was so focused on watching his face move closer, she didn't notice her skirt had hiked up again she tucked her legs up under her on the couch to avoid touching Trent's hairy calves. If they made contact she'd spontaneously combust. Her obituary could not read *burst into flames mid-conversation at Las Vegas casino hotel; horniness suspected as cause.* It would be a fitting end to her humiliating life, though.

He sat on the edge of the bed, facing her, beyond semi-erect and not caring that she could see it. That's what she got for trying to play it cool this morning.

Nothing you haven't already seen, girl.

She wanted a better view. She wanted to touch. She wanted him in her mouth. "I'll prove it to you."

Janelle leaned forward, her hands gripping the couch beside her knees, her feet back on the floor. Her lips closed chastely over his. Trent grunted softly and raised one hand to her face to pull her closer. Gently, he pressed his tongue to her lips. Janelle didn't try to resist. She kissed him back as dirty as anything as he'd done to her in the hallway. Lightheaded, she tasted him until they were devouring one another, wet and openmouthed.

He broke contact to move next to her on the couch and hauled her into his lap. "I'm not sure what you're trying to prove, Janie, but keep going."

She couldn't remember, either. Trent's hands kneaded her naked ass cheeks as her hips ground against his erection. Janelle hissed, so far gone that even minimal contact threatened to send her over the edge.

He tugged her tank top up. Janelle sat back to pull it over her head. She tossed it aside and hesitated. She wasn't going to have sex with someone she'd met barely twenty-four hours ago. But the way he was staring at her breasts in their pretty lace prison made remembering her boundaries extremely difficult. For the first time in her life, Janelle was happy to have been excessively endowed in the boobs department.

The tip of his tongue poked out from his sensuous bottom lip and licked slowly across before disappearing. "Janie. Jesus. You're incredible."

Then, he leaned forward to kiss his way over the tops of her breasts. If there was any blood left in her brain, it immediately rushed to swell them against the fabric of her bra. Trent sucked a sensitized nipple through the sheer lace, and she arched against him; Janelle clutched his short hair as every nerve sang and her nipple tightened painfully.

"Off," she gasped. "Take it off."

He fumbled with the clasp in the center of her back. "I can't figure it out."

Janelle almost laughed. "Aren't you an expert at this?"

Trent smiled, but the joy in eyes dimmed. "It's been a long time."

"Really?"

"Since Penny. Six years, maybe? I stopped keeping count."

Janelle pushed herself back and sat up, straddling his thighs. "You can't be serious."

He nodded once, the heavy fringe of his lashes shading his blue gaze. Nothing in his posture changed, but Janelle sensed the tension in his body. "Is there a reason?"

He laughed, startled. "You mean did Bad Penny give me some incurable disease?"

"I...Yes, basically."

"No, Janie, I've never had an STD. I was in a desert war zone for six years. There's no Tinder for active duty army grunts." His hands rested loosely on her hips, the only thing separating them the thin strap of her thong. Trent poked a finger beneath the edge and ran it slowly along her hip. She shuddered as the touch radiated through her abdomen.

Well then. Carry on.

Janelle couldn't. Not without more reassurance. "Can you prove it?"

Trent laughed again, for real this time. His arousal hadn't subsided at all during what should've been an awkward conversation. It wasn't, though.

"A condition of my enlistment was monthly drug screening and physical testing. There's random drug checks for all enlisted personnel, but I got special scrutiny. If they hadn't been desperate for warm bodies, I'd never have been allowed in. I have all six years of records if you want the full report."

"Later," Janelle replied, flicking her bra open. She tossed it aside. Once they'd gotten as far as exchanging their true names, he'd been nothing but honest with her; there was no reason to doubt him now. Besides, she had two condoms in her bag. Trent's big hands skimmed up her back, pulling her close. He buried one hand in her hair and tilted her body to one side to kiss her thoroughly. Unhurriedly. She pressed against him, her breasts aching and hard.

She hated it when men touched her chest, but the rough glide of Trent's thumb over her nipple brought incredible, short-lived satisfaction, and left a surge of desire in its wake. He cupped her full breast in his hand. Janelle moaned softly against his mouth. Her thong was soaked through, and she shifted away from the tempting ridge of his cock. If he knew what this was doing to her, they'd be on the bed screwing within seconds, condoms or no condoms.

She wasn't taking the risk. Not while her last few brain cells were still functioning.

"Janie," he whispered. His throat worked as he swallowed.

She had to do something to put out the fire raging between them, before she did something she'd regret. Lifting her butt, she moved one leg and then the other to the floor, her heart galloping. Trent's cool dark eyes were hooded and wary as she knelt between his knees. She hesitated, the muscles in her throat convulsing tightly.

She glanced down and Trent's dick twitched hard. The round head poked out of his underwear.

Her gaze trailed up from the intimidating lump at the apex of his muscular thighs to the corded muscles of his abdomen. Higher. His small nipples topping perfectly formed pectorals.

Higher.

Janelle forced herself to look at the broad spread of his shoulders, the clean delineation of bicep and deltoid. The sight made everything between her bellybutton and her mid-thighs turn to jelly.

His Adam's apple jutted above the hollow of his throat and led to the hard line of his jaw. Above, a sensuous mouth with a hint of humor at the corners. His mouth was moist at the center as though he'd licked his lips in anticipation.

Up again. The straight line of his nose came into view.

The last was the hardest part. Her eyes met Trent's and her entire body flared in response. His eyes weren't cool any more. They were incandescent.

"Will you let me?" A whisper, a plea.

Trent answered with an almost imperceptible nod.

Janelle hooked her index fingers into the waistband of his boxer shorts and inched them down until they cleared his narrow hips. He shifted to let her pull them over his ass, freeing his dick with a happy bob. Janelle sat back on her heels to pull the fabric down over his knees. From there, Trent kicked them off over his big feet.

Janelle wrapped her fingers around his thick length. She'd never been so excited about giving oral. She enjoyed it, but there'd never been an answering pulse in her body. Janelle ran her tongue up the vein on the underside of his penis as she ran the pad of her thumb down his tight testicles. Trent's raw gasp told her he hadn't been expecting that.

She followed the path of her tongue with her thumb, then licked the precum off the head. Then she wrapped her fingers around him and smoothed them up, followed it with a twist. Janelle's mouth fell open as part of his skin slid up and over the head.

What the fuck?

Oh. Trent wasn't circumcised. She glanced up. "You're not…"

"First time?" he rasped.

She nodded. "Do I need to do anything special?"

"Use the foreskin."

Janelle felt her eyebrows arch. How? Experimentally, she ran her hand up and down the shaft. A hood went up to cover the head, then slipped down again on the return trip. She did it again with more force. Trent's body relaxed, though the muscles in his hips flexed as she found a rhythm.

Now that she'd figured out how it worked, she licked the top again, tasting his salt. Then she opened her mouth and took his plump head into her mouth, working the foreskin with her lips and tongue. He dug his fingers into her hair, tense and hard as she took him further into her mouth, a ragged moan escaping his parted lips.

Her pussy tightened at the sound. She was so close. What would Trent say if she started touching herself? He might not notice. If he did, he might think it was weird. Better to focus on getting him off. She could take care of business later.

Trent's cock swelled against her tongue. Janelle gagged a little as the first pump of semen hit the back of her throat. She gagged, mastered herself and sat back on her heels, wiped a drip of cum from her chin and pumped her hand over him until it was sticky. That was a *lot* of cock. But apart from choking at the end, she'd done it. She collapsed with her back against the side of the bed.

I did it. She'd given a porn star head, and she was strangely proud of it.

"Janie, I…" Trent gasped. Milky fluid puddled in the grooves between the corded muscles of his abdomen. "Christ." He lay boneless against back of the couch, eyes barely open.

"Good?" Experimentally, she sucked a drip from her hand. He tasted good. Salty and clean, almost wholesome.

"You have no idea."

A slow grin of pride spread over her lips. Janelle crawled up from the little nest she'd made in the blankets and headed to the bathroom. Her need hadn't subsided at all.

"Where are you going?" Trent called after her, but if he couldn't figure it out, she wasn't going to waste breath informing him.

9

Trent idly listened to the water run as his heart rate slowed down. It was a good thing he was in peak condition, or the blowjob would've given him heart failure. Who'd have guessed not-so-sweet little Janie could suck cock like that?

He was still laying there gasping like a fish stranded on a beach when she returned. She'd either ditched the thong or covered it up with the silky shorts that barely covered her ass. Too bad; he'd spent the last couple of minutes fantasizing about tearing them off with his teeth. Janie curled up on the quarter of the loveseat he wasn't manspreading all over and dabbed at the mess on his stomach with a warm washcloth.

"What are you doing?" he demanded.

She glanced up, crankiness in her green eyes. "Helping you clean up. I'm nice that way."

What. The. Fuck. They weren't done. What about her? He might need a few minutes—debatable. It had only taken him three minutes of watching Janelle's ass to get hard again after jerking off in the shower. It was going to take more than one blowjob to work off years of celibacy, no matter how fantastic.

Trent captured her small hand in his and tossed the washcloth over the bed. It landed out of sight with a wet plop. He rolled up to pin Janie against the couch. She tried to scoot back, but there was nowhere for her to go.

Determined to keep things moving the right direction, he sank his fingers into her long hair and pulled her close for a kiss. She let him, but she held back, and her mouth tasted oddly minty.

Perplexed, he pulled back. "Did you rinse your mouth out?"

"Do you object?" She'd covered up her magnificent chest, too, with the white tank top that hid nothing. Resignation flattened her talented mouth.

"If it's good enough for your mouth, it's good enough for mine."

Janie's eyes hardened into emeralds. "You don't mean that."

"Good sex isn't clean and neat. Who the hell taught you otherwise?"

She pushed him away and opted for the chair in the corner of the room.

Someone, somewhere, had really fucked with Janie's head. A surge of white-hot blood lust to hunt the guy down consumed Trent, until he realized it probably hadn't been only one guy. This kind of messed-up didn't happen overnight. "You want to stop, we stop."

Her cheeks stained deep red beneath her tan. Janie's attention rested briefly on his naked genitals. Trent shifted so she could get a better look. When she glanced up, he grinned. "You should give me a try."

Janie unfurled from the chair and pointedly checked the clock. "We missed your afternoon session, and if we don't get ready we're going to miss the networking cocktail hour too."

"We could skip it. We should skip it. We're just getting started, Janie."

She tossed her hair over her shoulder and began to dress. "This is important, Trent. You can't miss it. I can't either. I'm on a mission this evening, and I can't duck it just because we decided to make out on the couch."

As badly as she wanted him, there was something else she wanted more. Just his luck. He finally approached a woman, and she rejected *him*. But no, was no, was no. It never meant anything different.

Trent pushed himself off the couch and headed for the bathroom. "Okay, doll. I'm not gonna fight you."

Let her stew in her own juices for the evening. Until she came around, he was in a quandary. He wasn't about to pressure her into anything she didn't want to do. But he owed her an orgasm or several. It had never occurred to Trent that Janelle might not let him touch her. At all.

"May I borrow your shirt?" Janelle asked the instant the bathroom door cracked open, brandishing the plain white dress shirt Trent had worn the day before like a shield.

"Sure."

He had every reason to be generous. He hadn't had to get her off. No, she'd panicked and now she vaguely regretted it because all she could think about was Trent's naked body and how good his big cock had tasted, which had her worked up with no release. She zipped into the bathroom, clicked the door locked and ran the shower.

"Don't take too long, we're running late," Mr. Hustle shouted through the door.

"Be right out," Janelle yelled back as she slammed the shower door closed and buried her fingers in her sex-starved pussy. A completely unsatisfying ripple took the edge off, but not much more. She didn't want her hand. Her vibrator wouldn't even have been much help. Her body wanted Trent, but she was terrified she'd end up more desperate and ashamed than she already felt if she slept with him.

Taking that step meant veering off the path she'd set for herself years ago, when she'd been naïve enough to believe that if she followed the rules of life, she'd be rewarded with love, a family, and a decent job. It meant charting a different course, one where her successes and failures reflected on her, personally. It meant owning her decisions. It meant finding a new path, one that wasn't cribbed from Crystal, Ben, or anyone else.

A path all her own.

She decided whether to fuck Trent. For now, her decision was not to. She liked him way too much already. There was no way he saw this as anything but a fling. Getting over Ben was the plan; getting hurt again wasn't.

Janelle toweled off, brushed her hair into a long twist and clipped it into place. A few strokes with her mascara wand, eyeliner, and lipstick and her game face was back in place. She wiggled into a clean thong, pulled the too-short skirt over her hips, and buttoned the white shirt over her green bra. It hung like a shroud over her frame. Janelle tucked the back hem into her skirt and tied the front in a knot. Then she worked the sleeves through the cardigan, rolled them up over her forearms and buttoned the cardigan over her chest. The extra fabric added fifteen pounds to her frame. Perfect.

The ensemble needed one final touch. Janelle exited the bathroom and grabbed her bag. Trent loomed near the door, relaxed and handsome in his dark suit.

"Ready?"

"Almost." Janelle yanked the final pair of shoes out of the bag. Technically, they weren't hers, but Alyssa didn't need them while she was off sailing with Marc De Luna. The black patent Louboutins added four inches to her height. Combined with the up-do, the pink reading glasses and the shirt, she looked easily ten years older. They probably wouldn't even card her at the bar, which was a good thing since Kyle still had her ID. Not that she had any money to buy a drink.

"What are those?" Trent demanded as she worked her feet into the gorgeous torture devices.

"Shoes."

"Stripper shoes," he commented admiringly.

"Watch it, Mace. They're my sister's, and she wore them at her office every day."

"Where'd she work, a brothel?" He held the door for her, openly ogling her legs.

Janelle tapped his chest with mock annoyance. "An advertising agency, you pervert."

"Were they advertising Viagra?"

Janelle tried to stifle a giggle, but it escaped out her nose in an inelegant snort. Trent grinned and shortened his step to match hers as she tottered down the hallway to the elevators. She'd gotten pretty good at walking in them, but his smile lit up his face and made her knees wobble. The air conditioning didn't seem to be working, either. She wished she could take off the cardigan without exposing her bra through the white shirt. "Remember, I'm Rachel now."

The elevator doors opened, revealing a packed car.

"We'll take the next one." Trent pulled her back, a possessive gesture that did nothing to tamp down her arousal.

"You'll wait ten minutes for another. We can squeeze you in." A family with teenagers jostled aside, leaving a small gap. Janelle stepped in, with Trent hard behind her.

Really hard. His hand rested on her hip, a fraction of an inch from grabbing her ass outright. His broad chest pressed against her back. With the added height of her heels, the top of her head came up nearly to his nose. The elevator door dinged open, and Trent brushed his lips along the rim of her ear. Janelle closed her eyes and swallowed. *Keep going.*

"They're fuck me shoes. Trying to tell me something?"

Her eyes flew open. "I use words to communicate, Mace. Not footwear."

How could he whisper that in front of kids? But no one had heard. The family was busily grabbing their bags and shuffling off the elevator. Now she couldn't get the thought of him banging her while wearing these shoes out of her head.

Olivia spotted them and waved as they walked into the buzzing conference room. She introduced them to a trio of men, two from government organizations and one from a major corporation. Janelle played up her Rachel persona, dropping her voice a bit so she didn't sound so young. Trent excused himself to the packed bar. By the time he returned fifteen minutes later, Janelle and Olivia were chatting up another group of technology suits.

"She's good at this. Seven cards tucked away in her shirt pocket already." Olivia accepted a glass of red wine, took a sip and pursed her lips. "Typical conference crap. How's the white?"

"Sour," Janelle reported back, drinking it anyway. She was a fake, but this was a networking event, and she was going to network her heart out.

"The whisky's not exactly top shelf either." Trent glanced around. "There's the Solomon guy we met at lunch."

"Let's say hello." Janelle beelined it toward the older man in the gray suit.

"Aren't you going to come say hi?" Olivia jerked her head.

"Go meet him, if you want to. I already have." Janelle overheard Trent's response and was of half a mind to drag him along, but he was a big boy and could handle himself. She positioned herself so she could watch him while introducing Olivia to Russ Solomon and his circle.

The instant they were out of sight, a curvy blonde woman sidled up to Trent. He bent to listen to something she said, and his expression shuttered. The stranger grabbed Trent's ass and squeezed. He angled sharply away, backing into a suit and causing the man to spill his drink.

"Excuse me." Olivia marched across the room, murder in her eyes.

Janelle hobbled after her, incredulous at what she'd just witnessed. Incandescent fury burned through her. "Did she just *do* that?"

"Not the first time I've seen it happen to him." Olivia said. The blonde woman skulked away, giggling, wobbling on her high heels. "Trent. You all right?"

"I'm fine." But he didn't look fine, his handsome features schooled into blankness, but anger etched around his eyes and mouth.

"You should've used your middle name…"

"I can't, and I'm not changing it no matter how much I hate it. My parents gave it to me." Trent's scowl deepened.

"Now you have to tell me what it is." Janelle set her fake glasses up on top of her head.

Olivia made a dismissive sound. "He'll never tell you."

"It's Rishi." Trent glared at his friend. "I'm not ashamed of it, Liv. My mom liked the meaning, but I'm obviously not Hindu."

"Rishi. Trent Rishi Mason." Janelle muttered the names quietly, trying them out. "I like it, but yeah, you're better off sticking with Mace for your cover identity."

Olivia glanced around. "Lady Grabby Hands left. Let's hope she gets the hangover she's earned, and move on with our evening."

An hour later, they were all into their second terrible drink, and the stack of business cards tucked into her shirt pocket resembled a cell phone under the pink cardigan.

"Look at this." She patted the lump over her breast. "I'm doing your job for you, Mace."

"I'm looking," Trent replied, his eyes dropping to the gap between the placket of his shirt where a hint of cleavage was visible.

"You'll be sharing those contacts, right?" Olivia gave Mace a sidelong look, but it was fake shade.

"A lot of good it'll do us having a mess of cards for people we barely met," he grumped.

Janelle stumbled a little on her high heels and grabbed Trent's arm to steady herself. She tapped her temple above the arm of her reading glasses. They weren't very strong, but they gave the room a fuzzy blur that made her feel more intoxicated than she was. "I have a system. The ones on top are contacts who mentioned issuing RFPs in the next few months. The ones in the middle are long-term prospects, and the ones at the back of the pack are unlikely to lead to anything. There's two flipped cards separating the sections."

Olivia laughed. "Rachel's a genius, Mace. I hope you're planning on keeping her around."

"For the weekend," Trent shrugged. His blue striped tie was askew and the first button of his shirt undone. He held his drink in one hand and his other stuck in his pocket, which made the hem of his jacket ride up to expose the narrow span of his waist and hips.

Damn. Of all the heroes in Las Vegas, she had to hook up with the one who'd starred in his own porn video. She'd given him a blow job, and the memory made her nerves buzz like a hive of horny bees. The lust was so strong she couldn't speak. Lady Grabby Hands had been out of line, though Janelle sympathized with desiring Trent enough to do stupid things.

"What are you two doing for dinner?" Olivia asked.

"No plans," Trent replied, removing his hand from his pocket. His suit dropped and hid the view. Janelle glanced away.

"I've been invited to a vendor event. You're welcome to come along."

"I don't have any—" Janelle snapped her mouth shut.

Olivia smiled and touched her arm. "Don't worry. They're always happy to flash the Amex for new customers. The rep pays. It's how the industry works."

"If Mace is okay with it." Janelle glanced up, uncertain.

"Everyone needs dinner." The look he gave her told Janelle he'd make her dessert, if she let him.

She smoothed her skirt with warm palms and shivered. Trent looked away, and Janelle felt as if the sun had set, a cool shadow replacing the heat of his attention. Her feet were starting to hurt, but the group was moving and there wasn't time to change shoes. She could only hope that the mix of bad wine, good company, and high heels didn't make her so weak-kneed she needed Trent's help staying upright. Because touching him was a short, slippery slope to sex with a man she still knew too little about.

HOURS LATER, Janelle and Trent stumbled through the door of the hotel room. Janelle scraped her shoulder against the wall until she was far enough inside the room to let the door bang shut, then kicked off the shiny high heels. Her toes expanded and stretched as she wiggled them. Bliss.

Janelle threw herself down on the bed without ceremony. If Mysterious Mace Mason brushed against her one more time, Janelle was going to pounce. During the cab ride back to the hotel, she'd been squished against his side in the middle of the back seat. She'd barely uttered a word, overwhelmed at the sensation of being pressed against his body for a full twenty minutes. Every bump and pothole threatened to send her into spontaneous orgasm.

Either she needed to make a move, or she needed to move on.

The bed dipped. Janelle propped her chin on her forearms. Trent had discarded his jacket and loosened his tie, leaning back against the headboard.

"Hey. You did great tonight." His touch was gentle as he pulled away the clip holding her hair. It was the first deliberate move he'd made since this afternoon.

"At what? Talking? Eating food someone else paid for? Drinking your wine?" She hadn't been brave enough to ask for her own glass without an ID, but she'd consumed most of his drink. She wasn't drunk. Tired, overstimulated, and confused, but her judgment was otherwise unimpaired. Which was why she tilted her head into Trent's palm as he ran his fingers through her hair, even though it drove her to the brink of *yes*.

"At learning the tech contracting business. At making connections. Even Olivia was impressed."

His hand sent sensual shockwaves through her body. Janelle relaxed physically, but her words were ruthless. "I got everything wrong. I always get everything wrong."

Trent's hand froze mid-stroke. "You get a lot of things right, Janie. You work hard. You've accomplished—"

"Nothing. I've accomplished nothing, Trent." She pushed back on her knees and sat up. She hiccupped. "I ran my mouth asking dumb questions this evening."

"You accomplished more tonight than I've managed this whole conference. Look at the stack of cards you collected." Trent leaned back against the headboard, kicked off his shoes and socks, and put one foot up.

Janelle glanced down and plucked the thick stack out of his shirt pocket. "The only reason they talked to me was because I wore four-inch fuck-me heels and a short skirt."

Trent accepted the stack of cards and placed them on the nightstand. Janelle unbuttoned the pink cardigan and fought her way free of it. His wrinkled shirt did nothing to conceal the dark outline of her bra.

Trent's attention flicked to her chest. "They talked to you because you're funny and friendly and you ask a lot of questions. You're interested, and interesting."

"I ask a lot of questions because I don't know shit about internet security."

"Yeah. Which makes you extremely compelling to a bunch of nerds stuck in a conference room talking shop about thwarting spam and I-D-10-T errors."

"What error?" Janelle liked learning this new field, but all the jargon made her feel like a half-wit. She didn't appreciate Trent trotting it out just now.

"It spells 'idiot.' User error is the nicer term." He loosened his tie and tossed it aside, his shirt collar framing his Adams' apple. She wanted to lick her way up to his jaw.

"Oh." Janelle stood up to prevent herself from taking action. His shirt billowed around her body, immersing her in a cloud of pheromones that hit harder than any drug. His scent had surrounded her for hours. She yanked the hem out of the waistband of her skirt, desperate to get the damn thing off. Aware of Trent watching her move, and still trying with vain stupidity to pretend she wasn't flirting her ass off. "I figured it was because I have boobs."

She flicked the first button open, then the another. Trent didn't take his eyes off her as the fabric gaped. Janelle tossed her hair over her shoulder and let the shirt fall a few inches.

"Janie." He spoke with coiled intensity, like a tightly leashed attack dog. "What are we doing?"

"Do you like watching me?" she asked, her voice an unintended purr. Okay, maybe her judgment wasn't a hundred percent, but it wasn't because of alcohol. She'd never been so turned on. Ever. Lust was a lot more potent than booze.

"I love it. I'd like touching you more." Trent's voice had dropped to a growl. It resonated within her body, even though she was pacing at the end of the bed and he was still where he'd been, at the head.

"I can't let that happen," she whispered, though her fingers disobeyed and set another button free.

"Why not, Janie?" Trent's voice sounded as desperate and confused as she felt.

She was being *such* an asshole, teasing him like this. Taking pleasure in it was horrible, it made her an awful person, but she nonetheless slipped her tortured feet into the fuck-me heels she'd kicked off and continued her slow strip tease along the foot of the bed.

Trent consumed her with his gaze. Janelle *wanted* to be dessert. She was on fire.

"Because I'm a good girl, Trent," she whispered. A taunt. Another button set free and she was exposed to the sternum. Janelle turned her back and slowly unzipped her skirt.

"From here, Janie, you look like you want to be a little bad. What does it mean to you? Being good?"

Janelle shimmied her skirt over her hips before responding. The hem of Trent's shirt covered her ass, but she hiked it up to give him a good view of her thong while she shoved her skirt down to her ankles and stepped out. Being good meant approximately anything other than what she was doing right now.

But being good didn't feel half as right as being bad.

"It means I play by the rules. I don't cheat, and I don't sleep with men who are in relationships with other people." Janelle licked her lips, thinking of Crystal and Barry, and wondering about Trent and Penny. She couldn't get a bead on their relationship. If Penny was disabled, they couldn't be seeing one another, could they? Yet Trent didn't act like he and his ex were completely over. Who went six years without a new partner?

You would.

"Being a good girl means sex is never meaningless to me, Trent. If I were capable of having sex without getting attached, I'd have done it by now." Janelle peeked over her shoulder, her heart fluttering in her throat.

Trent swallowed. She could see the way his throat moved. Janelle turned and let her skirt fall. He peeled off the bed like an advertisement for Pilates, vertebrae by vertebrae. He beckoned with lifted arms, and Janelle tumbled into them. Their mouths met, clumsy with need and unfamiliar terrain. Trent helped her get the rest of his shirt off, her touch sure but fumbling over the buttons. Before he'd freed his wrists, her hands slid up his chest. Warm muscles bunched beneath her touch. Liquid heat pooled in her abdomen. Janie gasped and ground her hips forcefully against his. Trent was hard, and huge.

Just get it over with. Stop living in the past and start making new memories to replace the old. Forget Ben, so pale and skinny and *young* compared to Trent's masculine worldliness.

She'd been so mad at her sister for once suggesting that she and Ben had been too young to be a serious couple. Here, away from everything familiar, it was easier to concede the point. The thought was gone as Trent rolled her onto her back and kissed her hard. Janelle opened, giving him everything, no longer wanting to be good. No longer wanting anything but him.

HIS TROUSERS CHAFED as all the blood rushed to his cock in a primal response. The only thing holding him back was Trent's sudden terror that he'd hurt her if he unleashed the full intensity of his libido.

Penny liked it when you let go. Trent shook away the intrusive thought. That was Penny. Janelle's body was a new experience, one he intended to savor, if he could manage it. The impulse to get inside her, right now, was overwhelming, but he held the line. Barely.

"Do you not want this?" Janelle pulled back, questioning. The uncertainty in her eyes dampened the raging fire of lust long enough for Trent to get ahold of himself.

"What makes you think that?" *Penny never had to ask.* Trent willed the phantom of his ex-girlfriend away.

"You're very gentle. I thought you'd be...I don't know, rougher?" Janelle bit her lip. "The way you kissed me this afternoon. On the couch."

Her words were gasoline poured onto a forest fire. Trent forced himself to breathe. "I want you, Janie. I'm trying not to hurt you."

"You're not," she whispered. Trent bent his head to taste the fine skin along her neck. "In the video you weren't gentle. With her."

Phantom Penny was back, louche and mocking. *We're not regular, normal people. We're stars, we burn bright and hot.*

"How do you know? You only saw a few minutes." Trent captured Janelle's breast with one hand, and she arched into his palm.

"I watched it all the way through while I was on hold with the credit card company." She whispered the confession into his ear, her lips brushing the rim. Trent wished she'd lick his ear, bite the edge just hard enough that he'd feel it. Suck his earlobe. The way Penny had known to do.

Comprehension muscled through Trent's erotic haze. "*All* the way through? To the end?"

Janelle nodded against his neck, her hair sliding over his shoulder, tickling him. His arousal whipsawed into horror. The last ten minutes of the video were Penny jamming a toy up his ass and sucking him until he came *everywhere*. The money shot was legendary. Early in his army career, his fellow soldiers had given him an untold amount of shit over it, insinuating that he was gay. That didn't bother him, and he'd never minded drawing heat away from the one soldier in their unit who did bat for the other team. The easiest response had been to grin and say, "did you see who I was fucking?" Yet his offhand bravado had never completely camouflaged the mortification of having his most private, intimate moments exposed for anyone to find in a few clicks. The way the blonde woman at the party earlier clearly had done.

Janelle made a feral little growl and arched against him. It was the hottest sound he'd ever heard, though with her face buried in his shoulder it was barely audible. She hiked one naked leg to his waist. His mind shorted out as he slid his hand up her lean, strong thigh to cup her ass.

"Touch me," she demanded hoarsely. Trent traced the silky line of her thong down the valley between her buttocks to the softest part of her body.

His fingers brushed the fine wire of her pubic hair, so unexpected it shocked him. He'd have sworn he felt the texture with his entire body. Penny had always been bare, almost every woman in the industry was. It had become normalized. The difference kept him wholly present as he slowly savored her most feminine parts. He slid a finger down her center, and Janelle shuddered in his arms. Trent pressed upward, wondering. Desperate to touch.

Christ. She was completely soaked. A tortured mewl reverberated over his nerves where she panted into the crook of his neck. So far, Janie was making this easy on him.

"You poor thing," he whispered, gliding his index finger over the thick folds of her sex to her clit. She gasped and angled against him.

Trent's erection hardened to the point of pain. "How long have you been like this?"

"Since I sucked you off," she mumbled, writhing against his hand. "I've had the girl version of blue balls all evening."

He groaned, circling her clit through wet fabric before tracing her outline back down to her center. Trent hooked his finger beneath her thong, edged it aside, and repeated the slow tease. Up to her clit, slow circle, down. This time, he easily sank his index finger to the third knuckle. She was so close, panting hot against his neck. His arm was trapped under her, holding her close as she arched and rubbed her tits against him. With his free hand, the one holding her open as he thumbed her clit, he curled two fingers to find the rough patch of nerves inside.

Janelle bucked and whimpered as he increased pressure. *That's the spot.*

"I want to be inside you," he gasped as her pussy clenched around his hand.

She didn't answer. She was riding out the longest orgasm he'd ever watched a woman experience. He drove her ruthlessly higher, the pulses slowing, then picking up again as he drove her right into the next one. Relentless. Until Janie couldn't hold back the sound of her pleasure any more, and let loose with a staccato scream.

JANELLE'S entire body shook as the remnants of the orgasm she'd been dying for subsided. All afternoon and evening, she'd been carrying on an imaginary conversation with Crystal and Rachel in her head, which went something along the lines of:

Pretend-Crystal: *It's been 36 hours and you haven't fucked your insanely hot roommate yet? Are you even heterosexual?*

Followed by pretend-Rachel's rebuke: *You can't have sex with a porn star you barely know. Even if you don't go home with a souvenir disease, you get attached, and you'll get hurt. Don't do it.*

On and on they went, imaginary good and bad angels perched on either shoulder. Yes, Rachel had basically ordered her to get laid earlier on the phone, but Janelle was certain Trent wasn't what she'd had in mind.

I want to be inside you. His words haunted her and brought Janelle back to the moment. Though her skin prickled with heat, she shivered. "I have condoms."

He stilled. "Good. I don't."

"I guess you didn't pack for this sort of trip." Rueful, Janelle unglued her face from Trent's neck and peered up through the mess of her hair. His shirt was twisted into a corset around her torso, but more problematic, he was still fully clothed. Janelle lost all fine motor control as she fumbled with the buttons holding his lapels closed. "Take your shirt off."

Trent unhelpfully attacked the buttons at her belly button.

"I meant the one you're wearing." She sat up and pulled his dress shirt over her head without further attempting to slide plastic disks through small holes. That level of dexterity was beyond her.

"You're not as nice as you pretend to be." Trent held up the hand he'd used to get her off. One at a time he licked each digit clean. Janelle's eyes widened and her mouth popped open. A puff of astonishment escaped without sound. Trent reached over touched her bottom lip. "You taste good. Try it."

Carefully, the tip of her tongue met his finger. Janelle made a face. "Gross."

He shook his head and tucked a strand of black hair behind her flaming ear. "I don't agree. Tell me what you want me to do."

"Kiss me," she whispered.

Trent chuckled. "Where?"

She glanced down, her neck muscles convulsing as she swallowed the words. "Everywhere."

He picked up her hand and pressed a gentle kiss to the inside of her wrist. "There?"

"Guess again." She licked her lips. "You're still wearing too many clothes."

Trent obliged her by removing his shirt and undershirt. "Now we're even. Where do you want my mouth, Janie?"

His lips quirked up at the corner as he pulled her down for a kiss. "On my body."

"Not specific enough. C'mon Janie, use your words. Tell me what you want and let me give it to you."

Why is this so difficult? Most guys would've been on her like a leech, forget the consent gymnastics. Ben wouldn't have pressed her to name what she wanted. He was nice, which was possibly the reason the sex hadn't been very good. It had been neat and polite. If there was a flavor blander than vanilla, it would've described their love life to a T.

Janelle didn't want vanilla anymore, but she didn't know what to do differently. Couldn't Trent just boss her around until she figured it out? Even a few pointers would've helped.

"I want you to go down on me," she whispered.

"Lay back." He patted the pillow.

Janelle stretched one arm toward the light on the nightstand and switched it off.

"How am I supposed to see what I'm doing?" Trent complained, though the room wasn't completely dark. Ambient light from the hall area inside the room door wasn't exactly mood lighting, but it wasn't pitch black, either.

"Legs open, Janie. I won't get far if you're suffocating me." Trent grinned. "Although that would be the second-best way to go."

"What would be the first best?" Janelle inquired, arranging the pillows. That was more like it. He was the experienced one, and she needed instruction. Desperately. The only thing worse than admitting, however privately, that her sex life was as limited as it had been disappointing, was her abject terror that she'd be a terrible lay. Trent's last partner had a set a high bar.

"Dying mid-orgasm."

"You've thought about it a lot." She wished she hadn't turned out the light. The darkness made every movement more intense. All she could see were their interconnected shadows. The head of the bed was in the darkest part of the room by design. Trent shifted his weight and nudged her thighs apart. She yelped and looked down as his hair brushed her inner thighs. He kissed the sensitive skin of her inner thighs, and it elicited a gasp.

"Everything okay?"

"Yes." Trent slicked his tongue straight up the center to her clit. It was the sexual equivalent of dropping a hair dryer into a bathtub. *Zap.* Her entire attention was on the sensation of his mouth at work. Her hands curled into the sheets, anticipating more.

Yet all he did was tease. Tiny licks, the barest contact, no fingers. It was the most maddeningly unsatisfying sensation in the world, driving her crazy with no hope of getting her where she wanted to go. She tried inching her body closer. "Trent?"

"Hm?" He poked his head out from between her legs.

"Harder."

His laughter between her thighs almost sent her over the edge. "Anything you say, Janie."

Trent tongue-fucked her with an enthusiasm she'd have sworn was feigned if he didn't sound so damn happy doing it. Her hands scrabbled in his hair as he latched onto her clit and sucked, making Janelle come so hard her nails nearly tore through the wadded sheets she clutched.

She couldn't speak. Trent grunted and shifted beneath her, moving Janelle on top until she was sitting on his hips. His hard cock a hard ridge under her. He still wore his trousers, and the friction of fine wool against her inner thighs was delicious. Sucking air into her lungs, Janelle ran her hands up Trent's chest and shuddered.

"You're hesitating." His voice was ragged.

"I keep having this imagined conversation. I have two friends, Crystal and Rachel."

"Is this the real one? Camping Rachel?"

Janelle nodded. "Crystal's the one who recommended the whole sugar baby thing. In my mind, Crystal's telling me to get a condom on you already. Rachel's telling me I'd be insane to take this any further."

"What would you tell Rachel or Crystal, in your situation now?" Trent asked.

Damn him.

"I'd tell either of them to go for it," she whispered.

"Well." Trent's hands anchored her hips. "What are you waiting for?"

It wasn't as if Janelle was protecting herself from loss, or hurt. She'd been falling for Trent since the moment he'd reluctantly saved her from being stranded in a strange city. Only the Penny question held her back.

"Are you still seeing her?" she blurted.

Trent started, and a wariness crept into his posture. "Penny? No. We broke up before her overdose."

His words were reassuring, but Janelle sensed it wasn't the entire truth. Still, it meant that this experience didn't need to stay in Las Vegas. There was a possibility for this to become something real. If he'd let it.

Before she could second-guess herself again, Janelle slid off the bed and scrambled for the two condoms in the pocket of her bag. Her hands shook as she tore open a packet. The first attempt, she tried rolling the condom on the wrong direction.

Trent tossed the damaged condom aside and held out his hand for the second one.

Janelle pushed her hair back. "I'm sorry."

"About what? A piece of latex?" He rolled on the condom, the right way.

She didn't answer. It was too embarrassing to admit she had almost no practice with using them. She'd gone on birth control right away with Ben, and she was still on it—not that Trent needed to know that. It was extra insurance.

Janelle straddled Trent's body and lowered herself over him. The sensation of his head pressing into her stretched her to the limit. By the time she'd taken half of him, her breath came in shallow pants. He strained upward, hips flexing beneath her and driving his cock deep. A sound emanated from her, unrecognizable as human.

He pulled back. "Like that?"

"Again." Janelle dropped her forehead onto Trent's shoulder as he surged into her body. She was so full of cock she couldn't do anything but sob with wordless gratitude. It didn't hurt at all. Pressure took her right to the edge of pain, but he was careful never to push her over.

Tight, controlled motions sent waves of pleasure cascading through her abdomen. It was *amazing*.

Trent dropped his hand onto her hip, finding her clit with his thumb. Janelle gripped his muscular shoulder with one hand as he stroked her. The orgasm hit hard. She was unprepared for the explosion radiating outward from her core as everything convulsed. For a moment, she was sightless, lost, completely interior. Then she pulled her head up and sucked air into her lungs.

Trent's still-hard cock moved.

"Oh, my god," Janelle breathed. "I didn't think that was possible."

"What wasn't?" His voice rumbled through her, a physical sensation more than sound.

"Orgasm during intercourse."

Trent laughed. "You're so clinical. And if you didn't know it was possible, you were absolutely doing it wrong."

"For once, I agree."

"I'm not done," Trent shifted so she was beneath him, face down. He pushed one knee up high and opened her legs as far as they would go and pushed the tip of his cock inside her. Only the tip, back and forth across the sensitive nerves just above her entrance.

Janelle gasped as her body strained to meet his. "More."

"More what?"

"I want your cock, Trent. All of it."

He drove himself into her, on a mission this time, the steady fill-with-draw rhythm driving Janelle higher again. She got there first, barely. He followed hard, pounding into her with a ferocity she'd feel later.

Spent, Trent collapsed on top of her, his weight pressing her body into the mattress. Janelle traced the outline of his shoulder with her finger. "Thank you."

"For what?"

Janelle framed his face with both hands and pressed her lips to his forehead. "I needed to feel good for once."

"So did I." Softly, he kissed her back. "But, if you want to have any more fun, one of us is going to have to hit the convenience store downstairs."

Janelle wiggled off him and into her clothes. "I'll go."

"You don't have any money."

"Oh. Right." Annoyed embarrassment flooded her, chasing away the last flush of arousal. Trent rolled off the bed and pulled on his wrinkled trousers.

"I'll go with you."

His words made her heart flutter, the way it had the day she'd arrived and been terrified out her mind, only in a nice way this time. Trent wasn't going to make her do the walk of shame alone.

In the small drugstore, Janelle peeled off down a separate aisle as they looked for the prophylactics. They met at the end, both spotting the perfunctory selection hanging on the wall behind a careworn, middle-aged woman missing a front tooth.

Trent leaned over and whispered, "Let's get the ten-pack."

Janelle fought a grin and lost. The box landed on the counter. Trent produced cash. Her smile wilted. Independence. She craved it even more than she did Trent's body. The kept woman thing wasn't her style. Why had she ever thought it could be?

It that moment, it was blindingly clear where she'd gone wrong with Ben.

At nineteen, she'd clung to him like a vine to a tree trunk as she'd struggled through college. After, she'd been determined to follow him to Texas, get married, and have kids. As much as he'd loved her, maybe he'd wanted to experience dating before settling down to start a family.

Maybe, she'd been a little selfish. A lot selfish.

It might've been good for her to give dating an honest try, too, instead adopting a defensive crouch. She'd have had some experience before she met Trent and not bumbled around like a fool. Not that he appeared to mind. Still...

"Janelle?"

Ice stiffened her spine as she turned to the man behind them and started. A middle-aged man, paunchy and balding, gaped at her as he held a phone dangling from his fingers.

She blanched, her knuckles white against the counter edge. Trent grabbed the shopping bag with one hand and her elbow with the other. "Excuse us."

"Wait. Janelle."

"This is Rachel," Trent interjected. There was no way for him to know this was her Rich Jerk. Running away would only arouse suspicion, even if she could move her leaden feet. What lousy timing. "Rachel Stone, business operations manager for TMS. We're here for the conference."

"Coincidence. Kyle Reygar, Sarasota Consultants." Kyle placed a magazine and a pack of gum on the counter. "Do you have a card, *Rachel?*"

Trent dropped his hand to the small of her back. "Here's mine. Nice meeting you."

Then he was propelling her forward, their rumpled clothes and hair leaving no doubt about what they'd been doing even if Kyle hadn't seen their purchase.

"That was him," Trent muttered tightly as they escaped to the elevator. "The guy who stole your wallet."

"Yes." Janelle sank against the wall, feeling every bit as dirty and used as she had when she'd stumbled out of the hotel after meeting Kyle.

Trent trapped her body against the wall with one braced arm. Janelle leaned her forehead against his chest and breathed. The shame dissipated, but a stain remained.

"We don't have to do anything tonight." He brushed a strand of her tangled hair away from her face, skimming her cheek with his knuckle.

"I want to," she said immediately. Janelle liked being with him so much. Too much. Trent wasn't for keeps. She couldn't make the same mistake she had with Ben. Which meant she had to make the most of their time together now.

The elevator dinged. Janelle took Trent by the hand and led him back to the cocoon of their room.

TRENT WOKE TO DARKNESS—VELVETY, thick, and complete. The red numbers of the clock on the nightstand read five-forty. He was hot, his body weighed down by Janelle's pliant body. She stirred beneath his arm.

He buried his nose in her hair. Last night, they'd made love again, slowly this time, savoring one another's bodies. They'd talked into the darkness about nothing, about everything.

Janelle's breathing changed. Trent skimmed his palm up her side, marveling at the fine strength of her thighs, the indentation of her waist, the ridges of her ribs and the generous swell of her breast. He ran his thumb over her nipple. She shuddered in response.

Janie was awake, all right.

He absorbed her gasp of pleasure with his lips. She tasted of sleep. A moment later she pulled away and reached across him, flattening her breasts over his chest as she pulled a condom out of the rapidly depleting supply. He tasted her gasp of pleasure, spiced with sleep. A moment later she kissed her way down his body to his semi-erect cock. She was voracious. So much for nice, sweet Janie. Fuck, he could get used to waking up like this.

All the more reason not to. This was only a distraction. Trent wound his fingers through soft dark locks, urging her on. His phone beeped on the night stand.

"Aren't you going to check it?" Janelle collapsed back onto the pillows.

"No. Are you?" Trent crawled up to lay beside her, tucking her soft body close.

"It's your phone, not mine." Janie was a champion snuggler. She slid one leg over his thighs and curled against him while running her palm over his erection, waiting.

Trent flopped over and picked up his phone. "Olivia. She wants to meet us at seven-thirty for breakfast."

"I'm skipping the gym. How about you?" Naked, Janelle sauntered to the bathroom. A minute later the shower started. Thirty seconds after that, he was under the hot water with her.

Janelle was like a sea otter with her dark hair slicked back. Her eyes glimmered playfully beneath the spray, eyelashes stuck together in triangular points. The straight, narrow angle of her nose dripped with fine droplets as she rubbed Trent's cock between her breasts.

"Janie." He closed his eyes, lost in the wet warmth of her skin against his. Trent fisted his hand against the tile, scraping his knuckle on the grout. Water sluiced over his back, dripping over him as he sheltered Janie's face from the spray.

Janelle didn't let up, teasing his balls with her free hand. "Is this all right?"

"Fuck, yeah." He let her keep going until he was close, then pulled her up and dragged her out of the shower. Without a towel, he laid her wet body across the bed, cool air prickling her skin with tiny bumps. Trent ran his palms up the inside of her thighs. Janelle grabbed his hair and squeezed as she moaned. A trickle of water ran down his temple.

"In a hurry?" he demanded, chuckling at her eagerness.

"I can't get enough of you," she panted. Trent licked her clean, sweet pussy until she came against his face. Only then did he let her take him in her mouth and suck. Her fingers dug into his ass as she pulled him deeper. She popped off as he finished, pumping him with her fist as his entire body shuddered.

They were startled by the pound of a fist from the hallway.

"It's nearly eight!" Olivia yelled through the door.

Reality intruded, as harsh as a ray of sunlight. The room was a mess of scattered clothing and rumpled bedding. The smell of sex permeated everything. Trent cast Janelle's naked, splayed body a regretful look and tugged on a random pair of boxers. He was possessed, driven by a need to consume her as often as he could for the short time they had together.

"I texted you three times, soldier." Olivia's expression was serious, but he caught a glimpse of amusement.

"I turned it off."

She sniffed. "Mmhm. Well, I'll leave you two lovebirds to it."

"Wait!" Janelle, wearing her leggings and V-neck t-shirt, poked her head under his arm. "Breakfast?" Janelle peered up at him. "You never mentioned food. Go get dressed."

"Atta girl." Olivia beamed approvingly.

Trent dropped a kiss on the top of Janie's dark head. Janelle held the door open. "Do you want to come in?"

Olivia wrinkled her nose. "No thanks. I'll meet you in the breakfast lounge."

They pulled themselves together quickly. Their friend was sitting with another woman, shorter and curvier with tawny skin and shoulder-length hair blown flat, when they made their way to the table carrying loaded plates.

"This is Stella, my conference roomie. She's been appraised of your situation, Janelle. Hope that's all right."

"It's fine, Olivia." Janelle

"Have you tried asking for your wallet back?" Stella asked.

"First thing. He threatened me with a tape he made in secret. Said he'd send it to everyone in my contacts list if I didn't go through with the…agreement" Janelle shoveled breakfast into her mouth. Trent caught her eye. Yeah, they'd worked up an appetite last night. Despite everything, she was more relaxed and happy than he'd seen her yet.

"That's illegal. First, he's in the wrong for taping you without written consent. Second, the instant he sends it to anyone, it's a felony." Stella sipped her tea as if she threatened people over breakfast routinely. Given her profession, she probably did.

"A felony?" Janelle's fork stopped halfway to her mouth. "Really?"

"It was when I still worked for a law firm." Stella laughed, a soft huff. "Intellectual property is my specialty area. This is 101-level stuff. Tech trademarking and patent infringement is my bailiwick now."

"If you call his bluff, you might get your wallet back. Easier than getting your driver's license replaced, if it works," Olivia added.

"It didn't protect me," Trent pointed out to Stella, as if she was responsible for any of this mess.

"Did you agree to be recorded?" she asked evenly.

"Yes. On camera. I didn't know she was planning to release it, though." Trent rubbed his jaw.

"If you consented to the recording, you'd have had a hard time winning at court. A few years ago, the law hadn't caught up with the technology. It still hasn't. Plus, you were famous. You had less expectation of privacy than a regular citizen." Stella folded her arms over her ample chest.

"Trent, may I borrow your phone?" Janelle held out her hand, palm up. She was already half out of her chair. His throat tightened. A desire to pull her back, take her away and keep her safe, surged out of nowhere.

You're not twenty. She's not Penny. She's not yours. But for a minute, he wished she could be. "I'll call him."

Janelle's stubborn chin tilted up. Her butt landed back in the chair, but her palm remained open.

"Give your girlfriend the phone, Mace." Olivia crossed her arms, peeved on Janie's behalf.

"She's not my girlfriend," Trent replied automatically. Janelle dropped her hand flat on the table with a smack. Her face went pale beneath her tan.

"Sorry," he muttered.

Janelle forced a smile. "It's the truth. Anyway, twenty-four hours from now I'm headed home."

Depressing thought. Going home meant leaving him behind, too. He shoved out of his chair, wishing it would screech across the floor instead of whispering over carpet with no effect. "I'll make the call. Man-to-man."

Janelle had always believed that finding the right man meant finding one who could protect her. From the indignities of casual harassment, to her financial problems, to the consequences of her foray into sugar babying, she'd been convinced that finding the right Prince Charming was all she needed to make her life right.

She'd been wrong.

I'll never let myself be this helpless again.

She couldn't have asked for a more perfect white knight than Trent. Yet Janelle's skin crawled with the need to stop letting him help her. Stumbling out of her seat, she stopped him with a touch.

"Trent. You've done everything. Let me do this piece." She

skimmed one palm along his muscular arm to his shoulder. "You can't fight my battles for me."

"Watch me." He left them, mulish determination turning his handsome face into a glower.

Olivia shook her head. "What has gotten into that man?"

"I think you mean, *who's* gotten to that man." Stella eyed her playfully. "You're lucky, girl, but watch out for yourself. Mace has more baggage than an airline in July."

"She knows, Stella. Come on." Olivia and Stella departed, hips swinging, leaving her to work out her problems. Janelle sucked the hurt into her abdomen, then tried to breathe it out. It didn't work. Her sister swore by controlled yoga breath, but it had never done a damn thing for Janelle.

Alyssa had charted her own path from the start. It had been such a shock a few months ago to learn that her creative, ambitious sister had made mistakes—mostly in the seemingly perfect fiancé she'd had so much trouble getting rid of. Janelle shuddered to think at how miserable Aly would've been if she'd taken Janelle's advice and stayed with Zach.

This trip had been revealing in so many unexpected ways. How many people had told her she had a princess complex? A million? Stepping back and letting him fix this problem for her was exactly what she thought she wanted. Except, she'd never been able to lie to herself. It wasn't what she wanted now. At all.

Quit being ridiculous. She preferred Trent's help. She just didn't want him doing everything for her, and she didn't how to say it without sounding ungrateful.

In the moment it had taken her to sort through her conflicting emotions, Trent had finished his call and returned wearing a cocky grin. "You'll get your wallet back, Janie. I'm pretty confident of that. Not much interesting happens at the conference this morning. While we're waiting for Kyle's next move. Is there anything you want to do? See the city?"

"Laundry. There's machines down the hall." No matter how many orgasms he'd given her, Janelle was sore this morning. They had to take a break. Besides, if there was ever a room that needed housekeeping, it was theirs. The sex hangover was starting to go stale. And some part of her needed to hold back a bit instead of gunning forward. The instinctive wariness cropping up now had tilted her entire world off its axis. Somewhere between taking off from Miami and sleeping with Trent last night, she'd changed in a way that was too fundamental and too *new* for Janelle to understand yet.

He laughed and kissed her cheek. "If you insist. I like you best naked, though."

10

"You've been cuddling that thing for the past hour."

"Jealous?"

"A little."

The way Janelle tucked her beat-up wallet close against her chest was enough to provoke envy in any red-blooded man. The hotel's front desk rang the room, and Trent had scooped it out of the cradle as Janelle came in the door with a stack of clean clothes. Her wallet was at the front desk.

"You'll get your turn," she grinned, deliberately tracing the worn leather between her breasts. Trent hooked his arm around her shoulders as they fell into step. In khaki shorts and a t-shirt, she radiated a preppy wholesomeness. This was the closest he'd seen of the real Janelle Carlisle.

Who's leaving tomorrow afternoon.

Reality kicked him in the gut.

"Are you going to tell me where we're going?" she asked.

"The Pinball Hall of Fame," he replied.

"Pinball!" Janelle squealed. They'd walked part of the distance, hopped on a bus and now they were sauntering along Tropicana

Avenue the last few blocks. Janelle's wallet was more like an undersized purse, complete with a wrist loop. "I love pinball!"

"Not as much as I do. I used to come here to come down from a coke high, before I was old enough to hang around in bars. I got a fake, eventually." Pinball was one of the few fond memories he had of this town.

"Five dollars. I'm going to kick your ass, Trent." Janelle cocked a hip as she plugged a ten-dollar bill into the change machine.

A sharp rock of pressure lodged under his ribcage. Janelle divided the quarters and handed him half. They chose adjacent machines and shot them into the slots.

"Highest score wins," she declared.

"You're on." Metal balls pinged manically. Lights whirred. Trent was rusty; he lost the first ball quickly, but he made up for it with the second.

"I win!"

Janelle jumped twice and pumped her fist. Trent didn't mind losing, considering what winning to her chest.

"Best two out of three," he offered.

"You're on."

They stayed for an hour, at the end of which Janelle handed him five dollars. "You gave me a run for my money."

"Nobody's been competitive with me in years. Either I've lost my touch, or you're good."

"I'm that good." She winked over her shoulder like a pinup girl. When she wasn't feeling low or cornered, Janelle's sass was playful, the kind of banter that drew male attention like a magnet.

After dinner, they went out for ice cream. It was only nine, but Trent wanted to get Janie back to the hotel room. Immediately. For one thing, her gait was less awkward than it had been this morning, which meant she might be ready to get back in the sack. He sure as hell was.

"You don't still have the green dress from Friday, do you?"

Janelle's expression closed. "Maybe. Why?"

Trent licked his cone. "No reason."

"I was going to toss it, but it's still in my bag."

Frozen milk product wasn't enough to douse Trent's interest. "Good."

"You want me to wear it, I assume?" Janie rolled her tongue suggestively around the line between her ice cream and the cone. Trent's balls tightened.

"With the shoes. And the glasses, and nothing else."

"Who would you be fucking, Trent? Me or Rachel?" Janelle's pink tongue swept over her bottom lip. Every muscle in his abdomen contracted.

"Both of you. All of you."

Trent knocked before using the key card, his hands a little shaky from nerves. He was used to being the one getting schooled, by Penny. Reversing that role, watching Janelle explore, was incredibly hot. But it was also nerve-wracking.

Janelle shooed him out of the room while she changed. After five minutes, he knocked. Janie cracked the door, a swath of dark hair falling over her forehead, which reached several inches higher than it would've if she was barefoot. A brief glance down revealed a lot of very naked leg and the shine of a patent shoe.

"Gonna let me in?"

She cracked the door wider. "Since it's you."

The green dress skimmed her body. Trent swallowed. Janelle wasn't wearing a bra. This time, she lifted her chin when she caught him checking. "What's on the agenda tonight?"

Trent pulled her close and brushed his lips over hers. It was so easy when she wore heels that solved the height difference. If this were real, he'd get her higher ones. The kind of shoes that weren't meant for walking. "You tell me."

"Hm?" Dazed, Janelle draped her arms around his shoulders. Anticipation stoked higher at the press of her breasts against his chest. Trent placed his hands on her hips to make her step back. He made quick work of removing his tie.

"You tell me, Janie," he repeated. He rolled the tie around his palm and placed it in her hands. "You're the boss tonight. Anything you want to try is on the table."

Her eyes widened. Her mouth formed an O. "Anything?"

"All you have to do is ask."

She licked her lips. The silk length of his tie unspooled to the floor.

"Are there any boundaries?"

"Not on my side."

Anything Janie dreamed up, he'd undoubtedly already done.

"Shouldn't we have a…a safe word or something?"

Janie was so funny. Straight as an arrow in her actions—mostly—and more than a bit adventurous in her thinking.

"If you want. You're in control. You decide if you need one."

"You're not worried my imagination will be too much for you?" she asked slyly.

"Should I be?" What in the hell was going through her head? Trent's entire body tingled with anticipation.

"I don't know. I've imagined a lot over the past two days." Janelle pulled the tie taut between her palms, the ends trailing loosely from her right hand.

"Quit talking and show me, Janie." Trent stepped closer, caressing her body with his gaze, a long, slow, appreciative down-and-up. The dress barely qualified as fabric. It was as thin as a whisper and showed everything beneath it, including Janelle's magnificent nipples and the outline of a very small thong.

"If that's what you want, Mace." Her tone was deceptively soft. "Take off your shirt."

His fingers weren't altogether steady. If they had been, he might've been too obliging. Instead, he did a slow tease, mindful of the time when she'd first arrived and he'd undressed, and let her know he knew she was watching. This time she didn't pretend to feel ashamed. Janie moved over him, propped with her arms on either side of his head. Their faces were mere inches apart, and for the first time, Trent felt uncomfortable. They were too close. The view was too intimate.

"What are you doing?" he demanded gruffly.

"I'm showing you what I think is good sex."

There was no avoiding the flutter of her lashes against his cheek as she slid the head of his dick along her center. Trent closed his eyes, that shouldn't have pulsed in his body, but did. He'd done every dirty

Say You Need Me

thing in the book, a fair number with Janelle. This slow tease was hotter than all of it. Combined.

This was subtle. Intense. So was the kiss she brushed across his cheekbone as she slid slowly over him. A slight smile touched her lips as Janelle cradled his face in her hands. Trent couldn't resist clutching her ass in an attempt to move her body faster.

"Quit trying take control, Trent," she whispered. Another soft kiss as her body ground hard over him. All he'd managed to do by digging his fingers into the swells of her ass was pull her close and tight against his body. They moved together, a single organism. Janelle's teeth grazed his ear lobe. Electric waves pulsed through him, and Trent gasped.

"Like that?" Janie's voice was hardly above a whisper, so soft in his ear he might've imagined it. He moved, the stubble on his cheek grazing her skin as she did it again. She ran her fingernail along the edge of his other ear, the twin sensations supercharging every nerve. The sound Trent made didn't resemble speech. She never let up the methodical grind.

Trent sank his fingers into her ass, frantic to increase the pace. This orgasm promised to be the fiercest yet, pleasure pulling from every part of his body and consolidating in the tight knot of his balls.

Janie went first. A shudder wracked her body as she buried her face in his shoulder and moaned. Trent's fingers wove into her hair, trying to bring her even closer.

"Now you can take over," she said breathlessly, nipping his ear again.

Trent cradled her skull in his palm and dug his toes into the mattress. He pounded into Janelle without finesse, beyond caring whether she liked this, too far gone to read signals. The orgasm was like jumping off a cliff or out of an airplane. Trent's spine flexed as he unloaded cum he didn't think he had left.

The storm abated slowly. Trent's heart beat pulsed so hard he felt its echo twitch in his dick, still buried in Janie's tight, hot body. His face, pressed hard against Janelle's shoulder, was plastered with bits of her long hair, those strands tickling him as always. Her scent permeated every breath. Their scent, redolent of sweat and salt. Their bodies, commingled.

Bliss. Trent was too spent to do more than notice the thought and let it go.

Janelle's fingers traced a lazy pattern at the nape of his neck. He cracked an eyelid enough to see her features relaxed with contentment.

All remaining stress seeped out of him. Trent relaxed into the aftermath.

If only he could stay here, like this.

If only this was real.

If only he wasn't still bound to Penny. In this moment, he hated her for the addiction that had nearly killed her, for releasing that fucking video, for the fact that he could never, ever shake free of her. Only a heartless jackass would abandon a disabled woman. Only a fool would accept anything less than his whole heart, and Penny had smashed it beyond repair.

Janelle was no fool.

Sharp resentment stung at how Penny haunted him even now. That this was his life. His dick began to soften, and he withdrew. The last thing either he or Janie needed was a condom fail.

"Good?" Janie asked, half asleep.

"Amazing," he replied gruffly.

"Plain old missionary sex. Don't knock it." She yawned.

Huh. The least kinky sex he'd ever had was also the hottest. On the edge of sleep, Trent traced the line of her shoulder with his fingertips. The motion soothed him into letting down his guard. "Can you change your ticket?"

"Mmm? Probably. Why?" Janelle snuggled closer, her hair cascading over his neck.

"So we can stay like this a while longer. I'd pay for it." Money didn't need to be a barrier. He knew she didn't have much. He did, though he was careful in how he spent it.

Janelle raised her head onto one hand, her features relaxed. "When do you leave?"

"Tuesday afternoon."

"I'll call the airline in the morning." She kissed him, and he rolled her over onto her back.

You're a dick for leading her on.

He should've established ground rules at the outset. But if he'd introduced a discussion about not catching feelings, Trent was certain she wouldn't have let him get anywhere near her. Tuesday at the airport, he'd make excuses about being out of practice—which was true—but he was still an asshole for asking her to extend her trip when there was no room in his life for sweetness and happiness. But Trent couldn't let her go, not yet. He'd cling to every second he could keep her. Even if it meant hurting her more in the end.

It was one of a litany of reasons he'd never deserve her. The idea of bogging down Janelle—with her romantic streak and newfound career interest—in the ongoing train wreck of his relationship with Penny was unthinkable.

He might be an asshole, but he wasn't cruel.

11

"I don't want to go back." Janelle's stomach was hollow. She'd skipped lunch. They all had, to make their flights. Even if there'd been time to eat, she doubted she could've, though.

"I thought you didn't like Vegas?" Olivia spoke over the middle passenger of the hotel shuttle van. Somewhere behind them, Trent was crammed into the back seat of the shuttle van with a bunch of other guys.

"I don't. But I need to make a big change. I've been spinning my wheels in Florida. Not that I have any idea where to go. I have no job prospects, no money, and my credit's Swiss cheese. I might have an idea about what I want to do, but I'm starting from square one."

"I hope you go for it, Janie. Thanks for organizing the cards and getting started with the introductions. I may need help with managing all the contact and follow-up. Are you interested in a freelance project?"

"I'm always interested in paid work. The faster I can move out of my parents' house, the better." Janelle grabbed her seatbelt as the van bounced over a pothole.

"Here's my card. Keep in touch, Janie. You have talent. You could go far in this business."

"You think so?" Janelle had gotten the taste, but she didn't know as much as she needed to if she wanted to make a go at this.

"Yes, I know so. Give me a call and we'll strategize." Olivia's expression turned pensive. "Where are things going with Trent?"

Janelle turned away. "I like him, but I can't figure out what's going on with Penny. He says she's not in the picture, but it doesn't seem like I'm getting the whole story."

"I doubt any of us are. I've known the man since his second deployment. He was getting his degree online and was transferred into his first intel support unit. I'd almost given up on getting my degree. It seemed like too much, but he pulled me across the finish line. I owe him for that. Everyone knows about his ex-girlfriend and that tape, but he never talks about her." The van pulled up to the curb and disgorged passengers like a clown car. Janelle bounded out, bag banging against her thigh. Last to emerge was Trent.

"Have you ever watched it?" Janelle asked curiously.

"No. My relationship with Mace is strictly professional. He's a good egg, just don't play cards with him. He's still a shark. Cleaned out my entire unit in a week. See you inside," Olivia waved, giving them as much privacy as she could.

Trent sidled over to her. Goodbye seemed too final. But what to say?

"Janie. I had a lot of fun this weekend," Trent began.

Her lids closed and opened, scratching like sandpaper over her eyes. "Me too."

"I'll miss you."

She couldn't stop the sniffle. "Me too. Call me when you get home?"

Trent stepped back and ran his fingers through his hair, refusing to meet her eyes. "I don't think that's a good idea."

Cold shock. She tried to speak, but words wouldn't come out. She swallowed, her throat thick. "Why not?"

"It was fun, but it's best to make a clean break. For both of us." His expression was sorrowful. Pitying. *Don't you fucking pity me.* She hadn't expected him to jump into a long-distance relationship but this? This was harsh. It stung to think he might've used her. Maybe all his sob stories weren't even true. They'd known each other for three days and were practically strangers. "You can't even make space for a phone call?"

Anger chased away tears, so she surrendered to it. *He's been planning this.*

"I have to focus on the business. And there's Penny...I'm out of practice with hookups. I didn't want to end it like this."

End it. Over. Janelle's heart expanded like it might explode, crushing her lungs from inside.

"Penny? You're not still with her, are you?" *What the hell is the story with them?*

"Not exactly. I mean, she's not well. I can't just abandon her."

The blow was crushing in its force. Trent was a good man. Not hers, though. He was Penny's and always would be. He'd gone six years without sex. Janelle cursed herself for not understanding the implications sooner. "There was never any chance for us beyond this weekend? Was there, Trent?"

"Don't be like this, Janie."

"I *am* like this. This is me. I get attached. I can't...do it if I don't care about someone. That's why I don't do hookups...I never meant to start with you."

"What did you think this would be?" Trent's expression was unreadable.

Her phone beeped. Janelle checked it, eager for any excuse to stop gawping at Trent while she waited for him to respond. Janelle didn't want these to be the last words they said to one another. She opened her mouth to speak and tasted cotton. Trent's strong arms wrapped around her shoulders. Her nose hurt. She had to get away before she started using Trent's shirt as a tissue.

Penny wouldn't like that.

She pulled away. Trent didn't stop her.

Well. You wanted to solve your own problems. Here's your chance.

"How was your trip, sweetie?" Catherine, her mother, folded Janelle into an embrace.

"It was fine." Florida's balmy warmth enveloped her, cloying and sticky.

"That's all you have to say?"

Janelle's body froze as if she'd been dropped into a plunge pool. "Why do you ask, Mom?"

They were in the car now, the highway an endless asphalt ribbon streaking beneath them.

"You were in Miami all weekend. We didn't hear from you once. I expected you to check in at least once or twice."

Janelle closed her eyes. She'd been faking happiness for so long, she hardly knew what it felt like anymore. Until Trent. On her birthday, she'd sworn something big had to change. She'd been willing to do anything—or almost anything, given she'd backed out at the last second—to avoid making the real changes that would make a difference.

"Mom." She swallowed. "I have a confession to make."

The story spilled out in fits. Janelle had to back up several times to give her mother the full context. She used Olivia's name as a proxy for Trent, neatly erasing him from her story. He was hers alone besides which giving her mom one heart attack was enough stress for the day. Pulling the driveway, her mother was ashen.

"Janie, honey. I wish you'd told us. I wish you'd come to me for help before flying off to do something so dangerous. What if he'd assaulted you? Or killed you?"

"I've thought the same thing a million times."

"Go unpack and relax. You didn't get into this pickle overnight, and you won't get out overnight, either." She paused. "I'm pouring a glass of wine. Do you want one?"

"Thanks, Mom. For listening." Even if her parents had been dismissive of her financial problems before, Janelle knew that half the reason had been her own bad attitude. She threw her clothes in the washing machine and set her toiletries on the bathroom counter. While the washer was working, Janie made herself a sandwich and ate it while printing out every account she had. Tomorrow she had to go back to the coffee shop and the warehouse, and this evening she needed the distraction from thinking about Trent.

Two months ago, before she'd left with Marc, Alyssa had tried to make Janelle sit down and get a handle on her finances. Janie cringed to remember how she'd thrown up her hands in frustration and given up. It had seemed so hopeless. The debt was huge. She'd been so locked into the idea of paying it off that she'd been too scared to consider other options.

Janelle wasn't scared anymore.

"You're diving right in, I see." Catherine pulled out a kitchen chair. She picked up a statement and released a slow whistle. "Janie, why didn't you tell us how much student debt you had?"

"I was ashamed, Mom. I told you it was a lot, but I was too scared to show you exactly how much it was."

Catherine placed her glasses on the wood table. "Janie, we wanted you to learn how to live as a responsible adult. If we were less than supportive, I'm sorry. Your dad and I weren't planning to retire as early as we did, and I've been worried we'd run through our savings. I never want to be a burden on my children. The financial advisor told us it was better for our children to borrow for college because you can't take out loans for retirement."

Janelle patted her mother's hand, unsure how else to respond. All this time, she'd been jealous of her sister's scholarship and success. Hitting the books a little harder might've won her a similar opportunity, but she wasn't gifted in any specific area the way Alyssa was. At nineteen, she'd been convinced she was going to marry Ben. College had seemed only a formality. "You did the right thing, Mom. It would've been a waste. I was too scared of succeeding or, more likely, failing on my own."

"Failing? Why would you say that?"

"Because it's what I do, Mom. I fail. I try and I fail. After a while, I stopped trying." Janelle's nose was hot and itchy. Allergies. Must be. She reached for the tissue box on the sideboard.

"You're not going to fail this time. Here. Look at this. The reason your credit is so bad is that you only have a single loan on your record. You should open a few other accounts to build up your credit profile."

"I tried! I was turned down for two credit cards, and the interest rates are sky-high." Janelle grabbed her wine glass, took a careful sip, and set it back down. This wouldn't be any easier with a headache.

"Interest rates don't matter if you don't carry a balance, Janie." Catherine sorted through her printouts. The plan didn't take long to develop. Janelle's parents would cosign for a loan to buy a car, and help her apply for a secured credit card through their credit union.

"I don't know whether to be horrified I didn't know how much trouble you were having or impressed you paid off nearly a third of your loans in three years. We should try to consolidate the loan into a smaller monthly payment. I'll make that call tomorrow."

The hour had gotten late. They set aside the paperwork to make dinner. Janelle hugged her mother and left a floury handprint on her back. "Oops."

Catherine hugged her back and whispered, "It's okay, baby."

And even though she missed Trent with every aching pulse of her heart, it was.

THE NEW PHONE'S preset ringtone was quiet, but it still made Jessie, her boss at the warehouse, poke her head up and glare. "You can use your phone at break, Janie."

"Sorry. It's new. I can't figure out how to put it on vibrate."

It beeped again, indicating a voicemail. She'd dropped her parents' phone line and set up her very own account, although she'd kept her old number. It was probably about the new-ish car. Though technically secondhand, saving her a few thousand dollars, the Honda had low miles and a good maintenance record. One Janelle fully intended to continue.

At 10:45, she took her bag to the grim break room and punched in her access code. The voicemail was only a few seconds long, but it left her statue-still with disbelief. "Janie? It's Trent. Give me a call when you can."

"Well if you ain't a sight for sore eyes." Her nemesis, the lead forklift driver, moved in too close and sniffed noisily. Still stunned, Janelle was slow to react.

"Mmm, you smell as good as you look, Janelle. Like coffee. Strong and bitter, just how I like my women." His eyes were locked on her chest.

"Rick, try looking down my shirt again and I'll report you to HR."

An empty threat. She'd done it once before, and the human resources director had laughed in her face. Janelle yanked her bag up and hustled down the hallway out the back door where two of the other warehouse guys were smoking. She waved away the cloud as she passed, hitting the number Trent had dialed from. He picked up on the second ring.

"Hi. It's me." Janelle's palms were sweaty, her heart racing. The moment was surreal. He wanted her. Trent had called to say he loved her. Right?

"Hi."

"So...were you just calling to say you missed me?" *Please say you miss me.*

"Not exactly. I was wondering if you could come to Virginia this weekend."

"Um, it's Thursday, Trent. Kinda last-minute." What the hell?

"I'll pay for the plane ticket."

"Why should I?" Her pulse raced giddily. There was noise in the background, as though he was in a cafe or a restaurant. "What happened to the clean break?"

"I'm not calling about us. Remember the Solomon guy from New York? He wasn't kidding about issuing a fast-turnaround RFP. I've been absolutely buried since I got back, and this response is due in New York by Monday. If we advance, there's a presentation in two weeks I'd also need help with. I'll pay you. Olivia says you're doing freelance work for her, and I don't have time to vet someone through word of mouth."

Disappointment sucked at her. "I don't know. I'd have to find someone to cover me at the coffee shop on Saturday."

"If we win this, you can quit the coffee shop. It's normal to build in a consultant's fee. I'm offering two percent on a million-dollar contract."

"What if we don't win?" *We. What's this* we *nonsense?* There was no *we*, no *us*. He was using those words to leverage their…hookup. This was even more calculated than the breakup at the airport. Part of her hated him for it. The rest of her yearned for his touch, no questions asked.

"I have a good shot, but I need help. Olivia thinks you can get the job done." Trent was so distant. So *professional*.

Olivia was such a dear. Maybe she could sneak in a visit with her during the trip. If she went. She'd hoped for a booty call from Trent, not a temp gig. Still, money was money. "I've got to get back to work, Trent."

"Is that a yes?"

"Janelle! You're three minutes over your break. Back at it." Jessie hollered from the rear door as she lit up.

"I'll make some calls at lunch. No promises." She hung up before he could respond.

It wasn't the opportunity she wanted. But if it was a step to getting a better job, Janelle would take it. Even if it meant wearing a chastity belt to work around Trent for a few days. She could probably find one to buy online. If she locked it on and left the key at home, she might be able to stop herself from shamelessly throwing herself at him.

It was a plan.

12

Trent spotted Janelle a full minute before she exited the security gate. She looked different. He couldn't say why, but the woman in the gray print shirt and jeans moved with a confidence that she hadn't displayed when he'd dropped her off at another airport, two weeks ago in Las Vegas.

She grinned and pushed her sunglasses onto her head. "Hi."

"Good to see you. Thanks for coming all this way." Should he kiss her? Fuck, no, he hadn't asked her to come so he could get into her pants.

Bullshit.

Janelle smoothed over the awkward moment by hooking her arm in his. Casual, friendly, not necessarily romantic. Trent's stomach did something spastic and uncomfortable.

"I brought the latest draft of the Solomon RFP. I worked on it on the plane, so there's notes in the margins." Janie's tone was light, preternaturally normal.

In the parking lot, she dropped his arm. Trent flipped through the stack of papers she handed him as he walked, putting a good three feet of distance between them. He shoved a sick feeling down as if he could bury it with work. Why had he brought her here?

You needed help.

She'd given it without hesitation. Though it had taken some convincing, Janelle had dropped everything to be here for barely twenty-four hours, and she'd been working past midnight both Thursday and Friday nights. They both had, though they'd communicated only over email.

"What you need, Trent, is a repository of boilerplate responses to make this process easier. We do something similar at the warehouse for bidding on contracts."

Her idea was a good one, but he'd never expect her to work for free.

You're paying her. It's not charity.

Except it was. Unless they won the business, she earned nothing. She'd refused to let him pay her hourly if he lost. He'd insisted on bumping her fee. Winning was imperative. Trent wanted to fuck her with his dick, not fuck her over financially.

"Maybe after the pitch." He'd resisted Olivia's recommendation that he call Janelle until he'd almost run out of time to finish the proposal. "Anything else new?"

"I bought a car."

Trent whistled. "Thought you were broke?"

"I am." Janelle sat up straighter, her sunglasses obscuring her eyes. "My parents cosigned for the loan. It's not new but almost. Mom says it'll help my credit score in the long run. I'm getting my financial house in order."

"No more sugar daddies?"

Janelle shuddered. "Never again. From now on, I solve my own problems. No more princess complex for me."

Subtext: I don't need you, Trent.

The sucker punch made him want to do violence, the way he'd raged at the world after his parents died. The way he'd enlisted in the army as much for the physical punishment as for the structure he badly needed, after Penny had come out of the coma and the extent of her brain damage was revealed. Trent was older now. Wiser, maybe. The jury was still out. He didn't react, just drove in silence until the parking garage of his building appeared. His jaw ached as he clenched his teeth against the torrent of words he'd die before speaking.

"We're home," was all he said and wished it was true, that it was their home. Together. It wasn't. It would never be. He'd always be the dumb shit whose ex-girlfriend had leaked their sex tape, who couldn't use his first name without the entire world finding out what he'd done. All they'd ever have was a few days of mind-blowing sex. He had nothing more to offer. It had been a giant mistake to bring Janelle here.

Trent's apartment building was modern and large, easily ten stories, with small trees poking over the edges of the roof indicating a deck. Janelle wiped her damp palms on her jeans.

"Nice building. How long have you lived here?"

Trent led her into an elevator, finally breaking his silence. "About eight months. It's zoned for commercial live-work residence, although I'm pushing it by having more than three employees."

"I don't understand. Is this your apartment or your office?"

"It's both." He unlocked a door to a sparsely but comfortably furnished, airy loft apartment with large windows. The view was over a parking lot, but they were placed high enough that Janelle didn't notice until she went to the window and looked down.

Trent was acting as if the weekend in Las Vegas had never happened. Janelle swallowed her disappointment. They'd only spoken on the phone once after that first, brief call, and she'd hoped the awkwardness would evaporate once they were together again.

If anything, it was worse. Janelle set her bag on a white leather couch and walked to a marble breakfast bar, where she laid out neat stacks of paper covered with sticky notes and red scribble.

"Shall we dive in?" Better to get to work. It was the only reason he wanted her here.

"Are you hungry? Do you want lunch?"

"No, thanks. I left sections four, nine, and twelve for you to fill out." Janelle barely glanced up. Looking at him made something sharp stab in her chest. He hadn't kissed her hello. She didn't want anything but to get their work done and go home.

Unless he'd changed his mind about their being together, she was here to prove her newfound skills. The sun shifted and set as they worked. Janelle almost asked him to put music on to break up the monotony, but even that felt like too far a bridge. What if he hated her music tastes? What if she hated his?

"You can't spell for shit."

Janelle's attention settled on Trent for a long moment. Was he annoyed? Amused? "No, I've never been good at it. Have it proofread before you send it out."

Several minutes of silence passed. "You make my company sound better than it is."

"Thank you?" It had been a mistake to come here. She needed to get out of this room. He'd been inside her body. Sitting in his apartment shouldn't be a big deal, but this stilted distance was killing her.

"It was a compliment, Janie." He leaned over the high counter. Janelle's face warmed under Trent's scrutiny. "Olivia was right. You have a talent for this."

"Lucky me. Of all the talents in the universe, I get the boring corporate-speak-crammed-into-Excel-squares one."

Trent huffed a laugh. "Come on. Let's take a break. I'll show you the roof deck."

The wide sky above them was streaked with pink and orange clouds. Janelle's relief was immediate. Air and light chased away her nervousness. She walked the perimeter of the deck, putting as much distance as she could between herself and Trent while looking out over the skyline.

You don't have to wait for him to make a move.

If he'd given her any indication he was happy to see her again, Janelle wouldn't have hesitated. The clean break in Las Vegas had been rough, yet it had been merciful. She wanted to believe he missed her. But he hardly looked at her, and if she came within arm's length he retreated as though she were a snake coiled to bite.

Maybe he regretted sleeping with her. Maybe she'd been terrible in bed. Janelle's eyes watered. She blinked to clear them and stretched her arms to the sky. All she had to do was finish the document, and if they made it to the next round, go to New York for a day to present in person. She could endure a few hours of awkwardness for the money; it was too good to pass up.

Janelle noticed Trent's shadow an instant before his big hand landed on the small of her back. She started.

"You must be hungry by now. I am. Do you want to go out?" he asked.

Her arm was around his waist before she could remember why she shouldn't touch him. Trent pulled her close. Janelle closed her eyes and breathed in his scent, the same unidentifiable spice that was all him. Her heart beat erratically, like a frightened bat trapped in her chest. Pain and pleasure pumped through her body, sweetly toxic.

Janelle could stand on tiptoe and kiss him. It would be reckless, but if Trent's hands slid around her ass and lifted her high against his chest, it would be worth it. She'd wrap her legs around his waist and kiss him, a succubus, desperate for him to love her back.

She did none of those things. The fantasy faded the instant she pulled away, leaving the warm memory of his palm cooling against her skin. "I'd rather order in. Let's keep working, and get this over with."

Trent went out to pick up their food. Janelle wandered aimlessly around the apartment, too curious to resist poking around.

It's not snooping if I'm not opening drawers.

The door to the large, windowed bedroom off the living room was crammed with long tables and desk chairs. Computer equipment and office supplies, including a large printer, occupied the closet. Janelle picked up the stack of printouts Trent had sent to queue before leaving. Excuse secured, she closed the door and tiptoed down the hall to the back of the apartment. At the end was a closet with a washer-dryer, a bathroom, and a door to Trent's bedroom. It was pitch black. Janelle flipped the light on.

No wonder. It was a windowless cell.

A plain, neatly made bed sat against the far wall. A large desk occupied an alcove next to the closet. Inside the closet was a small, cheaply made bureau. Beside it, on the floor, two pairs of shoes and a pair of army boots. Hangers with a monotonous array of dress shirts and suits occupied the long rod, an inch of space between the metal brackets. Everything Trent owned could fit in a large suitcase. The furniture was disposable. This apartment was nothing more than a crash pad at the back of his office.

Janelle reached for a photo in a silver frame. A much younger Trent, tall and skinny, stood with two people who must have been his parents. She set it down carefully, exactly as she'd found it. Now she *was* snooping.

Behind it was a second photo in a plain frame. Trent, a little older and broader in the shoulders, smiled next to a startlingly pretty, blonde woman. Janelle picked it up and turned it over. A note on the back of the picture written with purple ink in a round, girlish scrawl read: *I love your cock, Trent. XOXO forever, Penelope "Bad Penny."*

Janelle flipped the picture over again, a sad smile touching her. "It's a masterpiece, isn't it?"

On closer inspection, Trent exhibited an angry tenseness. Though it had softened, he hadn't lost his wary suspicion of the world. It wasn't evident in his teenage photo, before he'd lost his family. Janelle swallowed and set the picture back in its place. Lying flat beside the framed pictures was another photo, smaller, portrait layout. She picked it up by the edges and felt her eyebrows pop with surprise.

Trent had printed out the selfie he'd snapped of them at the Pinball Hall of Fame. The paper was thick, professional quality, not the cheap kind you did at home. Janelle ran her thumb over the surface, then placed it back where she'd found it.

Her self-guided tour had only taken a few minutes. A noise from the hallway made her dash on tiptoe past the kitchen and slide her ass onto a counter stool as if she hadn't been poking her nose into Trent's private life. Such as it was. The door didn't open.

Janelle glanced at the phone. Trent had only been gone for twelve minutes.

While her heart rate had slowed, Janelle cracked the front door to find a stocky guy, around her age, trying to jam a key into the lock of the apartment across the hall. A petite woman with dark hair leaned against the wall, clearly intoxicated. She froze, then tapped the man on the arm and pointed.

"Whoa. A chick! Look, Sean, the monk has a girlfriend."

"Hate to disappoint, but I'm not Trent's girlfriend," Janelle replied. Somehow, she'd hooked up with the one man who had less of a social life than she did.

The guy peered at her and winced. "Sorry. Hannah says anything when she's had a few."

"That's why you looooove me," Hannah responded, leaning on his arm.

"I'm Janelle." She grinned and stuck out her hand. Trent's neighbors were the first normal aspect of this entire weird visit.

"Sean. So, if you're not banging Mace, why are you here on a Saturday night?" The guy gave up trying to open the lock and pumped her hand twice. The key dangled from the door.

"Work. I'm consulting on a pitch due Monday." It was fun to say. True, too. Olivia kept saying she could make a career out of consulting, if she wanted to. And if Trent was right, she had some talent for spinning bullshit into gold. This was her test case.

"All that guy does is work." Sean shook his head and fumbled with the lock again.

"And work out. Your fuckhot neighbor's ripped," Hannah giggled. Janelle's cheeks warmed.

"Must be why you're moving in with me, not him." Sean managed to get the door open, not exactly sober himself, judging from how much trouble he'd had with the key.

"Other way around. You're moving in with me, toots." Hannah patted Sean's rear and held open the door. "Do you want a beer? I don't need any more."

"Sure." Janelle turned the lock on Trent's apartment door to prop it open and followed Trent's neighbors into a cozy studio. Sean's apartment furnishings were a step up from the cheap crap Trent favored for personal use, but the aesthetics were college dorm room. An unmade full bed was partially hidden behind a pullout couch that faced a huge

TV. The only wall hangings were sports team posters and jerseys. "When are you moving out?"

"Next week. I'm looking for a subletter for the last two months on my lease, if you know anyone who needs a short-term rental." Sean moved around takeout containers in the refrigerator until he found a bottle.

"I might," Janelle lied. Temptation. If she'd had a job lined up...

Great idea. Move in across the hall from Trent so he can politely ignore you all the time. Genius. Almost as good as the time you made your sister play The Bachelorette *in a dating contest, but less entertaining.*

"Here's my card. I'll post it Monday, when I'm back on computer. I can send you a link then." Sean fished in his wallet.

"Thanks. Nice to meet you, good luck with the move. I hear dinner arriving." Janelle held up the bottle in salute, and scooted out the door.

Trent came out of the elevator and did a double take. "Where'd the beer come from?"

"Your neighbor across the hall. Looks like you had the same idea." She nodded to the six-pack cradled in the crook of his arm.

"I've lived here eight months, and he's barely said hello. How'd you get so friendly?"

Janelle held the door to his apartment. "I said 'hi.' It was that easy."

Trent brushed aside a stack of discarded edits and set the beer and the plastic bag of food on the granite counter. He handed her a takeout container and a plastic fork.

Janelle hopped down from the counter and went into the kitchen. Opening the cabinets one by one, she found plastic cups, plastic utensils, cleaning supplies and paper towels. "Don't you have any dishes?"

Trent reached up to the top shelf of the first cabinet she'd opened.

"Paper plates?" Janelle cocked her hip. "No wonder they call you a monk."

"Who does?"

"Sean and Hannah. Across the hall." Resigned to eating out of a plastic tub, Janelle returned to her seat.

Trent ate standing up, next to the sink. "That's not nice."

Janelle shrugged. "I'd say you're more caveman than monk. At least monks sit down to eat. I bet they use real dishes, too."

Trent laughed. "I don't have time for cleaning."

True. The man barely had time to shave. She imagined how his three-day scruff might've felt on her inner thighs and shivered. Too bad about Penny still being in the picture. Or whatever was going on between them. It was weird her jealous streak hadn't kicked in, but then again, it was hard to feel envious when she was the one who was still able-bodied and in full control of her faculties. Janelle tossed her garbage in the trash can and popped two new beers, crossing the three-foot invisible barrier he'd maintained all day to hand him one. She tapped his bottle with hers.

"Cheers." She turned to pick up the stack of edited printouts on the counter. "Hannah had a nicer word for you."

"Yeah?"

"Fuckhot."

So why the hell do you live like this?

Janelle threw the word over her shoulder as she went to the living room and folded her body onto the white leather couch. The furniture in the front of the apartment was clearly where Trent had spent his budget. Like her, he'd buried himself in work.

Janelle pretended to focus on the papers in her hands, but the ink markings made no sense. She shouldn't have gone there. This was a business trip. *You and your big mouth.*

But there was the picture of them together. It was frameless now, but Janelle intended to earn one. Her romantic streak had kicked in, hard. She wouldn't force him into a relationship. Even if it were possible, it didn't work in the long run. She'd learned that lesson all too well, with Ben.

"That's not a nice word, either, Janie." Trent joined her, but as far away as possible, on the other end of the couch. No amount of money was going to salvage her pride if he kept on ignoring her.

"Kinda dirty," she agreed, placing an unread page face down on the empty seat between them. They worked in silence for a while, the question she needed to ask on the tip of her tongue. If they lapsed into flirting, there was a high probability they'd fall into bed again. She wouldn't do it unless she knew the truth.

"Are you married to Penny?" she asked quietly, holding her breath against the answer.

Trent rubbed his stubbled chin with one palm. "No. I'm her financial trustee. My agreement to release the video was conditional on my having a supervisory role over the distribution of the money. Penny has a guy she's worked with since her early days in the business who handles most of her accounts, including the royalties from her work. Her mother manages day-to-day spending. I guard the guardians."

"I thought...The only reason I could come up with for your celibacy and for the way you ended things was if you were married and couldn't divorce for financial or guilt reasons."

"I shouldn't have let you leave, thinking that." He placed the stack of papers on the floor beside the couch and faced her. "I'd never have made you complicit in adultery."

An avalanche of relief coursed through her. She'd carried so much guilt since Las Vegas, wondering if she'd been the other woman, like Crystal had been. Even though Trent had said as much, it had been hard to know for certain, and it had weighed on her more than she'd realized.

"Hey. Janie." At last, Trent bridged the distance between them, turning her gently to face him. "I was twenty when I met Penny. She was twenty-three. She looked angelic, but she was wild. I bagged my junk with her. Always. I hated the fact that she was screwing other men. It felt like shit. Even when there's open communication, it's not easy to know your partner is having sex with other people. I'd never put you or anyone in that position."

Kiss me, you fool. Janelle's eyes fluttered half-closed.

Silence. Stillness. He let go.

A bang against the wall behind her sent her heart rate into overdrive. A distinctly porn-sounding moan echoed through the vent. Trent exhaled and collapsed back against the couch as the sound of Sean and Hannah getting it on—loudly—echoed through the wall.

Giggles bubbled up through Janelle's chest and out her mouth. "Do you put up with this regularly?"

"More often than I'd like." A rueful smiled tugged at the corners of his mouth.

Say it. Janelle opened her mouth, but Trent got there first. "We could give them a run for their money."

Paper scattered as Janelle scrambled across the couch. "I thought you'd never ask."

Janelle threw one leg over him and moaned as she ground against the ridge of his erection. Trent's hands were under her shirt as she flattened her palms on either side of his face and kissed him.

"We shouldn't do this." He tugged her shirt up and over her head.

Janelle sat back on his thighs. "Is Penny going to be upset?"

"She has no say in what I do." Trent waited, as if he wanted to say more but couldn't.

"Fuck it, then. We *are* doing this."

Trent squeezed her breast so hard Janelle's nipple edged over the lace as she ground her hips against him. Her back arched and a sound rivaling anything from next door came out of her mouth.

"Don't hold back, Janie." Amusement. It turned his voice from whisky smooth to smoky hot seduction.

"I'll scream your name so loud they'll hear it on the roof deck if you keep doing that."

Trent tucked a finger inside the lace up and popped her other nipple out. He sucked the tip between his teeth and bit gently. Janelle moaned, loud even to her own ears. Her fingers were buried in his hair, the texture tickling against her chest.

"Too hard?"

"Do it again. Harder."

He anchored her hip with one hand to grind her pelvis harder against him, sucked and bit while squeezing her other breast. Janelle let go of his head long enough to reach behind her back and flick the clasp of her bra open. Trent feasted on her breasts: sucking, licking, squeezing, biting.

"Off," she demanded. He let go and sat forward. Janelle tugged his shirt over his head and flung it away. They were naked from the waist up. Trent tipped sideways, pulling her down on top of him as they crawled onto the couch in a writhing, grinding bond of shared physical need. She maneuvered beneath him so Trent's body crushed her into the leather. Skin-to-skin. Pure sensation.

Trent ground against her. Janelle squeezed his cock through his jeans.

"Off." She fumbled with the button.

"You first." Trent pulled her up. Wordlessly, they stripped off their remaining clothes. Hannah and Sean were still making porny noises through the vent. Competition.

Janelle closed her hand around him. *I love your cock. And everything that comes with it.*

"Condom. Now," she ordered breathlessly.

No questions. No protest. Trent yanked his jeans off the floor and produced one. He tore open the package and rolled it on. He rubbed the head of his dick against her clit, slid down and inside her without resistance. Janelle's entire body relaxed.

"Janie."

Trent's low moan reverberated through her body. His body shook with the effort of holding back. Janelle kissed his jaw, tasting his rough stubble. Neither moved.

I love you.

"Fuck me," she whispered. "Make me feel it. Give me something to take home tomorrow."

Trent pulled out. Wordlessly, he moved her onto her back, head propped against the opposite arm of the couch. He scissored two fingers into her and opened her wide.

"More," she gasped. "Is that all you've got?"

Trent knelt on the white leather, pushing her legs apart. He chuckled, the warm sound flooding her body with desire. "Are you in a rush, Janie?"

Son. Of. A. Bitch. "You kept me waiting all day. Yeah. I want you to get me off, right now."

"Anything for you, sweets." He inched his way out. Then ground into her, hard. Janelle's mouth dropped open.

"Yes. Like that." She groaned.

Slow out. Fast in. Trent's control was incredible. His skin was damp where it met hers. Pleasuring her like this came at a cost, one she was more than happy to make him pay. Trent picked up momentum. Janelle had no room to move, ratcheting up the sensation exponentially. He braced himself against the wall, his arm solid above her shoulder. She was thoroughly trapped. All she could do was take him, over and over.

Janelle forgot to care whether Hannah and Sean could hear them. The sounds coming out of her mouth were senseless and explicit, half coaching and half begging but mostly incoherent. Trent got the gist or didn't care, seemingly lost in his own storm.

They came down slowly, riding the high. Spent, he gently pulled out, leaving her wistful at the loss.

"Shit."

Janelle laid her forehead on her crossed forearms. "Something wrong?"

"The condom broke." The panic in Trent's voice was unmistakable. Janelle rolled over and eyed the split condom hanging from his fist. A milky droplet fell onto the white leather. She wiped it away with her finger. "So what?"

A beat of astounded silence. Janelle rolled over and stood up, sated and content for the first time since they'd parted in Las Vegas.

"I just dropped a payload of cum straight..." He broke off, clearly terrorized. "You could get pregnant."

"I've been on birth control for years, Trent. If you're clean, there's nothing to worry about."

"Why the hell, if you weren't having sex?" His confusion was almost endearing.

"I use it to skip my periods. Hormonal contraceptives. Not just for sex anymore." Janelle blew a kiss over her shoulder and went to clean up.

"You could've said something when we were in Vegas." When she came back, Trent had pulled on his boxers and jeans, and he sat with half his tight ass hanging off the side of one of the counter stools. Naked, Janelle went to him and kissed the head of the tattoo in the middle of his back.

"I wasn't going to screw a guy I'd just met without a condom. No matter how many medical records he had on file." She let go of him slowly, sliding her hands over his still, tense muscles. "What are you thinking, Trent?"

He almost spoke, then stopped himself. Her shoulders tensed. *Give me something to work with. Let me in.*

Instead, he guided her to stand between his knees and kissed her. Janelle opened and gently bit his lower lip. Trent nipped and licked the spot on her neck below her ear that was like an on switch for her girly bits. With a shuddering exhale, she pulled away and sauntered down the hall toward the bedroom. "It's a different story; now we're acquainted."

His chair scratched against the floor.

Trent caught her as she opened the door to the bedroom. He spun her around and picked her up, her legs locked around his waist. The room was pitch dark and silent, the only light coming from the kitchen. His knees hit the edge of the bed and they dropped together in a tangle.

With great deliberation Trent pulled out a condom package and rolled it on. Janelle's vision clouded until she looked away. Message received. He wasn't going to fuck her bare, even with an outright invitation. It was probably better that way, even if it hurt now.

13

"I don't think you should come to New York."

Trent's words slashed through Janelle's sleep-addled brain. He could've at least let her put some clothes on before going there. "You're firing me for sleeping with you?"

"No. I still need you to help with the pitch. I don't...you're a distraction, Janie. I need this contract."

"I need it, too." Janelle wasn't talking about the contract. "You're telling me this now, why?"

He rolled away, stood up and pulled on a plain white t-shirt. Even as he cut out her heart with a butter knife, Janelle couldn't help but admire his body. The man was gorgeous, extravagant, maudlin tattoo and all. *Mine.*

If he thought he could brush her off now, Trent had underestimated her. He'd fucked her as if desperate to pour everything they felt for one another into a single night. It wasn't as if he hadn't given her a preview of this conversation once before. Janelle hadn't expected it so soon, but ever since he'd made clear that all boundaries were still in place, she'd known this was coming. She pushed. He let her in a step or two, then Trent closed down.

Nothing about their pattern had changed.

"We should've stuck to the clean break." His jawline hardened. Though he visibly strained to project calm control, the straight line of his shoulders and his refusal to meet her eyes gave him away.

"There wasn't a clean break. Not on my side." Why couldn't he see it? Janelle kicked away the blanket. The airless room reeked of sex and sweat, of his body and hers. She wondered if it could be turned into a perfume. If so, she'd bathe in it. "You're the one who called me. Not the other way around."

"You'll still get your money, Janie. I'm not gonna stiff you."

Flippant replies on the tip of her tongue stayed caged by her clenched teeth. *Jagged wounds never heal right.* "I'm taking a shower and a walk. When I get back, we'll finish the last section of the proposal. Olivia's picking me up for lunch at eleven. You're on your own after that."

"You're quitting?" Trent demanded.

Janelle chuckled humorlessly. "I'll never quit on you, Trent. When're you going to figure that out?"

WE ADVANCED. Trent hit send, the buzz of his employees drowned out by the turmoil in his mind and body. Janie was so far under his skin, it physically hurt to be separated from her.

Sixteen days. More than two weeks had passed since he'd fucked her on the couch two of his developers were currently sitting on, arguing over a snippet of code. On the wall above, a faint smudge where he'd braced himself and driven his cock into her like a jackhammer.

Give me something to take home, she'd demanded.

Bad enough he'd mixed business and his personal life. The live-work space had been a good solution when he'd been starting up eight months ago. Now, it was a mess of too many interconnected threads.

Work was inseparable from Janelle.

Janelle was inseparable from his heart.

His heart was in his work in a way that hadn't been true a few weeks ago. They'd beat out five other companies to get to the final round. They had a fifty-fifty chance of winning. Losing was unthinkable, and very possible.

Trent's phone vibrated in his palm. **Congratulations.**

He'd fucked up. Massively. He couldn't exist in the same room as Janelle without being one hundred percent focused on her. Olivia had been right that she had a knack for this work, but she'd been completely wrong about their ability to work together. Trent knew, had known it before he'd called Janie. If he were being honest with himself, he'd used it as an excuse to contact her when he'd known damn well it was a bad idea.

Going into a high-value, high stakes pitch with Janelle at his side meant his mind would be on what she was wearing, on her faint, feminine scent and the throaty sound she made when she came all over his cock. There was too much at stake to risk having her standing next to him. It didn't matter that she could talk to anyone, while he struggled to find words. With her around, his dick was fully in control of his brain. He had to be present in the room or risk losing.

"Excuse me, Mace."

Trent shook his head to clear it. "Yeah. Priya?"

The first thing he'd do if he won the contract was rent office space. This arrangement wasn't working anymore.

Send me the final and your branding. I'll work on the presentation this week.

Janie had said she wouldn't quit on him. He was holding her to that promise, but she was staying in Florida. Where she was safe —from him.

"Can you see me?" Janelle tilted the screen on her computer.

"You're pixelated. Wait. Okay. Better." Her sister Alyssa's face swam into view, a loose braid trailing over her forehead and down one shoulder. Below that, she wore a bikini top and yoga shorts.

"You went back to blonde?" Janelle asked.

"That's all the sun's doing. No more dye. It's so much easier to keep up." Alyssa shifted on the bed. "Hey, look. I got a tattoo!"

"You did not! Who are you and what have you done with my sister?" Janelle's shock was mostly sisterly teasing, but considering how corporate Alyssa had been only a few months before, the change in her appearance was disorienting.

"Don't tell mom and dad. I'll tell them when I'm ready. See? It's a *pedorrera*."

"A what?" Janelle summoned her high school Spanish from the depths of her memory. "A farting bird?"

Alyssa's smooth laugh hadn't changed since she'd gone off on her sailing adventure. "It's a Cuban tody. They're adorable, tiny birds, and they do make a farting sound when they're hunting insects. We saw them when we were visiting Marc's family."

"Saw what?" A masculine voice that Janelle knew all too well floated in from offscreen.

"*Un pajarito bonito*," Alyssa made a kissy face. The screen went dark as Marc De Luna's form blocked the camera. When the image came back, Marc had tackled Alyssa back onto the bed. She was smiling up at him.

"Hey. I don't need to see this. Get a room!" Janelle called out.

"Hi Janie." Marc sat up. If anything, he looked more ripped than ever. Alyssa, too. They'd turned all lean and muscular from sailing and, presumably, a lot of sightseeing and sexing along the way.

It would've been easy to summon a pang of jealous longing, but Janelle felt only warm affection. "Marc, can I have a few more minutes with Aly before you get her back?"

"Only if you're not plotting some ridiculous contest," he smirked. Not long ago, his casual cockiness had irritated the hell out of Janelle. Her dynamic with Marc had always been big-brother-little-sister-ish. In retrospect, it shouldn't have been a surprise that he and Aly had shacked up, on a sailboat or anywhere.

"Oh, come on. It wasn't that bad. I need some big-sister perspective, so scram." Marc obliged her, after a lingering kiss with Aly.

That is what I want with Trent. Janelle thought wistfully.

"Okay, Janie, what's up?"

"I've, um, been offered a job, and I'm taking it."

"Yay! That's terrific!" Alyssa bounced and clapped. Again, not a reaction Janelle would've expected from her sister only a few months ago.

"It's in Washington, D.C." Janelle's smile faded as her sister cocked her head, puzzled.

"D.C.?"

More or less. "Virginia, technically. D.C. area. It's a business development role with an IT contractor."

"I…" Alyssa played with the end of her braid. "How did you land it?"

"I networked and made connections. The company's owner was willing to risk hiring me for a contract role, and I found a short-term sublet. Mom's helping me clean up my finances, the way you tried to get me to do. In a few months, I'll be in better shape." Stretching the truth was easy. Too easy. Janelle swallowed. More than anything, she wanted to be able to speak the truth freely. Without shame. She'd wallowed in it for way too long, and she had no more time for that emotion. But before she went blurting Trent's name, she had to know if there was a future for them, and the only way she was going to find out was to take a big leap of faith. "I was wondering if you could make a fancy PowerPoint template for me. For a pitch. I want to go into this job looking like a rock star."

"Sure. Of course. Send me the branding and a sense of what you want it to look like." Before she'd set sail with Marc, Alyssa had worked at an advertising company as a graphic designer. Janelle's relief was immediate and short-lived.

"Janie, are you sure you know what you're doing?" Aly asked.

"Not really. But I have to try something new. Maybe I'm gravitating toward the corporate world, even while you're running away from it. Wouldn't that be funny?" Janelle injected false confidence into her tone.

"I'd be shocked beyond belief and yet somehow not surprised. I can totally see you running a big company someday. You're decisive, you have vision, and you work hard for things you want. I think you'd be good at it, honestly."

Janelle and Alyssa affectionately signed off.

Say You Need Me

WE WON.

Two words of relief. An undefined ache as Trent popped open the bottle of champagne Olivia had brought. She chatted with Priya and Chaitu, the developer and project manager for the new account respectively. Olivia was cool in her lime green sheath dress and gold jewelry. April had been warm, and today was glorious, all promise and hope.

Congratulations.

One word. How many did they have left to say to one another? Trent's thumb slid over his phone screen. **I'll mail your check this afternoon.**

In the hall outside the apartment, the door banged closed. The new tenant. If he hadn't been in New York, he might've snapped up the studio across the hall. Instead, someone else had beaten him to it. Now he *had* to look for real office space instead of taking half-measures. The signed contract with the retainer deposit had arrived from New York that morning.

"To *winning*!" Trent raised his glass.

Keep it short and sweet, and get everyone back to work. All five employees, and Olivia, raised glasses of champagne. Trent's phone buzzed, ruining the moment.

Don't bother.

Trent choked. *What the hell, Janie?*

I'm paying you. A phone in the hall beeped. He could hear it through the door. For a second, it sounded like Janie's. Lots of people had that ring tone, though.

I'll pick it up.

Trent stared at his phone. Olivia raised her glass with a knowing smile, then turned back to her conversation. *No.*

The ache morphed into dread. Liftoff. A crash was inevitable.

When?

The signal from the hall was immediate and unmistakable. **Next time I see you.**

His phone tickled his palm. He typed a response. Deleted it. Tapped the same word—a plea, a flutter of hope he wanted to crush under his heel like a butterfly. What kind of sick bastard wanted to kill butterflies?

When?

The same beep. A soft knock on the apartment door. Trent depressed the handle and cracked it open.

"Hi." Janelle stood on his welcome mat in a knee-length black skirt and green patterned blouse. It turned her eye color a brilliant emerald. Mischievous yet collected, she searched his face, waiting for him to react.

Oh, fuck.

He let go of the handle. The door slammed closed. Heart racing, he turned to find six pairs of eyes focused on him.

"Who was that, Trent?" Olivia's dark eyes speared him with pity and amusement.

"No one," he declared, panic rising.

Olivia's sharp inhalation cut deep. Betrayal. She'd known about this massive clusterfuck and hadn't breathed a word of warning. "Let her in, Mace."

"I didn't invite her here."

"She worked on the pitch. You wouldn't have won if it weren't for Janelle's work on the presentation. Give the girl a glass of wine and a handshake."

Winning doesn't give her license to live across the hall.

Beneath his panic, Trent couldn't deny a thrill of anticipation. Not long ago, Janelle had stood naked in his windowless, shitty bedroom while he did his damnedest to scare her off. She'd told him she'd never quit on him. He hadn't believed her until this moment.

Janie. What the hell do you think you're doing? He hadn't been the one to declare war, but he was sure as hell going to win. Even if it meant losing everything he wanted. Fuck, he was so messed up. He wanted her. He couldn't have her. She wasn't supposed to be here.

When she finally got it through her stubborn skull that he wasn't good for anything but sex, it would end. She'd hate him, but it was better than letting her care. After all, Trent had no heart left to break. It had been shattered three times. Each time, he'd glued it back together, and buried the damaged thing farther down to protect it. No one got close. Janie was beyond naïve if the believed she could show up and turn them into a happy couple. There was no fixing sheer stupidity.

He stalked down the hall to the desk in his windowless bedroom. When he returned a moment later, Olivia had filled a plate and poured a glass of champagne. Chaitu was helping her with the door.

"Where are you going?" Trent demanded.

"If you won't invite her in, I'll take the party across the hall." Olivia radiated cool disappointment.

"Great, do you mind giving her this?"

Olivia stared at the check in his hand. Her gaze bounced to his, sorrowful and shocked. "I'm not your errand girl, soldier."

She let the door slam closed behind her. A rebuke. The training wheels were off. He couldn't count on Olivia's help indefinitely, anyway.

It was better to make a clean break. Always.

"I DIDN'T THINK he'd react like that." Olivia speared a piece of ham with her fork. "Trent's either scared shitless, enjoying the drama, or some combination of the two. You sure hit a nerve, Janelle. I hope you know what you're doing."

At lunch during her visit a few weeks before, Olivia had offered her a part-time, temporary job. Janelle had handed in her resignation letter at the warehouse the next day. Once Jessie had finished alternately berating her for leaving and crying about how she was going to miss the only other woman at the warehouse, Janelle had fired off an email to Sean about the sublet.

Olivia had expected her to work from Florida. Janelle had other plans.

"I knew it was a risk. It's only for a few weeks. I needed to start fresh." The only thing keeping her in Florida was her family. Between the temporary job offer and the temporary apartment, it seemed her stars had aligned. Proximity to Trent was both an inducement and a concern. "I figured the worst that could happen is I move in, he starts seeing someone else, and I have to suck it up and deal for a few weeks before I move back home. At least I'd know, right? And I'll have made more business contacts, too."

Saturday morning, she'd loaded her shiny new two-door hatchback with everything she owned, hugged her parents goodbye, and driven eight hours. Sunday evening, she'd stayed with Olivia. Monday morning, she'd picked up the keys from the leasing office and moved her few suitcases and boxes into the apartment, half-hoping, half dreading they'd bump into one another in the hall. But she didn't see him all day.

Tuesday, the news had come about the win. Olivia had texted to invite her to the party. Janelle had knocked on his door with her heart in her eyes, trusting he'd see her bold move for what it was: a declaration of love.

Slamming the door in her face had been Trent's equally non-verbal, unmistakable way of literally shutting her out. Janelle sipped the champagne Olivia had brought over. "Thanks for including me in the party."

"You belonged at the real one, but I do what I can. I should get back to the office. You're coming in tomorrow?"

"Yes, I'll be there first thing."

Olivia patted her shoulder. "Hang in there. He might come around. Though I wouldn't blame you if you told Trent to suck an egg after today. If everything else is working out, you'll have time to look for a new apartment."

"Exactly. See you tomorrow, Olivia." Alone with her unpacked boxes, Janelle's confidence leached away. This was the first time she'd ever lived alone. No roommate. No family nearby to fall back on. Her one friend in the area apart from Trent was Crystal. Olivia, now that she was Janelle's boss, didn't quite count. Janelle flopped onto the couch that turned into a pull-out bed, which had been delivered the previous afternoon. A small table and chairs sat next to the door. A bright upholstered side chair, rug, and coffee table from Ikea completed the setup.

No TV. She'd get by with streaming shows on her computer until she could afford one.

Janelle gathered the cardboard from her newly assembled furniture and dragged it down the hall to the garbage room.

"Need a hand?" A Southeast Asian man, gestured to the heavy cardboard. "I'm Chaitu. I work for Mason."

"Thanks, Chaitu. Janelle. I moved in yesterday."

"Did you really consult on the RMS pitch?" he asked curiously.

Janelle used her foot to jam the cardboard into the garbage closet. "Yes."

"It was really good. Priya presented. She said they basically awarded it on the spot. What happened with Mason?"

"Nothing," Janelle replied, a little too quickly. "I was only a consultant. He didn't expect me. I just moved across the hall, and I don't know anyone in the area. I was assumptive in stopping by. Lesson learned."

Chaitu didn't appear convinced, but he didn't press her for details. "The team goes out for Taco Tuesdays. We're moving the party down the street later, if you want to join us."

Janelle beamed. "That would be great. You know where I am. Knock when you're ready to go."

Might want to stay out of Trent's way for a while.

Nah. She hadn't come all this way to politely maneuver around his delicate sensibilities. She wasn't going to force him into anything, but she wasn't going to let him pretend there was nothing between them, either.

Back in her little studio, Janelle finished washing and putting away the dishes and hanging up her clothes. Once she had a more permanent address, she'd send for the rest of her belongings. For now, the closet was only half-full. She'd taken every single high-necked, oversized blouse to Goodwill before she moved. Only her best clothes, including the things her sister had given her after quitting her job in New York, had come with her to Virginia. She was done hiding anything, including her body. Hiding hadn't protected her from harassment anyway.

Around four, she made a quick visit to the grocery store. Janelle had just set the bag of food on the counter when a sharp rap on the metal door startled her. Early for Chaitu.

It was Trent. Janelle leaned against the frame, waiting. "Do you need something?"

His mouth was a flat, angry line. "Here's your check. What the fuck are you doing here?"

"What does it look like? Moving in."

"You could've told me."

"I can imagine how the conversation would've gone. 'Trent, I'm thinking about moving into the apartment across the hall.' You'd mumble something about a clean break, fuck me until I couldn't see straight, and pat my ass right before you let the door hit it on the way out. I let you do that once. You're not getting away with it again."

"Keep it down, would you?" He glanced behind him, at the hive of busy coders working away in his more-work-than-live apartment.

She snorted. "Are you ashamed of fucking me?"

"Of course not. Can we have this conversation inside?"

Janelle crossed her arms and sank deeper against the door frame. The edge bit into her back where she propped it open while blocking the entrance with her body. "Sure. Invite me over."

"Can't." He bit the word out. With exaggerated politeness: "May I please come in?"

Janelle backed up. "Since you asked so nicely. Unlike some people, I don't slam doors in my unexpected guests' faces."

Trent's body was coiled and taut as he stepped two feet over the threshold. He examined the room for a long minute. "Sorry. For slamming the door."

"Are you?" Janelle poured two glasses of water and held one out. He took it and looked up at the light fixture. Trent examined her handiwork without moving a step further into her apartment.

"I was planning to rent this place. No wonder Sean gave me a weird look when I asked about it."

"Am I supposed to be sorry I stole it out from under you?" she demanded.

"Are you?" Finally, he looked at her. Janelle tried to read everything in his eyes, but there was too much.

"No, I got here first." She grinned sweetly.

"So you did." He rubbed his jaw. A three-day scruff covered it. Janelle wanted to rub her face against it.

"I'm not going away, Trent." Janelle leaned against the counter, waiting.

He ripped his attention away like a Band-Aid left too long on delicate skin. "What do you want from me?"

Love, you moron. Hearts and rainbows and kids and minivans and arguing about bills over leftovers for dinner. "Who says I want anything?"

A knock at the door. She placed her water carefully on the counter, identical to the one in his place, only smaller.

"Expecting guests?" Sarcasm dripped from his tone, but Janelle thought she detected a hint of concern beneath.

"I have plans." Janelle opened the door and pasted on a smile. "Hi, guys. Give me one minute. I'll be right out."

Trent's body tensed with smoldering fury. "Taco Tuesday. You're going out with my team?"

"Yes, I am. And there's not a damn thing you can do about it." Janelle picked up her handbag and walked out. Let him stay. Let him snoop. The only potentially embarrassing thing he might find was her vibrator. He could claim her or he could leave her alone, but he didn't get to use her for sex and pitch help and then push her away on every other level.

If Trent wanted a fight? Game on. This battle was going to be epic.

THE SOUND STARTED SHORTLY after nine, right after Janelle stepped out of the bath. Low voices talking. Music swelled and fell, followed by the increasingly loud sounds of people having sex. Like Sean and Hannah getting it on, the vent connecting the two apartments served as a conduit to whatever movie Trent was blasting.

In her bathrobe, with her hair dripping and her face free of makeup, Janelle propped her door open and rang the opposite bell. It chimed, loudly, but he didn't answer.

"Trent, could you turn it down?" Janelle used her fist on the door. No response. Not even an angry one.

Janelle returned to her apartment, unfolded the couch and made up her bed, then lay in it. This was low, even for Trent. He fought dirty, she'd give him that.

All the porny sounds being piped into her apartment started her imagining everything she was going to do to him if he ever saw reason. Janelle turned on her vibrator and gave it a good workout. She was in this to win it and confronting Trent with sex on the brain would only lead to throwing herself at him. Last time, she'd jumped him the minute he'd suggested sex, and it had been a mistake.

An hour later, the movie was still playing and her vibrator had run out of battery. The situation wasn't funny anymore.

"Trent Mason, you are a flaming asshole," she muttered, punching her pillow into a tent to cover her ears. Thirty seconds later, she was hot and couldn't breathe. She lay there, listening to too-loud movie sex for another half-hour. Then Trent's voice sneaked under her door.

"Yeah, just got home. Gotta go. Bye, Aunt Susie."

Janelle flung her door open as he stuck the phone in his pocket and pulled out the key. "You weren't even here, all this time?"

Your outrage isn't helping.

Neither was Trent's smirk. "Miss me?"

"Not at all. My vibrator and I had a lovely evening."

That wiped the smile off his face like Windex took smudges off glass. For two seconds, Janelle would've sworn he was going to barge into her apartment and fuck her brains out, and if he did, she'd let him. Resisting his touch was a nice fantasy.

Then one of his muscular shoulders lifted and fell in a half shrug, as if he couldn't be bothered to produce a full one. He turned back to the door and spoke without looking at her.

"Next time, come over and watch it with me. Bring your toyfriend."

The door banged shut behind him. She'd moved in barely seventy-two hours ago and this new door-slamming phase of their non-relationship was already getting old.

With a little growl, Janelle stalked into her place. A moment later she emerged with a piece of paper, a marker, and a roll of packing tape. The sound of plastic and glue ripping off the reel echoed along the hallway. Satisfied, she stood back and admired her work.

Score: Janie 2, Trent 1.

Priya and Chaitu could fill her in on Trent's reaction later.

The next morning, Janelle found her sign crumpled and taped to her door. With her lower lip caught between her teeth, she smoothed it flat.

Keep my employees out of this.

Fair enough. Janelle added a black streak under her name and scribbled *You're loosing* across the bottom. Then she took her shower, dried her hair, and dressed in a violet blouse and black trousers. In her purse was the check he'd brought over yesterday. In the car, she ripped it open and gasped.

Twenty-two thousand dollars. It was more than they'd agreed to. She turned it over, heart fluttering, then spotted the message in the memo field. *For services rendered.*

Oh. That. Asshole. The affront hit her like a boxer's glove to the temple. "You can't turn me into a prostitute just by cutting me a check, Mace. You might not have a problem with it, but I do."

Her tires squealed a little as she drove out of the garage. He was trying to turn this into something shameful, the way he felt about his video. Too bad she was done with feeling ashamed. Cutting, witty retorts wheeled through her mind all morning as she worked. By lunchtime, she'd settled on one. Janelle made a quick stop at the bank. At the mailbox, she hesitated. Across the street was a shipping and packing store. Janelle grinned.

Make him sign for it.

Oh, yeah. Trent couldn't scare her off her that easily.

TRENT SCRIBBLED his name without thinking, preoccupied with the unexpected cease-fire with his new neighbor. He should be concentrating on nailing down the details on the other three pitches he was working on. Or onboarding the New York client. He trusted Priya and

Chaitu, but they were young, this was their first big account, and he couldn't afford mistakes.

Instead, all he could think about was nailing Janelle. She kept him walking a razor-fine line between irritation and adoration. The woman refused to take a hint. He didn't want a relationship. Not right now, not with anyone.

Want isn't the right word.

Of course, he wanted to be with her, but he had other priorities. Janelle wasn't the casual type. When she wanted something, she gunned for it with everything she had. But she had the wrong target in her sights. Technically, there was nothing wrong with renting an apartment near him. It was a free country and all. He could understand, obliquely, how being close to one person she knew in the area might have been appealing. If she'd told him about it…well, Trent couldn't deny he'd have told her to find somewhere else to live. With her credit history that would've been difficult. He tossed the torn envelope onto the desk in his windowless bedroom and pulled out the single sheet of printer paper wrapped around a personal check.

What the…?

The check was for over five grand. She'd returned the bonus he'd included, plus some. The paper was an itemized list of everything he'd paid for since finding her outside the hotel in Las Vegas.

Pink reading glasses.

Lunch.

Gin from the hotel mini bar.

Vodka from the hotel mini bar.

10-pack of condoms.

At the bottom of the page, a handwritten scrawl. *I said I'd pay you back. We're square.*

Trent sucked in a breath. He'd never expected her to repay him. It was the kind of thing people said to make borrowing money easier, when they didn't have a choice. He knew she didn't have much—they wouldn't have met if she hadn't been broke and desperate. What kind of jackass did she think he was?

The kind who fucks her and leaves her. Repeatedly.

For the next seven weeks, this was his reality. Their ongoing feud, while entertaining, was as much a distraction as screwing her would've been. Trent suspected this was the point.

EARLY ON THURSDAY, they bumped into one another coming out of their apartments. Trent wore a light t-shirt, shorts, and running shoes.

"Morning," was all Janelle said. "Out for a run?"

Bet he loses the shirt after a mile or two. She sighed.

He side-eyed her but fell into step. "No swimming pool in this building."

"True."

"Maybe you should've looked for a different apartment."

"A pool wasn't the first item on my checklist. An affordable short-term lease was. In seven and a half weeks, I'll have a landlord reference and better credit rating if I need to re-evaluate my living situation. Are you going to make me do that?"

Trent responded to her pointed commentary with another sidelong, assessing glare. Janelle poked the call button for the elevator. He headed for the stairwell, then stopped short. "You really didn't move in because of me?"

Poor man, so puzzled by the notion she had reasons for moving here exclusive of him. The elevator dinged open. "Believe me, Trent, you were a huge incentive, but, no, you were not the reason."

He caught the door as it closed. Janelle bit back a smile. "Thought you were taking the stairs?"

"Thanks for holding the elevator," he glowered.

"I didn't." Oh, the hell with concealing her amusement. A grin took over her face. Janelle couldn't help it.

"I got the check. I'm not cashing it." Trent's glower transformed into an answering smirk.

"It's a money order. The funds are gone from my account no matter what you do with it. Frame and put it on the wall. Use it for toilet paper. I don't care. It's yours." Janelle brushed by him, levity evaporated.

He followed her out the building, a step behind. By the time they got outside, he'd found a retort. "A-plus trolling, Janie. Notch another point on that scoreboard you're keeping, for now. You misspelled *losing*, you know. I'll find a way to get you back."

Trent pulled his shirt over his head and took off in the direction of the nearby park. Janelle stared after him, longingly admiring the play of his tattooed muscles. Then she headed the other way for her morning walk. She wouldn't want Trent to think she was stalking him. For a moment, she wished she could do it all over—the move, the apartment. It wasn't working out the way she'd hoped. Another one of her dumb schemes gone wrong. But at least now, she knew they were headed in opposite directions.

14

He had to end the game.

Trent waited until after his employees had left for the weekend before knocking on Janelle's door. Soft music played from inside.

Janelle peered through the crack. "I can turn it down if it's bothering you."

Trent wondered when the last time he'd listened to music for pleasure. His life was airless, like his sleeping cell. No wonder Sean and Hannah had called him a monk. He'd been living like one ever since his discharge. Before that, too, only in a different context. Deployment in Afghanistan hadn't exactly been luxurious.

"Do you want to come over for a few minutes?" he asked, running his hand through his hair.

Wary, she glanced at her laptop on the table. "It's Friday."

"So?"

"I'm going out soon. I was working on a new proposal. It came in today, due Tuesday, so I want to get ahead."

"Where are you going later?" he demanded.

Her pretty face shuttered, and Trent's body knew the answer before he'd finished the question.

"Out. I have a date."

"You make fast work." Raw jealousy streaked through him. *Maybe you should give this a chance.*

"Have you changed your mind about dating me?" Janelle crossed her arms beneath her magnificent tits, framing them.

"No." Pride. He'd pitied her for it once, because he recognized it in himself.

"Then it's not your business what I do with my free time." Janie's pink mouth pulled at the corners.

"So you're not going to complain if I start seeing someone?" he demanded.

"I'll be hurt that you didn't choose me, but it's your decision. I knew it was a possibility." She started to close the door. "If we're done here…"

Trent stuck his hand into the gap. "Tomorrow. Dinner."

"I have plans."

"Another date?" *I'll murder any man who sets hands on you.* He wouldn't, not really, but the thought was there and it wasn't going away. At least she hadn't slammed his fingers. Trent couldn't fault her if she did. He had no right to both ignore her and prevent her from moving on.

"Yes, in fact," Janelle replied evenly.

"Brunch, then." Maybe they could find a halfway point to meet. Everything south of his waist sure liked that idea.

"I'm working on my RFP."

"Sunday."

She was silent for a long minute. "I cook. And we eat on dishes, not paper plates."

"Deal." He moved to kiss her, but caught himself. "Have fun tonight."

JANELLE MIGHT'VE BEEN a little disingenuous in describing her plans for Friday and Saturday as dates. Hannah had invited her to meet some friends for drinks, and in the spirit of making new friends, she'd said yes. Then, Crystal had popped up on Facebook and asked to meet up in the city. She hadn't hesitated to accept.

Staying busy was crucial to avoiding the sit-home-waiting-for-Trent syndrome she could easily fall into. Janelle had made herself a promise to say yes to every invitation. So far, she'd kept it.

Still, *date* implied she was meeting up with other men, and that wasn't the truth. Her dishonesty had been spur-of-the-moment, but it had been a lie nonetheless. If her ploy to inspire jealousy had worked, Trent hadn't shown it. Why would he? He'd dated an actively working adult film star. He wasn't likely to get possessive, no matter how much she wished he would, at least a little bit.

Sunday, she slept in, went for a run, and drank coffee over an actual paper newspaper. For a moment, Janelle suffered a pang of longing for the time she'd spent discussing the Sunday news with her parents, first as a teenager, then when she'd lived at home again for a few months. A call home soothed the vague sense of loss, especially when they offered to come and visit her soon.

Shopping accomplished, Janelle debated fashion choices. Too sexy and there was a not-insubstantial chance they'd fall into bed without having the hard talk they needed. But if she put in no effort after pretending to go out on dates, she was sending him the message she wasn't interested. One untruth was bad enough.

Janelle settled on a pleated skirt that fell to her knees and a lace blouse worn over a bra. It wasn't quite sheer, but the bra was visible if you looked hard. Trent rang the bell a minute after she'd wrapped an apron over her clothes, concealing the sexiness.

He'd dressed studiously casual in jeans and a t-shirt that outlined his biceps and hid nothing of his ridiculously defined pectoral muscles. Intentional? Just a little. Plus, he'd brought flowers. Janelle hated the way her heart pitter-pattered at the sight. "Pretty. Thank you."

"Not as pretty as you."

Janelle turned away to hide her smile, searching for a glass large enough to hold the bouquet. "Aren't you full of compliments today."

"It might be the first one I've ever given you," he said. His mouth quirked up ruefully.

Janelle found a vase and ran the tap to fill it. "It's not. But it's the first time you've brought me flowers. My neighbor might be a romantic after all."

"Don't get your hopes up, Janie." Trent leaned against the counter. Janelle remained behind the granite barrier, chopping and boiling water. It was safer there. Silence stretched between them as she popped open a bottle of wine and poured them each a glass. "I don't want to fight you anymore."

"Yeah? Do you concede?" she asked without glancing over her shoulder.

"What am I conceding, if I say yes?"

Janelle bit her lower lip. Her hands gripped the countertop, her stance wide. The battle, sure, but the battle was about how he kept trying to shut her out. She wasn't having it. "That you care about me enough to let me into your life."

The words came out in a whisper. Hot embarrassment flooded her as he stood there, watching her. Janelle picked up her wine glass stirred their dinner before it caught fire.

"Is that why you came here?" he asked quietly when she turned back around.

"No. I came here for me. To make contacts and get more experience. If I'd stayed in Florida I wouldn't have been as motivated to make this work. I'd have fallen back into my old habits." She swallowed. Better to get it over with. "I also came because I want us to…give it a try. If it's not working, my sublet is up in seven weeks. I'll move out, and you can take over the studio like you'd planned to. But if it is, we could…" Her tongue was like a dried-out sponge. "We could figure out the next step. Together. I'm not asking for forever or hearts and diamonds. All I want is a few weeks to see if what we have works in the real world."

Say something. Janelle ran water over the dishes in the sink, but he didn't speak. "If you want me to leave you alone, all you have to say is say so. I'm not here to force you into something you don't want. After the New York pitch, I thought your objection was the distance. So, I eliminated the distance problem."

"Unilaterally," he countered.

"If all you wanted from me was sex, say so." Janelle stirred dinner a little more forcefully than necessary. A shrimp fell out of the pan. She picked it up and tossed it back in, burning her finger in the process. She stuck her finger in her mouth, wishing he'd say something, even if it hurt.

"I can't give you what you want, Janie." Regret laced his voice.

Janelle plucked the wine glass he was swirling, but not drinking from, out of his hand and handed him a beer. She poured the contents into her own glass. Another useless piece of information to cling to: Trent didn't like wine.

"I told you from the beginning, I don't do hookups. I get attached easily." Janelle carried two plates to the table.

"On the day we met, you were running from a hookup."

"I did something foolish, but it didn't change anything fundamental about me. Maybe, if Kyle had been a decent human being, I'd have gone through with it and convinced myself it was okay. But having sex once in a while with no affection or expectations? I can't do that. Not with him. Not with you. Not with anyone."

"I can't keep my hands off you, Janie. I've tried. It doesn't work." Trent spoke to his beer. The food sat untouched before them.

"You're doing a damn good job of it right now," she complained, stabbing her dinner without raising her fork to her mouth.

At last, he looked up. "It's torture. You should've stayed in Florida, where you were safe." He pushed his food away.

"If I'd wanted safe, we'd never have met." Janelle traced the painted rim of her plate with the tip of one finger.

"You've boxed me in. I can't stay away, knowing you're right across the hall. Distance was the only barrier I had. You've taken away the decision."

The selfishness of her move hit her with sickening force. Though she hadn't meant to, she'd forced his hand exactly the way she'd done with Ben. Janelle dropped her fork. "You can always ignore me."

Wait. Trent's responsible for how he reacts. He hasn't left you alone since you arrived, either. You eliminated the distance problem without asking him, true, but he's the one who walked the last yard into your apartment.

"You first," he grumbled, the first acknowledgement he'd given her that this wasn't completely one-sided.

Yeah, that was going to work. They'd been crackling with chemistry since the minute they'd met. Still, she called his bluff.

"All right. I'll leave you alone, if that's what you want. I wish I could tell you I'm sorry, Trent. I can't. If I'd talked to you about it, asked permission, you'd never have given me a chance. I'm here, and I'm staying so I can figure out how to crush this business development thing. The New York pitch gave me a taste of success, and I don't need your approval to go after more. What you do about my presence for the next few weeks is up to you." Janelle shoved back her chair and removed both plates, mostly uneaten. She put the leftovers in containers and began cleaning up in the kitchen.

Trent stood up and walked out the door.

Well. She had her answer.

Janelle slammed the dishes into the dishwasher. Her eyes hurt. Her heart ached. She'd gambled and lost. She pulled the apron over her head, rolled it into a ball and slammed it into a drawer.

The buzzer rang so loud she almost screamed, followed by a pounded fist. "Janie. Open up."

She swung it open, angry words dying on her lips. He propped up a heavy mattress with his broad shoulders.

"You don't have a bed," he observed.

Janelle gaped. "I—the couch pulls out."

Trent pushed passed her. "I'm not sleeping on a couch for the next seven weeks. Where can I put this?"

15

Janelle gaped at him as if Trent had lost his mind. Maybe he had. He'd meant it when he said he was tired of resisting. This woman was pure, high-grade temptation. He was done holding back, and there was going to be a proper platform for everything he planned to do with her for the next seven weeks.

"You're moving in? Just like that?" Her green gaze was luminous as she searched his. Trent's heart squeezed, the pressure of her expectation tectonic.

"I don't want you wandering around my apartment with my staff there, and I'm not sleeping on a couch for seven weeks." It was the only practical solution. "You want to play house, let's play house. Unless you don't want me here."

Her expression shuttered momentarily. Then a wide grin spread over her lips, her even white teeth above pink lips. "This is better than I'd hoped."

Janelle's pink nails dug into the fabric of the mattress as she tried to pull it into the room. Trent brushed her away and hauled it inside. Janie bent over to shove the chair out of the way, giving him a good view up her skirt. It stopped just short of the main attraction.

Trent leaned the mattress against the wall.

Janelle advanced toward him. Late evening light filtered through the high windows and glinted off her hair, streaking it with red and purple, the colors of sunset. His breath caught, and an unfamiliar feeling swept through him. Whatever it was—happiness was too much to ask—her determination to have him was glorious.

Who could resist her?

Not him. Few men would've stood a chance, and his moral compass pointed every which direction but north. And yet, nothing had changed. Penny was still an anchor in his life. Janelle had a jealous streak, and the last thing she needed was his shitty life decisions holding her back when she was trying to make a leap forward.

Janelle didn't appear to care about any of it. She ran her hands over his chest, backing him against the bed. "Thank you."

Her lips were soft, her breath warm, her body tensile and yielding as Trent pulled her hard against him. "For what?"

"Giving me a chance."

Self-loathing popped the air out of his joy bubble. Yeah, they'd spend the next few weeks reliving their Vegas hotel sex, but when their time was up, Trent knew he'd walk away again. Janie was too much, too close to everything he'd ever wanted, too perfect, and now she had unfulfilled ambition that might take her anywhere. Letting himself care about her and then losing her would pulverize every remaining shard of his heart. He couldn't protect himself and give Janie the love she wanted. He couldn't protect *her* anymore. All he could do was delay the moment of reckoning and try to enjoy the ride. The final drop was bound to be vomit-inducing for both of them.

Janelle's fingers worked his jeans open and sprung his cock free. Trent's butt pressed against the mattress as she licked the tip. He couldn't say no. He didn't want to. He wanted to say yes until he was hoarse and spent and they were so tangled together they couldn't be undone. He couldn't do that to her, any more than he could abandon Penny.

Her jaw loosened, sucking him deeper. The mischief in her eyes as she looked up almost made him come. He thrust into her mouth.

Janelle pushed forward to meet him, and Trent dug his fingers into the silk of her hair until her lips almost touched his balls.

She popped off and grinned up at him. "I'm going to do this every day."

Then she went back to work, until Trent was forced pull out.

"Easy, Janie. We have all evening."

She sat back on her knees, still fully dressed, her expression both innocent and utterly debauched. "It's been weeks."

Damn the consequences, there was no stopping this.

Janelle pulled his jeans down over his hips, past his knees, and kicked them aside. She rose and tugged his shirt up, though she remained fully clothed. Trent suspected there was a very nice surprise beneath that swishy skirt. The lace top was sexy enough, sheer enough to see the outline of her bra but otherwise covering her from neck to elbow. Combined with the apron she'd worn to cook dinner, Trent had been fighting a hard-on since he'd arrived.

Naked, he pulled her close. The rough texture her shirt scratched over his chest. Janelle wound one arm around the back of his neck. He tasted himself on her lips as he cupped one hand around the sweet curve of her ass. She hopped up. Trent swiveled and pressed her into the mattress as it tried to sag away from the wall. His hips flexed and his heart rate kicked up as Janie sank her teeth into his lower lip.

"I'm not sorry I came here." She gasped as he nibbled his way across her jaw, tasting the smoothness of her skin with his tongue. Janelle locked her legs around his waist. Trent shoved her skirt up, the rough tips of his fingers following soft skin all the way to her crevice. Her breath was hot against his skin as she moaned.

"You will be." But not yet. Not now. He traced the curve to her center and found nothing, no barrier. An animal groan tore out of him.

"Inside me, Trent."

It would be so easy. *I can't do this to her.* He couldn't *not* do this with her, either.

"Condoms," he bit out.

Janie wriggled out of his arms. On the floor, she yanked open the drawer of the small table next to the bed. Trent braced the mattress against the wall.

"Come here." She tossed her shirt over her head. Her hair was a mess, sticking up every direction. Her bra was sheer and embroidered. Trent's balls tightened harder. Closing the distance was almost painful. Tugging one off in the shower every morning and again at night hadn't done more than take the edge off his need for her.

She tore the foil open with her teeth and rolled it over him, one leg tucked up under her wrinkled skirt, the bra barely containing her amazing breasts. The rough texture of her shirt over his chest had been so good. No wonder she ground against him when he teased her through the fabric of her bra.

Janelle lay back on the couch. One elegant foot was propped on the arm, the other leg dangling off the side, and her hair splayed out over the cushion. Her pale pink fingernails curled into the dark fabric, working it up over her tan thighs.

"Janie," he pleaded.

Her full pink lips twitched as she smiled. "Make me sorry, Trent."

She didn't believe him. Trent knelt between her legs, her sex glistening in the lamplight.

"Not tonight, Janie. I meant it. I'm done fighting."

He teased her with the head of his dick. Janie squirmed, pushing herself up on one elbow trying to get enough leverage to slide over him. Trent's thighs were on fire holding back from the pounding he desperately wanted to give her, but he laughed. She growled.

"Are you sorry yet?"

"I'll never be sorry."

She leveraged her hips as his head tipped into her glistening folds. Trent grunted, pulling back. Bliss was a thrust away. He slid two fingers inside her to the third knuckled and crooked them against the rough spot. Trent gave her just enough pressure to make her squirm and cry out, long neck arched. Not enough to satisfy.

"Sorry yet?"

"You're still fighting."

Janie's green eyes glittered with frustration. There was no better sight. It made him harder than he'd ever been, his dick straight out, balls tight. That was why he was drawing this out. Once he got inside her, it wasn't going to take more than a few thrusts to blow.

"Say you're sorry and I'll let you come."

"I'll never be sorry," she said again, but he heard the desperation.

"Never?"

He circled his thumb over her clit, too gently. Her teeth captured her lower lip and she arched against his hand.

"Maybe a little."

"Say it out loud."

"I'm sorry I cornered you," she whimpered. Trent slid three fingers inside her this time, stroking the sensitive spot as he pressed the pad of his thumb over her clit. When her expression softened and the pulse throbbing along her elegant neck evened out, Trent pushed her knee against the back of the couch and pressed his cock into her with a smooth motion.

Janelle clutched his arm and moaned. Lost as he was in the sensation of her tight, wet body, Trent still remembered to help her out with his fingers. The orgasm reverberated up his spine like a shockwave. Janelle arched her back, meeting him with a wild moan. Not completely in sync but close enough. He didn't deflate right away. Trent kept going for a few extra thrusts to make sure his woman was cared for.

His woman.

For a few weeks.

"Now I'm especially not sorry I cornered you," Janelle snuggled against him. She would be, though. Janelle deserved better than anything he had to offer. Maybe proximity with his damaged self would help her arrive at that conclusion on her own.

There was a whoosh of air, a thump and a crash, and darkness all at once. Trent dove down onto the couch, covering Janelle with his naked body. His heart hammered. At first he thought she was crying, so he stroked her hair with his free hand.

"Are you all right?"

She let loose with a whoop of laughter. "The mattress fell down. I think it hit the cord of the lamp and pulled it off the table. We should finish moving you in so there's a place to get it on without breaking things."

And they did. After which Trent made her say she was sorry again, several more times. And again, in the morning, for good measure.

"My parents are visiting next weekend."

"Is that right." Trent wound his arm tighter around her waist until Janelle's body was pressed hard against his, her hair sticking to his shoulder where her head was tucked against his neck.

"Can we stay in your apartment for the weekend, so they can sleep here?"

The windowless bedroom had been transformed into an office to accommodate his growing team, but lately he and Janie had been working together in the studio. On days when she was at Olivia's office, he had all the space he needed, but with Janie was around it quickly became a competition—one they usually resolved through midday sex. Four weeks of near-constant intimacy hadn't diminished their need for physical connection.

"You should stay here. I'll sleep across the hall." Trent kissed her forehead.

Janelle turned to him with a full-on pout. "My dad snores. Besides, I don't want to hide you."

Trent pulled his arm out from under her and padded to the bathroom. "You want your parents to meet the ex-poker-pro porn star you're fucking? I don't think so, Janie."

Hot water sluiced over his body. The bathroom door slammed open. Two seconds later, Janelle yanked on the shower door.

"I want you to meet my family."

Trent knew that uncompromising glint. Under other circumstances, he adored it. "You're letting out the steam."

She closed the door behind her, eyes narrowed with irritation. Janie had a wonderful habit of barging in on his showers, which usually resulted in her practicing phenomenal oral skills on him. Not a bad way to start the day.

"If you want me to suck your cock ever again, you'll come to dinner with me and my parents."

Trent laughed. "And then what? They google me and find out who you're hooking up with?"

Janie stood back against the shower wall, her tan body sprayed with droplets. "I wish you'd stop being self-conscious about the video. It happened. Nobody cares."

"I care."

"Trent. Look at me."

He didn't. As no blowjob was forthcoming, he washed his hair and soaped his body, hogging the water. She was the one who'd crashed his shower. Let Janie be cold.

"Everyone knows about it. Your staff. Olivia. Nobody cares. Who do you think you're hiding from? People like that woman at the conference who grabbed your butt?"

Myself.

"I'll risk no more oral sex." Janie loved it as much as he did, as she'd declared only an hour ago. *I love your cock in my mouth* had been her exact words. As if he was going to resist when she caved.

"Your call." Janelle stepped into the spray and began washing her body, lingering over all the good bits. There weren't any not-good bits where she was concerned. Janie was the total package.

But if she thought she was going to pull some *Lysistrata* shit on him, she was out of her mind. Her parents didn't need to know Trent Mason, former professional gambler, whose erect dick was available for anyone with Internet access to see plowing another woman's pussy, was currently screwing their daughter multiple times a day.

How could she think this was a good idea? Any of it? Sleeping together, shacking up. Meeting her family was out of the question.

She showered quickly while he toweled off, spending a little extra time on his erection since he knew Janie was watching even as she fumed. True to form, Janelle popped out and knelt on the bath mat.

"Empty threats," he taunted.

Janelle beamed slyly as she ran her tongue up his length. "Not empty. I thought of a better way to persuade you."

"Oh?"

Trent went from hard to bursting as Janelle massaged his balls. She then moved lower, finding the sensitive spot between his sack and his anus. She popped off long enough to give him a cocky grin and ask, "Do you like this?"

He responded with an incoherent grunt and dug his fingers through the slippery strands of her wet hair to pull her back into place. Janelle worked the puckered rim before edging her finger inside. Trent stiffened at the intrusion.

"Do you want me to stop?"

"Keep going," he managed through gritted teeth. Janie didn't fight fair.

She worked a second finger into his butt. That alone would've been amazing, but she kept going until she found the sensitive spot about two inches in. Janelle worked the lump, each stroke sending waves of pleasure through his pelvis. Trent gripped the towel holder in a desperate bid to remain standing. Janelle sucked and stroked and massaged until his entire body turned to jelly.

The orgasm reduced Trent to mindless gasps. His ass hit the edge of the bathroom counter as Janelle pulled off and stroked him rhythmically. There cracking sound, and the towel bar gave way in his hand. Trent came like a volcano, jizz landing everywhere. The sheer quantity of it was almost disturbing. A splotch had hit the wall, another gush spread across the floor. Smaller puddles had hit the shower door and the toilet seat.

Trent's legs threatened to fail. Janelle pushed his chest and he fell back against the cold counter for support, her expression torn between triumph and concern. "You okay?"

"Holy shit," he mumbled.

Janelle's eyebrows were two astonished arcs. "It looks like a poltergeist exploded in here."

Trent summoned enough energy to laugh. His entire body felt amazing, like he was glowing from the inside out.

"So you'll meet my parents?" Janie smirked.

"Sure, sweetie. Whatever you want."

Janelle kissed him softly and held up the broken plastic. "We have to fix this before they get here."

"On it." He hauled himself up.

"I'M NOT sure about your new boyfriend." Janelle's father relaxed into the sofa, stretching his feet. They'd walked half of D.C. that morning, visiting two Smithsonian museums and the Washington Monument before taking Metro back to Alexandria.

"You've met him for all of fifteen minutes," chided her mother, who'd collapsed into the side chair.

"Cathy, Trent didn't even want to tell us his name. Are you certain about him, Janie?"

"I'm sure." Janelle forced her jaw to relax before she cracked a molar. She wasn't, not at all. In her head, this was supposed to be easy: Trent would adore her retired teacher mom and engineer dad, with their offbeat sense of humor and rock-solid affection for one another. It would be utterly banal. If Trent could see himself as normal, one half of an unexceptional couple, he'd begin to see the future they could have together.

As usual, when it came to her ideas about how the world should work, Janelle was disappointed. Another normal fatherly response—one she hadn't counted on—was to take exception to their daughter's boyfriend. If she'd been upfront about the relationship, her dad might not have felt blindsided on meeting Trent, who in turn, might not have run away at the first sign of disapproval.

Janelle no longer had the heart to tell her parents she'd be sleeping across the hall at Trent's.

Suck it up, buttercup. You're sleeping on the couch this weekend—alone, unless you count Mom and Dad snoring two feet away.

"Trent is...introverted, but he's smart, talented and ambitious. I know you'll like him once you have a chance to talk." Janelle fumbled in her closet for fresh clothes while awkwardly trying to conceal the masculine clothing on Trent's side.

"I'm sure we will, honey. Mind if I take a short nap before dinner?" Catherine yawned.

"Go ahead, Mom. I'll go see if Trent's ready." Janelle left her parents to rest and took her bundle of clean clothes across the hall.

All I want is to love you out in the open. The thought burned like a sparkler in her chest, blistering and painful. Yet introducing Trent as her boyfriend had made his brow furrow in a scowl of disapproval. Even that word was too much of a label, apparently. Never mind they'd been living together for weeks.

Red flag.

Janelle let herself into Trent's apartment without knocking. "Hello?"

"Here." Trent's voice echoed down the hall from the windowless room he'd converted to an office for three. He was nowhere near ready, staring at a jumble of incomprehensible code on a black screen, wearing nothing but a pair of black boxer briefs.

Janelle zeroed in on the outline of his package for a long moment. Her eyes followed the treasure trail up to the divot of his navel, a delightful waypoint nestled between the rippled muscles of his abdomen. By the time she'd lingered over his pectoral muscles and reminded herself how much she enjoyed clinging to his broad shoulders while naked and climaxing, a long minute had passed. Her attention snagged on the sharp line of his jaw. Trent's mouth curved in a smirk as he leaned back from the keyboard.

It never got old, seeing him like this. Relaxed, in his element, a little arrogant. It only happened when they were alone. For one unsettling moment, Janelle wondered if her unquenchable lust was clouding her judgment.

Maybe it only happened when *he* was alone, and she was an intruder.

"Like what you see?" he asked, pushing back from the desk.

"You know I do." Janelle trailed her gaze back down to where his cock had grown. She shoved aside self-doubt and tugged her shirt over her head. In her bra, she knelt between Trent's knees and pulled him free. The wood floor bit into her knees as she slid his cock between her lips and sucked. Trent's fingers wound into her hair.

Too soon, he pulled her up and slid his hands into the waistband of her pants. Janelle straddled him as he curved his palm over her ass, bringing her sex into contact with his hardness. He nipped her lower lip. Janelle gasped, ready, breathless. His tongue teased hers, and she sank her fingers into his hair to pull him closer.

I need you so badly it scares me.

She poured the thought into their kiss, taking it deeper. Trent flicked open the button on her jeans, and Janelle shifted enough to let him shove them down over her ankles. Naked but for the bra, she freed his cock and sank down over him. They exhaled as one.

He filled her and retreated again and again, driving her higher, their faces a breath apart as the arms of the desk chair bit into her thighs. Trent picked her up and shoved her against the door, his body dragging wave after wave of pleasure from hers. Helpless, Janelle explored the bunch and release of his shoulders with her nails and her mouth as he took her against the door. She came hard.

"Set me down," Janelle demanded, gasping for oxygen. She laid her forehead against the smooth surface of the door and held her hands above her head. Trent covered them with one big palm and entered her from behind.

"Janie," he gasped, raw.

Say you need me. As if he'd ever voice such a sentiment. Trent's body bucked. Janelle arched into him, taking everything he could give her as he came inside her.

It wasn't enough. He always left her empty, aching for more, when he withdrew. They'd stopped using condoms regularly. She'd taken that as a sign he trusted her, but now doubt crept into the aftermath.

"We should get ready to meet my parents." Janelle picked up the bundle of clothes she'd set on the desk, leaving the jeans she'd been wearing in a heap on the floor next to it.

Trent rubbed his hand over his stubbled chin. "I need to shave. If I'm going with you."

Dread cut through the afterglow of sex. "You said you would. It'll be fun. My mom likes you."

"Your dad doesn't," Trent replied in a flat tone. "Can't say I blame him."

"Trent. My dad's opinion doesn't matter." But it did. Janelle knew her dad hadn't quite adapted to seeing his baby girl all grown up. It rattled her to discover that the people she loved best didn't automatically care about one another.

"It does to me." Trent kissed the tip of her nose, and went to clean up.

The past several weeks had been more than anything she'd hoped for. She loved having Trent up in her business all the time, whether it meant phenomenal sex on tap, or tripping over him as they were about their lives. The tiny studio was constantly messy, but they tried to keep their work lives contained.

Saturdays they spent long mornings in bed, then tried to get out and do something interesting. Last weekend they'd gone to a winery. The weekend before, it had been flying drones. Sometimes they went to movies or out to dinner. It was never not fun.

Until her parents decided to visit. Janelle had held off from telling Trent about it for as long as possible. He'd reacted the way she'd feared, and it had stung worse than she'd wanted to let it. But she wasn't backing down now. This was an interim step toward something bigger. Maybe it wouldn't lead to kids and a minivan in the suburbs, but she was more and more confident in their relationship.

Except in the uneasy moments when Trent went distant, like now. Janelle kissed his shoulder, right above Icarus' wing.

"He doesn't know you. Once he does, Dad will be fine. You'll see." Still, Trent hesitated. Janelle tried a new tactic. "If you act as if you're hiding something, Dad *will* get suspicious. Are you going to make me explain your life story without you? I'll do it for you, if it makes this easier for you."

"No," Trent replied hastily. "I'll go clean up."

Janelle kissed him again, and Trent pressed close to nuzzle her.

"Thank you for coming with me," she whispered. "My family is really important to me. I don't feel right hiding you from them."

"I said I'd go." He pulled away, leaving Janelle with the vague sense that she was pushing again. Was it so much to ask that he share one casual meal with her parents?

He said he wanted to live a normal life, but Trent avoided doing anything about it. He hadn't rented an apartment other than the one he used as an office, he didn't cultivate friends, he hadn't tried to date. If she hadn't blundered into his life, Trent would still be living as a workaholic monk.

Dinner started awkwardly. Her father wasn't outright hostile, but he asked pointed questions all through the appetizers.

"How long have you and Janelle known one another?" Janelle's father speared an avocado from his salad.

"A couple of months. Since she moved in." Trent picked at his shrimp skewer. They'd agreed to leave out any mention of Las Vegas, which Janelle now regretted. It was exhausting to cover up the truth.

"He was attending an IT security conference, Dad." Janelle patted Trent's knee under the table. He kept his hands studiously within view.

"Whoosh, over my head." Her mom laughed, the only one at the table having a good time. "I can check email, pay bills and look things up online, and that's about it."

"You went to college for computer science?" Mr. Carlisle's tone dripped with skepticism.

"I got my degree online while I was in the army," Trent replied tightly.

"Impressive," Catherine held up her wine glass. "That takes determination."

Mr. Carlisle snorted dismissively and set down his silverware. "Online degrees aren't worth much."

"Dad." Janelle kicked her dad under the table. "Quit being rude."

"Where'd you get your degree?" Trent demanded, a challenge.

"Carnegie."

"Good school. My uncle went there for physics." Trent glanced at her, his jaw tight. "Aunt Suzie's husband."

"Tell us about your aunt." Catherine took over the interrogation, and dinner proceeded along a friendlier path. Janelle sighed. It was too much to ask the men in her life to get along.

But by the time dessert menus were placed on the table, Trent and her dad had found a common language in sports.

"I like your boyfriend, sweetie. Don't mind your father. You moved too fast for him to feel comfortable. It'll be all right." Her mom squeezed Janelle's shoulder reassuringly.

Until he finds out about the poker and the porn. Oh, and the drugs.

Maybe Trent was right to be wary of the world. Janelle had let him into her life and her heart, but to everyone else, Trent was still the guy from that video.

A FEW DAYS LATER, a thick envelope arrived in the mail. There was no more avoiding the subject, so Janelle brought it up as they walked back from the park where they ran together in the mornings before work.

"My lease is up for renweal." There were three weeks left on the sublet. Janelle licked her lips, anxiety seeping in. "If I make appointments to check out apartments, will you come with me?"

There was so much loaded into the question. What was their future together? Trent had long outgrown the work-live space. He'd been in technical violation of the lease terms before she'd arrived. His employees spent as much time offsite as they did in his apartment, but it was a matter of time before someone noticed. He needed to rent actual office space, and soon.

Which meant living in a studio apartment together made less and less sense. They were tripping over one another, especially on days when Janelle worked from home. Her fledgling consultancy was picking up steam, and when she needed to work late she used Trent's apartment so he could sleep. It was okay for a few more weeks, but they should be searching for a new apartment now—a topic she'd been avoiding because every time she edged close to the subject, he shut her down.

"When?"

"Next Saturday? I can look for apartments while you scope out office space."

Trent was quiet for a minute. "I have plans."

Janelle peered at him questioningly. "Can you tell me what they are?"

He said nothing. Trent had closed down, gone wherever he went when she pressed him on something he didn't want to talk about. "Not really."

Janelle was unsurprised by his response, but she swallowed past her disappointment. "Is it an all-day plan? Or could I schedule appointments in the morning?"

"Janie..." Trent stretched his broad shoulders and rubbed the back of his neck. "They're all-day plans."

She waited. "Is it a big secret? Engagement ring shopping, for example?"

One could hope. Foolish as it was. There was a long pause as he punched the elevator button with more force than necessary. "I'm going to see Penny."

"Penny." Janelle absorbed the word like a blow. How stupid and assumptive could she be, flippantly suggesting they get engaged? "Where does she live?"

"About an hour and a half from here." Trent's back was stiff as he stripped off his sweaty clothes.

A flutter of panic beat inside Janelle's chest. "Is that why you moved here, after you got out of the army? To be close to her?"

Trent nodded tightly. "She's the closest thing I have to family, Janie. Penny and my Aunt Susie in New Jersey. A couple of cousins. I hardly know them."

You still love Penny. Janie sucked in a tight, hot breath. A firecracker of jealousy exploded inside her. It made no sense. Penny was no longer able-bodied, from what Trent had said. Yet there was more to their relationship than looking over financial documents to keep people from cheating her out of her money.

How else to explain the intangible distance between them?

What if he's only putting up with you because you barged into his life and wouldn't take no for an answer? What if Trent's only here for convenient, high-quality sex?

"Can I go with you?" Her body flashed ice cold, as it had when they'd said goodbye at the airport in Las Vegas. She'd listened, but not heard.

"Why would you want to?" Trent's bafflement was etched over his sharp features.

"I've never met a porn star. I'm curious." It was true, although she wasn't interested in Penny. It was Trent's behavior she wanted to observe.

"I'd rather you didn't." Trent paused at the door to the shower, his eyes sliding past hers. Today, she wouldn't be joining him.

"Please? I really want to meet her. You've met my family, and I want to meet yours." Janelle peeled off her sticky shirt and tossed it into the overflowing laundry bin.

"Penny's not really family." He rubbed his bristly jaw, usually a good sign he was about to give in.

"She's almost family. You said so yourself." Janelle hated herself for pushing, but something was off. She needed to know the truth if there were still feelings between Penny and Trent. It could explain the moments when they were together, yet she felt alone.

No more professions of *love*. That word wasn't crossing her lips again unless she heard it from him first. The burn of embarrassment licked through her.

"I guess. I know you won't laugh or anything."

"Of course, I wouldn't, Trent. I'd be thrilled to meet someone who was part of your life."

But she wasn't, not entirely. Not in the moment and not on Saturday when they climbed into Trent's car and headed out of town on a bright late-May morning.

"Do you think you'll take the California gig?" Trent asked. On Friday afternoon, a sizable opportunity with an energy company in Sacramento had come in. Janelle had until Monday to accept. Sunday afternoon, Trent was taking the train to New York for two days to work on the new client.

"No. It's worth five million, but there's four companies involved and if it all blows up, I'm the one who'll take the reputational hit. The risk is too high, even for a one-percent commission upfront. I'd rather play it safe and stick with smaller jobs for now." Janelle tried to focus her attention on the work, but all she could think about was the barrier between her and Trent.

The landscape gave way to country, then to bare fields of freshly planted green shoots. They turned down a gravel road, the tires kicking up a plume of dust and rocks behind them. Low, modest houses on neatly maintained green yards passed the window. Janelle's hair felt tight on her scalp, tingling with anxiety. The past week had torn Janelle between optimism and the unshakable sense something was terribly wrong, and that it was her fault.

"This is it." Trent parked and cut the engine. A shadow appeared in the door.

Janelle unbuckled her seat belt. "I can't wait to meet her."

16

A dog barked as a form obscured by the screen door struggled to open it. Janelle's heart rate skipped, then settled as a blonde woman pushed it open. Her fine hair was pulled back in a loose ponytail. She wore a zebra print blouse with jeans and matching zebra slippers. "Who's this?"

"Penny. This is Janie. Remember I told you she was coming with me?"

"Did you?" Penny's features mostly relaxed, except for her full lips, which twisted up at one side. A touch of saliva had puddled there, and she wiped it away with a tissue from her pocket.

"Come in." Penny limped to a walker. She leaned on it while ushering them into a modest but clean and well-appointed kitchen. Her movements were slow and poorly coordinated. Though she still had curves, Penny's form had become rounder and softer.

A large, bearded man stood in the kitchen. He nodded to Trent, then brought them soft drinks.

"This is Bob," Penny waved a hand and lit a cigarette. "He takes care of me."

"Shouldn't be smoking, Pen," the man growled.

"See?" Penny blew a kiss behind her, then her attention seemed to fade. "Remind me your name?"

"Janelle. Janie for short. I work with Trent."

"Not like I used to work with him." Penny's leer brought out all the humor that had made her so appealing in the video. Janelle laughed, but Trent's mouth twisted with irritation so she bit the insides of her cheeks to make herself stop.

Encouraged, Penny leaned over and cupped her hand to whisper, "He'd never work with me. Trent was always too good. But now, I have Bob. He puts even Mace's package to shame."

Penny winked. Her hand came away damp from the paralyzed side of her mouth. "Oh, damn, I hate when that happens."

"How long have you and Bob been together?" Janelle asked. Spotting a box of tissues, she passed it silently across the table. Trent gave her the side-eye, but Janelle ignored it.

"Couple years. Time gets away from me." Penny blew a puff of smoke. Trent waved it away.

"Pen, let's sit outside."

"Oh, Trent. Army beat it out of you, didn't they?" Penny lurched awkwardly out of her seat.

"I watched you hooked up on a ventilator once. Bob's right. You shouldn't smoke." Trent took her elbow, much the way he'd done that first day, steadying Janelle outside the casino hotel.

"You're no fun anymore." Penny clutched her walker and paused "Where are we going?"

"Outside."

"Right."

The early summer day was warm. The lawn backed up to a forested area. A concrete pathway wound between the tress.

"C'mon, Pen, let's walk. Get you some exercise." Bob had followed them out, carrying a lightweight fuzzy jacket.

They ambled beneath the silver-barked trees, Penny setting the pace. A pink child's scooter lay on the ground, forgotten.

"Bob's daughter's." Trent moved it aside so Penny could pass easily.

"Is he her caretaker?" Janelle asked as Bob hovered at Penny's side.

"Yes and no. They started seeing one another a while ago, and he's taken on a lot of that role. Turns out he was one of her biggest fans, back in the day. Even with the brain injury, she's a dream come true for him. I was skeptical at first, but he's all right."

Janelle hung back to observe Trent talking with Penny. He was affectionate and considerate, but mostly she noticed his relaxed movements. He was open with Penny in a way he'd never been with her, unless their bodies were entangled. Janelle sucked in a lungful of cool spring air.

When they'd completed a circuit of the path that curved around a small pond, they finished their drinks. Penny offered food, but Trent caught her eye and jerked his head toward the door.

"I have a lot of work to do; we should get going." Janelle squeezed Penny's hand and stepped back.

Trent leaned in and kissed Penny on the cheek, whispering. Penny lost focus for a minute. "You take care of the new girl here. She's pretty."

Janelle smiled tightly and pulled the collar of her spring jacket closed around her neck. It would smell of cigarettes, and she couldn't wait to take a shower and wash her hair. Yet she'd liked Penny. Even in her diminished state, it wasn't difficult to see the liveliness that had made her so much fun on camera.

It was Trent who worried her. Watching them together had opened up a pit of devastation in her stomach she couldn't explain. It wasn't her jealous streak kicking in. It was worse. All she knew was that the crater was expanding, swallowing her heart with every step.

"Penny's pretty messed up." Janelle didn't speak until they were back on the highway. Trent hated her stillness. It meant her clever mind was spinning, and when that happened, Janie got ahead of herself. He imagined she'd looked just like this when she'd planned her surprise rental across the hall.

"Yeah. She'll never recover." Now Janie would understand why what they had was temporary. He couldn't lose someone he cared about as much as he'd loved Penny. Not again.

"Especially if she keeps smoking like that." Janelle stared idly out the window.

"Don't fucking joke about it, Janie. It's her only vice now." How could she make light of it? He'd tried to get Penny to quit cigarettes with about the same success he'd had convincing her to stop making porn movies. Or heroin.

"That and Bob." She smiled.

"He's a good guy." Trent's tone was gruffer than he meant it to be. He hated the way Janie's offhand comment cut, though he knew she didn't mean anything by it.

"I don't doubt it. She'll need care for life; I hope they can stay together." She was quiet a moment before continuing, and Trent had the sense that Janelle was testing him. "I set up two appointments to look at apartments tomorrow afternoon."

"Cancel them."

Janelle's body tensed as if he'd slapped her. "Why?"

"It was great, but I never meant things to go on this long. It would've been better to make—"

"—a clean break," Janelle finished bitterly. "Saw that one coming."

"Yeah. I can't let what happened to Penny happen to you."

"That's the dumbest thing I've ever heard. First, I don't plan to take up heroin. Secondly, you're not in control. Everyone gets hurt. Penny went on a wilder ride than most people, but she seems happy, all things considered."

"What the hell does that mean?"

Janelle startled at his harsh tone. The tip of her tongue appeared between her lips. A bolt of white-hot desire nearly made Trent lose control of the car. How could he want her so badly when she was so blasé about his life?

"Penny's well cared for, and Bob seems like a good man. It doesn't sound as if she regrets anything she's done, except the drugs and releasing the video without your consent. You're the one who can't let go."

"Because I'm the one who has to live in the real world." Trent swallowed. "Fucking hell, Janie. If I had the option of living in the sticks with everything paid for and a nice little family, you think I wouldn't take it?"

She was silent for a beat. "No, Trent. You wouldn't."

"Really." The speedometer hit ninety. Trent eased his foot off the accelerator, though he wanted to smash his foot down on the pedal.

"You're too ambitious. You'd never be happy with the sweet little wife and family living a quiet life in obscurity. You're always aiming higher."

"The hell I am."

"It's not a criticism, Trent. You've accomplished so much."

Trent snorted. "Yeah, fucking on tape is an awesome credential."

Janie stayed silent, for once. No teasing, no sass, no smart comeback. "Nobody cares about the tape. It's history."

A mile ticked by, then another. "Penny might be the one with the walker, but you're the one who's broken."

"What the fuck did you just say?"

"You are the most emotionally damaged person I've ever met. If you want to wallow in misery over your mistakes, have at it. I won't play along anymore. Penny's made her peace. She's moved on. But you're still stuck in the past, and I don't want to be stuck there with you. I lo—I *care* about you, but it's not enough to fix what's broken in you."

More miles ticked by. A semi-truck pulled in front of him and Trent was forced to hit the brakes. Traffic slowed to a halt. Trent's blood pressure spiked so high he didn't need a cuff to know it was through the roof. "It's not your job to fix me."

"Someone needs to, Mace."

They each stared straight ahead, blindly focused on the river of red brake lights stretching into the distance. Janelle side-eyed him, a fact Trent only caught because he was doing the same. As if they were enemy combatants peering over walls.

After ten miles of stop-and go traffic and thick, sullen silence, Janelle screwed up her courage to strafe him with words. "You still love Penny."

"You're only figuring that out now?" Trent returned fire. He didn't.

He loved what she'd been, what they'd been. What they could never be again. His affection for Penny was as bittersweet and faded as a vintage photograph.

"Then *why* did you move in with me?" Janelle demanded, fighting a useless battle to control her wail. "Why lead me on?"

"You knew I wanted to end it." The words came out in a menacing growl. He'd known this moment would come. He'd braced for it. He'd *planned* for it. This wasn't supposed to feel so raw.

"You're the one who called me here to help you with the New York pitch." Janelle punched at buttons on the dashboard in a futile effort to blast more air conditioning into the car. Between the traffic, the sun beating directly down and the anger simmering between them, the car interior was stubbornly stuck at eighty degrees. "You're also the one who initiated sex. I was trying very hard to leave you alone until you suggested we give Hannah and Sean a run for their money."

"It was a hypothetical statement, Janie. Not an invitation. You're the one who pounced on me."

"Oh. So, I'm the one responsible, is that it?" Janelle's face was tinged red under her tan, and it wasn't from the heat.

"Any man with a pulse would've taken you up on sex. You started it in Las Vegas, and you did it again when I asked you to help on the pitch. I wasn't planning to sleep with you." Trent spotted an opening and gunned the engine, yanking the car into a narrow space. The driver he'd just cut off laid a fist on the horn. Two minutes later, the car he'd been in front of passed by. So much for shortcuts.

Across the center console, Janelle stared out the window at the river of cars. Her jawline was set hard. Trent thought he saw her chin tremble, though it might've been the vibrations from the car.

"You're saying I forced you into dating me." Her tone was flat and barely audible.

"I'm saying you're the one who wanted this. You're the one who moved in across the hall. How would you have reacted if I'd moved across the street from your parents?" His throat was tight and his palms slick on the steering wheel.

"I'd have brought you food and introduced you to the neighborhood, like any normal human being," Janelle replied. "All you did was slam the door in my face."

"Yeah. Because no matter how you've been building this up in your head, I never said I wanted more than a few nights in Las Vegas. You just showed up and refused to take no for an answer."

"That is not fair." Righteous indignation undergirded Janelle's tone. Good. Angry was better than tears—although sometimes you got both when you pushed hard enough. Angry tears were the worst. Penny had always zoomed right past yelling to screaming and crying, and this conversation had him flashing back to the awful, drug-fueled fights that had been the flipside to their tumultuous relationship. When things were going well, they'd been better than any high. But with Penny, the good times had never lasted.

Janelle must be calling on every resource she possessed to keep her temper under control, despite his deliberate prodding of all her most vulnerable places.

Jesus. He wasn't twenty anymore. He couldn't fight like this. Despair crept over Trent. Even if what he said was true, it wasn't the entire truth. He hadn't fought that hard to keep her out of his life, because he'd wanted her in it. He just didn't want *this*. Arguing over who and what they were.

Janelle choked back a sob. "I wouldn't have slept with you in Las Vegas if you hadn't made me rethink my experiences and try new ones. I also never asked you to move in. You dragged in the mattress like a…like a *troglodyte* claiming a new cave."

Penny never used fancy words for caveman. Up to this point, Trent had been hearing an echo of this fight in his head. Arguments about who did or didn't do or say what, when. Fights about who they were. As individuals. Together.

You said you'd give up making films, Penny.

It's my job. You knew that when we got together. You said you loved me anyway. Being able to see me, not my work, is what made you special.

You said you'd quit when you made enough money. So, quit. We'll go live somewhere quiet. We have enough for a house in the suburbs. We can have kids, travel.

Trent, baby, I don't want to quit acting.

Penny. It's not acting. It's fucking other men on camera for money, and if it doesn't stop, I'll leave.

She'd forced him to make good on his ultimatum, but the temporary separation had been worse than he or Penny could bear. She'd adopted heroin as a substitute for him. Trent had doubled down on poker and cocaine. They'd been as dysfunctional lovers as Sid and Nancy, or as Heathcliff and Catherine. But instead of dying tragically, he and Penny had lingered on into maturity and adulthood, long enough to regret their mistakes and make new ones. As he was doing now.

Trent slammed on the brakes. Instinctively, he flung out his right arm to keep Janelle from hitting the dashboard, his forearm connecting solidly with her chest.

She slapped the back of his hand. "Those are off limits during arguments."

Trent couldn't sort out where he'd gone wrong. There were so many choices. His emotions were too raw, too Technicolor bright, blinding him. He'd been wrong to get involved with her from the start, not that he'd let it stop him. But the real travesty had been in letting her believe that there was hope for them. For him. Janelle had pried and dusted off his crusted-on armor, letting light in through the chinks and cracks. It had been nice to believe, for a little while, that he could have what he wanted: a normal life.

In that moment, he knew how to end things for good. To prove to Janelle that he didn't care, that she couldn't hurt him. Trent had protected her for long enough. This time, he had to protect himself.

"What makes you think I'd want to touch you again?" he asked softly, detached. The traffic jam began to clear. His heartbeat slowed in his chest. Trent could feel his blood pressure falling so rapidly, he was on the edge of passing out.

"Which is it, Trent? Am I a siren you can't resist, or a disgusting blob you're trying to scrape off the bottom of your shoe?" Janelle's voice shook. He'd never heard her break like this. Not even with the Rich Jerk. Disconnected, shut down, Trent could sympathize with her. He *was* being a monumental asshole. It was for the best, though. She'd ignored his warnings. This wasn't a clean break, but it was final. He'd take it.

"You kept telling me how you were a nice girl, Janelle. Remember? A good girl. I can't tell you how appealing that was, after the shit I went through with Penny. But now I know better. You're not a good girl. You're not nice at all. You like dirty sex, the rougher the better. And you say I'm ambitious? Who's the one who started a brand-new consulting firm that's taking off like a rocket?"

"We've both been successful out of the gate, with a lot of help from Olivia. Your company's barely a year old." Cold fury made Janelle's voice sharp as an ice pick, but Trent heard the glacial, subsonic crack of pain underneath.

Pity. It was the first emotion he'd felt for her, and now the last. Fitting. "Janie. When I start dating seriously, it's going to be a girl who's everything you said you were but aren't. She'll be nice, and sweet, and any kids will take priority over her job. Always."

Janelle was silent. Still. Trent finally glanced over when she sniffed wetly and bent forward to rummage through her handbag. Tears streamed down her face, wide rivers polluted with mascara.

"I hope you're as happy with her as I was with Ben," she replied softly, never glancing at him. "I would never have asked you to give up Penny. I know you never will. But I won't be your third wheel."

Trent pulled the car into the garage. Janelle slammed out of the car and was gone. He sat there, drained but amped for a screaming match, frozen with paralyzed shock as he tried to understand what he'd just done, and why. Janelle never looked back.

17

Four days later, desperation was getting to him. Trent had slept in his apartment the night of their fight, returning to the studio only long enough to pack for his overnight trip to New York when he'd heard her leave and lock the door. He'd been too pissed off to see straight, tossing his clothes into a box and hauling them across the hall.

When he'd arrived home on Monday evening, Janelle had disappeared from the studio, leaving only his bed in the middle of the empty room. A few pathetic paper dishes and plastic cups were all that remained in the cabinets.

Everything was disposable. He'd been disposed of, as he rightly deserved. She hadn't left a note, just disappeared from his life as quietly as she'd come.

He'd swallowed past the hollow place in his chest. Trent couldn't ignore how badly he missed her. Nor could he stop mulling over what he'd done—not only in the car last weekend, but ever since Janie had showed up on his doorstep with an open invitation to a future he claimed to want, but been afraid to reach for.

"Do you have any idea where she is?" Trent forced his body into stillness. The trendy bar around them buzzed with activity. Earlier, he'd had a meeting with a client in the city. Olivia had been there for a pitch, and to have lunch with Stella. Trent had asked her to meet for a drink because she was the one person who might know Janie's whereabouts. He'd tried calling her parents, but they hadn't called him back. Presumably, Janelle had told them it was over. An amber Scotch sat untouched before him, his stomach unwilling to accept it.

Olivia sat back and popped an olive into her mouth. "Yes. Why should I tell you, though?"

"I need to see Janelle." Trent ran his fingers through his hair. He was pretty sure it stood up every which direction.

"Why? So she can tell you off like you so righteously deserve?" Trent toyed with his drink. Olivia softened. "How in the world did you screw it up so badly? That girl adores you. Or did until last weekend."

"I was trying to protect her."

"From what?"

"From me." Two words, cut jaggedly from his core.

"You mean the sex video? *Nobody cares.* They're practically a rite of passage."

"Where's yours, then?" he shot back. He hated how other people dismissed the impact of that damn video on his life.

Olivia pursed her lips. "Are you crazy? Me? No way. But come on, Trent, you're a guy, you were famous, and you dated a porn star. Anything less than a video and everyone would be wondering if there's something wrong with your dick."

"This isn't the conversation I wanted to have with you."

"Likewise." Olivia regarded him with warm, dark eyes. "Seriously, Trent. Janie's beautiful, and she's crazy about you. How'd you mess that up?"

Trent's body was nothing but a seething mass of regret. Self-sabotage was a bitch. He'd done it by burning every bridge he could find after his parents died. He'd done it again when he enlisted, hoping to get himself killed because he didn't quite dare to do the job himself. Pushing Janelle away was the only way to destroy the joy and light she'd brought into his life. Another way of killing himself.

"Same way I always do." Silence stretched between them.

"Trent." Olivia's hand closed over his, a bond of friendship and trust. "It's worth the risk. Yes, you might get hurt. But you're hurting now. You haven't protected anyone. Not Janie, and not yourself either."

His friend's words sank into his gut like a sword. "Do you regret getting married?"

"Not for a second. I love my kids and I loved my husband. I wasn't the one who ended it." She hesitated. "I do regret getting pregnant and married so young. I had a partial scholarship to Columbia. I made it through a year, but the second semester my grades were terrible and I had to drop out. I wonder what would've been if I'd stayed in it." Olivia shrugged, as if to shake off the heartache.

"But I'm going to stay true to myself. I know me a little better than I did as a teenager. You're older than you were when you showed up in my unit looking like a kicked puppy." She squeezed his hand and let go. "Janie's in California. I don't think she wanted to take this job, but if they win, it'll launch her career. Don't go messing with her."

"Where's she going after that?"

Olivia hesitated. "I'm not sure I should tell you. She's moved in with someone she knew in college. A law student at Georgetown. Crystal, I think her name is."

Oh, fuck no.

Crystal, who'd gotten Janelle involved in that crackpot sugar baby scheme. Who knew what trouble her friend would get her into? She had a budding career now. He couldn't let her ruin it before she even got going, just because he'd been too terrified to grab hold of his good fortune. She was everything he'd said he wanted and more. He didn't want a clean break. He wanted to be with her.

Janie had needed him to make a commitment—he knew she would've accepted the tiniest of baby steps forward—and he'd dug in his heels, stubborn ass that he was. The way he always did.

No more.

Trent had lost enough. All the pieces in his heart had shattered over, and over again, but Janie was the glue he needed to start fixing it for good. He'd get her back. He just needed to figure out how.

Janelle rolled her carry-on suitcase over the crooked hardwood floors into her room. The bedroom was small but bright, with her couch on one side and boxes of dishes, clothes and books on the other. The other end of the room held her table, which also served as a desk. In between lay the cheerful rug, onto which she dropped her suitcase. Then she dropped her tight, tired body onto the couch. She hadn't opened it once since moving into Crystal's spare room.

"Hey, how'd it go?" Her friend tapped the frame before poking her head in.

"Horrible. There's a reason this company's been shedding clients. They're a dysfunctional mess. If they don't land this client, they're staring at bankruptcy. So, they bring in a twenty-five-year-old consultant to tell them how to do things they should already know how to do." Janelle rubbed her eyes and yawned.

Crystal grimaced. "That's rough. Why don't you get cleaned up and come out to lunch with me? We have a surprise visitor. One you might want to see, now you're over with Trent Sizzling Hotness Mason."

Janelle snorted. "I'd rather sleep, honestly."

"You sure? It's someone you might like."

"Okay, Crys, I'll bite. Who's crashing on your couch this weekend?" Crystal was plugged into a vast network of international couch surfers, which was one reason she'd had trouble finding a roommate for the summer. At least once a week, Janelle stepped over bodies in sleeping bags on the floor.

"It's Ben. Apparently, the engagement is off with the Texas blonde. And no, he isn't crashing here. Not unless you want him to." Crystal winked suggestively.

Janelle's body stilled like a clockwork toy winding down. "I don't know if I want to see him."

"You missed him for years. Why not?" Crystal crossed her arms, cool and inquisitive.

"Because…"

"Janelle, you've changed. So has he. Come and say hello. I won't leave you alone with him. You can have a conversation and see where things go."

Nothing in her heart stirred. She'd shaken free of Ben's hold on her. But since the one her heart ached for wasn't an option, maybe she ought to explore it. Just see what happened, as Crystal suggested. "Okay. Give me fifteen minutes to clean up."

JANIE WAS EASY TO SPOT. Her polka-dot blue dress was both modest and sexy, a line she walked so well. She wore her dark hair up in a ponytail, her eyes concealed behind sunglasses, and her lips were painted his favorite shade of dark pink.

He was so busy checking her out, Trent almost tripped over a shorter, brown-haired girl walking a few steps ahead of Janelle nearly stopped in her tracks.

"Ohmigod. It's you, isn't it?"

Trent's muscles tightened. Behind the human road block, Janie stopped mid-step. A guy bumped into her, knocking her forward. He put one arm around her waist to steady her. Trent's vision hazed red.

"Trent Mason? From the video?" The brown-haired woman's question snapped his attention back like a rubber band.

"You know about it?"

"I'm Crystal. I *love* your video."

His esophagus lurched. Getting sick in the middle of a D.C. sidewalk was a distinct possibility. This was a disaster.

"Aren't you the one with the sugar daddy?" he snarled.

Crystal's mouth curved into a grin. "Not anymore. He started making noises about leaving his wife, so I ended it."

Okay. His attention was already back on Janelle.

"Trent, what are you doing here?" Janie's tone was the opposite of friendly. She'd pushed her sunglasses on top of her head, and her eyes were jewel-like in the bright sun. Her pink mouth was parted, showing even teeth. Not in a smile.

"Is this guy bothering you?" The man at her side edged closer, his arm around her back.

"No, it's okay, Ben."

Ben. No. Her ex was here?

"Janie." *Great plan, Mace. Dump your girlfriend and then get all worked up when she goes back to the guy who loved her.*

"Crystal. Ben. This is Trent. We…worked together. Temporarily."

Ben didn't leave her side. He was modestly good-looking, clearly intimidated by the prospect of facing down a larger man, but glued to Janelle's side despite the distinct possibility Trent was going to break his face.

His polo shirt, khakis and clean-shaven chin telegraphed upwardly-mobile stability. The kind of guy Janelle deserved. The kind of man he'd never be, but wanted to be so badly it made his teeth ache.

"I need to see you, Janie. Alone." Trent ground out.

Janelle pursed her lips. "Then call and ask. Don't ambush me on the way to brunch."

"We're late. We'll lose our reservation." Ben took her elbow, possessive, and Janelle moved forward. She glanced back over her shoulder as they passed, then lowered her sunglasses and kept walking.

"Can I get your phone number?" The brown-haired chick stared up at him. She wasn't as pretty as Janie, but she exuded confidence. It was sexy, in its way.

"What?"

"Hi. Crystal over here. Remember me? I know you and Janelle are over. She's my roommate for the summer. I'm completely, one-hundred-percent available, no strings attached, for all your rebound needs. Can't happen at my place, though, cause, you know." She jerked her head in the direction of her friends. "Here's my card. Call anytime. Literally any time. I love your work. Bye."

So, that was Crystal. She didn't seem like the sugar baby type, but she sure had an instinct for trouble. Maybe there was a way to point her at Ben and get both problems out of the way.

"I'll have a Bloody Mary."

Janelle observed the steadiness of her hands as she passed the menu to the waiter. It was this bizarre sense of disconnection that had powered her through the past week, between moving out of the studio overnight while Trent was in New York, barely unpacking in Crystal's apartment, and then flying to California for three days. But her armor was cracking. What she needed wasn't alcohol. It wasn't Ben. She'd known within two seconds of greeting him in Crystal's lobby that the love she'd clung to for years had been a mirage.

What she needed was Trent. But she couldn't have him. Appearing out of nowhere changed nothing, no matter how hard her heart pounded at the sight of his muscular frame.

"Are you okay?"

Ben's hand on her arm was warm and gentle. As was his gaze. Not long ago, she'd have given anything in the world to have him touch her like this. Now she wanted to slap his hands away.

Which made her pathological. Emotionally unavailable men were her kink. Clearly.

"I'll be fine." Her drink arrived as Crystal burst into the restaurant and scanned the room. By the time she reached their table, it was half gone. Crystal ordered a mimosa, and Janelle ordered another Bloody Mary with an extra shot.

"You're really not okay," Ben observed.

"Trent won't follow us here. I went out of my way to make sure he didn't see which restaurant I went into." Crystal tucked her hair behind her ear, avoiding Janelle's direct gaze.

"Thanks." *You hit on Trent, didn't you? Is that why Ben's here? To get me out of the way?* Her friend was such an opportunist. Yet she was living with Crystal for the rest of the summer. Making a stink about her suspicions wasn't a bright idea, unless she wanted to go back to Florida. She'd come this far, and there was no way Janelle was backing away from what she'd built here. For the first time in her life, her career had momentum.

However much she wished Trent hadn't let her believe they had a chance, she'd prepared for this outcome. If it had happened earlier—before he'd moved in—she'd have been better prepared to handle the loss. The remnants of her Bloody Mary gurgled in the bottom of her glass. She downed the shot the instant it hit the table.

Why was this her life? What was *wrong* with her?

Ben reached across the table and took her hand, rubbing his thumb across the back. His hazel eyes were warm with concern beneath furrowed brows. Janelle fought the urge to pull her hand away. She'd wanted him, once upon a time. She could find desire for him again.

Maybe.

But watching Trent move on with his life? Janelle didn't have the strength. She wouldn't be able to stem the tsunami of jealous rage. Not where Trent was concerned.

Janelle closed her eyes and ordered something random off the menu, along with another Bloody Mary. The dreadful state of her stomach couldn't be muted with alcohol or absorbed with food.

Stop being ridiculous. There was no reason to suspect Crystal of anything. Her phone beeped. Janelle answered automatically, in case it was a client.

"Janie, come outside and talk."

Janelle sobbed once as the sound of Trent's voice grated over her nerves. Crystal and Ben glanced at one another, then began patting her back from either side of the round table.

"Why?" *Why are you doing this to me? Why can't you love me? Why can't I stop feeling this way about you? Why won't you go away, if you won't give me what I need?*

"I have a few things to say in person. Will you come outside?"

Janelle hung up and chugged her beer, gagging. Her head swam. The alcohol was hitting all at once. She got out of her chair and staggered backward, tripping over it. The chair fell over and hit the one behind it. "I'll be right back."

The ladies room was cold and anonymous, with tall doors from ceiling to floor. Barricaded inside, Janelle vomited into the toilet. Her skin cooled, bumps rising in the air conditioning. She stayed there for a long time, her head pressed against the tile.

"Hey Janelle? Are you in here?"

"Yeah." Her voice echoed hollowly. Janelle's body hurt. Her head hurt. Most of all, her heart ached within her chest.

"Ben got rid of Trent. He came inside, but Ben threatened him with a restraining order if he comes near you again." Crystal kept her tone matter-of-fact.

Janelle couldn't hold back the tears any longer. She was exhausted, stupidly drunk, it wasn't even noon, and the man she no longer loved was acting as a human roadblock to the one she did, but didn't want her. Not on any meaningful level. Every time she tried to untangle this knot, she only succeeded at pulling it tighter.

"I hate it when Ben solves my problems for me," Janelle whispered, but Crystal didn't hear her over the stall door. Relief coursed through her. She hadn't been the only one to make mistakes in their relationship. Ben had tried to fix everything, and she'd let him because adulthood had been terrifyingly complex. Avoidance hadn't saved her from having to deal with it, though. It had only set her back.

Aly was right: she and Ben had been too young. Now, she'd grown up. Ben hadn't changed, though. No wonder Janelle couldn't find the attraction she'd once felt for him.

"I gave Trent my number and told him to call me if he wants to talk to you. I'm happy to be the intermediary until this blows over."

I bet you are, Crys.

"Thanks." Janelle blew her nose and splashed water on her face. Crystal held out her arms, and she stepped into the warm hug knowing she'd never be able to face leaving the restaurant bathroom without Crystal's support. Thank goodness she'd remembered to wear her sunglasses.

TRENT CONTEMPLATED the little rectangle of ivory paper framed by his thumb and forefinger. A name. A phone number. An email address.

No response from Janelle. A week since the scene at the restaurant, when he'd needed to know if she was all right and Ben Cockblocker had gotten in his face threatening to call police. As if he'd ever hurt Janelle. Physically.

Crystal wasn't unattractive. He could hit that. A straightforward way to cut the yo-yo string on his relationship with Janelle. But then, what would he do with all the feelings she'd stirred up and refused to go away simply because she was absent?

He called once a day to leave a message he was pretty sure she deleted without listening to. *Please call me. You said to call and ask if I wanted to talk to you.*

The voicemail message played in his ear. Trent said his piece and disconnected. *Don't make me give up.*

"Boss?"

"Yeah, Chaitu?"

"Russ from the New York account is on the line."

"Okay. Thanks." Trent picked up the office phone. Midway into the conversation, his mobile phone beeped.

I don't want to see you.

Disappointment slashed through him, cut with a surge of excitement. She'd responded!

"Are you there, Mason?" Russ's annoyance was plain.

"Yeah. Sorry."

"Do you charge extra for paying attention or something?" he demanded. New Yorkers. They were a breed apart. Trent forced himself to focus on the conversation.

I'm sorry for what I said in the car, he texted back after he'd gotten off the phone with his client.

A minute passed. **I am, too. I shouldn't have said you were broken.**

Trent swallowed. **It's true.**

It had been, anyway. It wasn't now. He was finally pulling himself up, and forcing himself to see what had been right in front of his face all along. Penny didn't need him. He hadn't done as well by her as he'd wanted to, but thanks to Janelle's visit, he'd seen her life through fresh eyes. Penny was nicely set up. She didn't need to be the beneficiary of a company he'd never wanted to run. He was free, and at the same time, adrift.

The phone beeped again. **It hurt when you said you couldn't be with me because of my work. I know it was an issue with Penny. I didn't understand it would be an issue with me, as well. I do now.**

Shit. Owning up to his problems hadn't made fixing them any easier. Why the hell had he said that? He didn't see Janelle's career as an impediment to a relationship. He'd reached for the familiar, and everything he knew about romantic relationships was poisonous.

Fighting through this was hard, maybe harder because text messages were so short and impersonal. He typed words and deleted them, but was interrupted by another text message from Janie.

Be well.

Two gentle words to say good bye. Trent didn't hesitate. His thumb slid over the keypad of his phone. Janelle didn't pick up.

Trent hung up. "Fuck."

Then, he did pause. There was no way to make this look good. This time, his call was answered on the third ring. "Crystal?"

A pause. "This is she."

18

"Don't get all silent on me, now." Olivia hooked her arm into Trent's and pulled him into the room. It buzzed with industry types. The same government flacks in poorly cut suits and slick sales people who'd populated the conference in Las Vegas.

"You're sure she's here?"

"She said she'd come." Olivia steered him in the direction of the bar. "Have a drink. Relax. She'll be here."

Half an hour and a beer passed. Olivia worked the room, confident in speaking with anyone. Janie did it well too. And was doing it, now, not twenty feet away. The first sight of her in weeks made Trent's body ice over. As it thawed, his abdomen clenched hard and blood sluiced south to his dick.

Janie wore a black dress with a clingy cardigan and the high heels that made her look tall. She chatted with two men and a woman of Indian descent. She didn't glance up.

"Trent. Go talk to her." Olivia was back, her dark eyes encouraging.

"You first."

"Coward." She elbowed him.

He was. Despite this, Trent moved, his body gravitating toward Janie over his mind's objections. Which, to be frank, weren't that strong. All of him wanted to bask in Janie's presence. Being without her had been like going through open heart surgery without anesthetic. Like it was pumping outside his body.

He's been a real shithead, thinking he could protect his broken heart when all he'd ever done after losing his parents, and then Penny, had been to sweep the bits into a box and shove it down in a dark corner. Janie had been gluing the pieces back together from the minute he'd met her. She'd lanced wounds that had festered for years, simply by listening and never taking no for an answer.

There was a long beat of silence as the group noticed him standing nearby.

"Hi, Trent. Is there something you need?" she asked evenly.

"You."

Janelle's eyes flared, and the smooth line of her jaw tilted upward as she spoke to her companions. "If you'll excuse me."

She turned to him with a determinedly placid expression. "Why are you here?"

"Same reason you are."

"I'm not taking any pitch clients right now. I have my hands full," she said.

"Good for you. Olivia says you're forcing her to add staff."

Janelle smiled, reluctantly, but with pride. "All her own fault. She's great at identifying which opportunities are a good fit. I just manage the procurement process. It's not so different from the warehouse, to be honest."

Her grin faded as quickly as it had come. The tip of her tongue appeared briefly between her lips. "What are you working on these days?"

"A pitch," he responded, a little grin creeping over his face.

Janie's pretty face was so expressive, her eyes incapable of hiding the minutest flash of emotion. It was damn sexy. Especially to him. Trent had been dead inside until he'd met her, a fire nearly gone out. She'd poked him and breathed on the coals of his soul, forcing him back to life. Now he read wariness, but he'd counted on Janelle's curiosity.

"A big pitch?" she asked, as if she couldn't help herself.

"The biggest of my life." Trent's gaze never wavered. Janelle peered up at him, a foot and a half away, a distance too far to bridge.

"Good luck. I'd offer to help, but like I said, I'm booked. Besides, working with you usually ends…badly for me."

Guilt. It gnawed at his bones. He was ash. Icarus falling from the sky, understanding his folly and his hubris too late, as he fell to earth. It was Trent's story, tattooed in his flesh. He hadn't meant to repeat it.

"I should go." Janie made a show of checking her phone.

"I'll walk you to your car."

"Trent…" Janie pushed her hair back.

Here it comes. She's gotten back together with the ex who can't fuck her worth a damn.

"It's not that I don't want to see you, or talk to you, Trent. It's just… You were right all along. A clean break is for the best. I apologize for pushing. For trying to make us into something we aren't."

She shouldered her bag and clicked away on those high heels he loved. Taking his half-mended heart with her.

Olivia was at his side in an instant. "Didn't go well?"

Trent shook his head, despondent. "I don't know what to say. I'm an asshole?"

"That's a good start. Follow up with an 'I love you even though I was a jerk' and it should do the trick."

"It won't. This mess is going to take more than a sentence to fix." Trent rubbed the back of his neck, stymied.

Olivia touched his arm, a friendly gesture. Comforting. One of those small mom-moments she doled out sparingly. "What were her exact words?"

Trent repeated them verbatim.

Olivia frowned. "Why are you standing here? Go after her."

"She doesn't want to talk."

"No, Trent, she doesn't want to get hurt. You made her feel like you didn't care about her. If you're serious about fixing this, go talk to her. You've got your work cut out for you. Make it good."

Another small touch, on his back, and he was in motion.

Janelle had been caught waiting for the elevator. He caught sight of her disappearing inside and headed straight for the stairway, taking them two at a time. The exercise cleared his head.

Trent had pushed Janie away because he thought he couldn't withstand another loss. It was true. He couldn't. He needed her back. Now that she'd figured out what she wanted to do with her career, watching her take wing and soar was a thrill. Why couldn't he have said *that* in the moment?

Because he'd been terrified her work would take her away from him. His fear had been magnified in the raw aftermath of letting her into his past. She'd pushed, because that's what she did, but she'd been friendly and even kind with Penny. Whereas he'd been like a guard dog throttling itself on a chain toward her ex. Janie had compared him to a cave man, and it was an apt comparison. He'd behaved like one. No wonder she didn't welcome him back with open arms. Trent knew he couldn't force her to change her mind, but somehow, he had to get her to listen.

Trent's feet pounded on the stairs, leaping the last four and crashing against the metal door. He was a little winded as he caught sight of Janie's heels flashing out the sliding doors to the parking garage. Trent's feet slowed. He stopped. The glass doors closed behind Janelle.

What if she listened, and said no?

"OH, MY GOD."

That was fast.

Usually it took Crystal longer than five minutes to get anywhere near climax—a fact Janelle could've lived in peace without ever knowing. Moving in with Crystal had meant a hearing a regular loop of Trent and Penny's stupid sex tape. Good thing this arrangement was only for the summer. Janelle was so ready for a long-term lease.

No more temporary rentals, she promised herself.

"Janelle! Come here. You have to see this."

"Are you wearing clothes?" she shouted through the wall.

"Hold on. Okay. Come in."

Janelle pushed open her roommate's bedroom door. The laptop was hooked up to a larger screen. Featured prominently was Trent's naked ass, covered by the credits to his sex tape with Penny.

"I've seen it before, Crys." Janelle turned around, though her heart rate picked up at the sight of Trent's perfect body. Misadventure though it had proved to be, she had zero regrets about the sex.

"Don't go. I know you think it's weird I watch your ex's porn tape all the time, and maybe it is, but his dick is fucking godlike. I can't believe you got to ride that for months. But that's not why I called you in here."

Crystal had to click several times to get the video going again. The sound of Trent's voice was equal parts pain and longing for Janelle. She loved him. He didn't love her. These things happened every day. It wasn't a tragedy. A hollow ache filled her chest whenever she was reminded of him. Yet she stayed and listened.

"Eight years ago, I made this video. It was never meant to be seen publicly. Since you're watching it, I hope you've enjoyed it, because your prurient interest supports the woman who starred in it, Bad Penny. But for me, this has been a tough past to shake."

Janelle opened her eyes. Instead of Trent's godlike cock plowing into a very happy Penny, the image was frozen in the background. Present-day Trent, fully clothed in a t-shirt and jeans, spoke directly to the camera.

"I thought this tape meant I could never have the woman I'd dreamed about. A woman who's ambitious and intelligent, forgiving and generous. A woman like you, who'd want a family. I tried to protect this woman from myself, but all I did was hurt her. I once asked her, what if there's no good or bad, only the things we desire and dare to ask for?"

He looked down. "I'm asking you for another chance. I don't want a clean break. I want you to call me. You know who you are, and you know where to find me. I'm waiting for you. I love you. The rest of you…enjoy the show."

Stunned, Janelle collapsed onto the edge of Crystal's bed. If her mind hadn't been blown all to pieces, she'd have wondered how recently the bedspread had been washed.

"You've got to see the comments. 'Mason I'll marry you and have your baby.' A zillion phone numbers. A whole bunch of topless photos, and those are only the first page." Crystal scrolled gleefully down.

"Did you know about this?"

"I had an inkling."

"You didn't say anything."

Crystal shot her a glare over her shoulder. "Of course I didn't. I'd hoped Trent's godlike dick would find me an acceptable substitute, but it wasn't happening. And you didn't get back together with Ben, either."

Janelle released a shuddering sigh. "What the hell am I supposed to about this?"

Crystal handed over her unlocked phone. "Pick up the phone and call him, dummy."

Janelle's face reflected back at her. Black mirror. She tossed it onto the bedspread. "I can't."

Her friend shifted her weight until her legs dangled over the edge of the bed. Crystal sank to her knees, her oversized t-shirt hiked up around her thighs. She placed one hand on Janelle's forehead.

"No fever. Are you insane?"

Janelle swatted away her hand. "Crys. Trent's cut and run on me three times."

"Three times?" Crystal's hand dropped to meet the other one on Janelle's knee.

"We met in Las Vegas, after the horror show that was my sugar daddy experience."

Crystal winced. "I never thought you, of all people, would go for it. I mean, I knew you were curious enough to email me about it, but I figured you'd finally decided to stop mooning over Ben. I'd have warned you away from it if I'd thought you were serious."

Janelle examined her nails. There was a chip on her right index fingernail. Easily fixed. "It probably wouldn't have changed anything. I was determined to make an ass out of myself."

"But it led you to Trent. Why didn't you two stay together after Las Vegas?"

"He told me it was best if we made a clean break, because he could never give me what I wanted."

"What did he think you wanted?"

"Respectability. The kind of life Ben would've given me. Quiet. Unambitious. Happy and settled. It's what I said I wanted, but it's not true. Not anymore. Maybe it never was."

Crystal's voice was soft with compassion. "I always thought you tried to be something you weren't to be with him. Honestly, I didn't always like you in college, but you're different now."

"What does that mean?" Janelle demanded. Curiosity softened her outrage.

Crystal exmined her nails. "You're more authentic now. Before, it was like you tried to be someone you weren't because Ben likes a certain kind of girl. He's got a boner for the princess type, and it was never you no matter how hard you pretended it was. Which is why I ask, what do you want, now?"

Janelle swallowed. "I want to crush this consulting business. I want to make millions or die trying. I love it, even the crazy, boring parts. The thrill of the chase gets me thinking in a thousand new ways. I love hunting new business."

"Then go do it, and don't fuck around with Trent. He's not going to be lonely." Crystal flicked her hair over her shoulder.

Janelle flopped backward onto the bed, too mixed-up to care about hygiene. "I still want a family, and a house in the suburbs and a dog. I want that with Trent. But he told me outright that he doesn't want a wife with a career. He gets both. It's not right to ask me to choose between the two. Like Ben did, if I'm being honest."

"Hey. Janie. You're overthinking it. Trent's looking for a girlfriend, not offering a ring on bended knee." Crystal patted her leg and headed for the bathroom. "I'm going to go finish what I was planning to do before Trent's surprise announcement. I plan to use up all the hot water. Go call your man. Tell him what you just told me. Don't go easy on him."

Janelle retreated to her own room, hands shaking as she picked up her phone. She set it face down on the desk.

Later. She'd call after her work was done. Maybe. Just because he'd decided to stop running from his past didn't mean he saw a future for them. It made more sense to give Trent what he'd wanted from the start: a clean break.

19

Janelle wore her favorite lace shirt to the office the next day. This time, she paired it with a sheer lining to keep it safe for work, and ankle-length silk trousers with flats for easy commuting. It still felt edgy and fun to wear fashionable clothing at the office, after years of dressing in shapeless tops to avoid too much attention—not that her strategy had worked.

Working as a consultant gave her a certain degree of latitude. Her contract was up in two weeks. Olivia wasn't going to fire her for mildly risqué fashion.

She was, however, about to make an announcement. All thirty-five employees were gathered in a conference room with the company logo that Janelle had had redesigned by Alyssa spinning on an animated loop. A few were in wheelchairs, and when she looked carefully Janelle spotted several more with missing limbs.

And then there was Trent, dressed in a crisp button-down shirt that defied sweaty July-in-Virginia weather, and freshly shaved. On the rare moments when their gazes brushed, she jerked away, willing the warm zing of longing away.

Not calling Trent had been the right thing to do. She wasn't ignoring him. He'd made a plea to everyone who watched his porn video. Not to her. He hadn't wanted to move in together, after they'd already been living together for two months. What more did she need to know?

She'd said *I love you*, repeatedly, and all she'd gotten in response was a shrug. Or a kiss and spectacular sex, which was no small consolation prize. Still, she was holding out for more. If it took another three years to mend this heartbreak, so be it.

At the front of the room, Olivia clapped her hands. The room hushed. "Team. Welcome and thank you for joining us over the lunch hour. Food is waiting for us in the hallway as soon as I finish speaking, so I'll talk fast. You've all been working hard these past few months, thanks to Janelle Carlisle's outstanding work in business development. She's knocked it out of the park and we're feeling it. So today, I'm making your jobs easier."

A whoop and applause. "Some of you know Mace, owner at TMS, our partner for more complex security projects. As of today, he is out of a job. I've acquired TMS and his team of five talented developers and project managers." The screen behind her flicked to headshots of Priya, Chaitu, and the rest of the TMS employees. "Let's give them a warm welcome. You'll also see Mace from time to time, because he'll be consulting on high-level projects. Any questions?" Olivia paused for effect. The only response was more clapping. "Great. We'll start with a celebratory toast, and then let's eat!"

The team began pouring prosecco and non-alcoholic cider into clear plastic cups. Janelle's fingertips wrapped around the cool fake crystal to raise it, but she didn't drink. Watching Trent put a lump in her throat she could hardly breathe around, much less swallow.

He shook a few hands and came to lean against the counter next to her. Janelle inhaled. The familiar odor of his soap set off a bomb of longing in her chest. Her eyes went hot and itchy, and her chest squeezed tight.

"Why'd you sell?" Janelle kept her words succinct to prevent her voice from cracking.

Trent glanced sideways, and she dropped her gaze, unable to meet his. Two short, calming breaths helped. A little. For a moment.

"I never wanted to run a business. Managing people, growth strategies, that's all Olivia's skill set. I've decided to specialize. Olivia will run the business, and I'll focus on security consulting for high-end clients, like the New York job. It frees me up to pursue what I really want."

"Which is what, Trent?" Janelle's heart beat like it was going to explode. The wine shook, so she set it down, untouched.

"You, Janie."

She swallowed at last, trying to keep her emotions in check before they erupted all over Olivia's party. Straightening, Janelle turned on her heel and headed for her desk. "You have a weird way of showing it, Trent."

She grabbed her bag off her chair and strode toward the stairwell. The door flew open so fast behind her that it nearly whacked her heel. Janelle's heart pumped in her throat.

He's coming for you.

She didn't know whether to be angry or happy. If he didn't back off, Trent was going to get the brunt of all her loneliness, all her sadness, all her fear and hope from the past few weeks in one unfiltered gush. Janelle picked up the pace, hating herself for running away. Hating him for not listening when she'd still had enough control to talk about how she felt without yelling.

Great. They were going to have this fight in the middle of her office. Since they were clearly going to have it out, the best course of action was to get as far away from her colleagues as possible, before she couldn't hold back anymore.

"Did you get my message?" he demanded.

"Which one?" Walking helped release some of the tension electrifying her body. She strode past the elevators and headed for the stairway. Trent had no trouble keeping pace.

"Any of them."

"All of them. I got all of them, okay?"

"You saw the video?"

"Yes. That one too." Janelle leapt down the last two steps and landed with a skid. Her teeth snapped shut on impact. "Crystal made sure of it. Which I bet you knew she'd do."

"It was the only way I could get to you. I wish I hadn't made it—"

Janelle stopped on the landing. Trent bumped into her raised fist. Extending one finger, she poked him in the chest. "I have never cared about the damn video. It's permanent advertising for your godlike dick. The video is all your hang up, not mine."

"Godlike dick, huh?" A smirk crooked up the corner of his mouth.

Janelle deliberately tamed her hand before she smacked him. He knew exactly how to push her natural inclination for drama to the limits. If it weren't for Trent, she might never have learned how to leash it.

"Crystal's words, not mine. She's your biggest fan. You know how many times I've had to hear it through the walls this summer?"

"Glad my advertising worked on you." Trent's cockiness grated against her one remaining nerve.

Janelle glared. "Congratulations. Now go find a fresh victim. Crystal's extremely interested, in case you hadn't noticed."

She wouldn't put it past him to be completely oblivious.

Janelle turned on her heel and kept going. They couldn't keep fighting in the stairwell. Their voices echoed up six stories. She had to get them somewhere alone, or at least private enough that when everything she was holding back erupted, she wasn't going to embarrass herself in front of anyone but Trent.

Hell, she'd been embarrassing herself in front of him since the moment they'd met. What was one more time? Her cheeks burned at the memory. The lace of her shirt rubbed her skin, the flats were giving her blisters and the backs of her knees were damp with late-July air humidity. Trent had done this to her since the moment they'd met.

He'd made her vulnerable. He took all the shit she doled out without blinking, then flipped her on her back like a turtle, belly exposed, feet flailing. Helpless. But then he left her there. He couldn't open up emotionally, and she couldn't fill the chasm by feeling too much for both of them.

Janelle yanked the sunglasses down onto her nose. Hidden, her eyes leaked a few tears. Then she was at her car, keys in hand, fished out of her bag from habit. She yanked open the door and grabbed the wheel, laying her forehead against the hot plastic. The door behind her opened and slammed.

Every time I close a door, he opens it.

The odd thought calmed the storm long enough for her to raise her head. "Okay, Trent. You want to talk? Let's talk."

Janelle turned sideways. He peered at her through the trough over the center console.

Worried. Maybe he did feel something, after all. Trent cupped her chin gently and rubbed a rough thumb over her damp cheeks. "I love you, Janie. Please stop running away."

Her eyelids squeezed tight, but the tears came anyway. Janelle leaned into his hand, absorbing the warmth of Trent's touch. She kissed his palm with lips that weren't completely steady, leaving a faint pink lip print on the heel. For a few minutes neither of them said anything.

"I miss you. I sold the business because despite what I said that day, I didn't care about it the way I care about seeing you succeed."

"Don't feed me lines, Trent." Janelle sniffed and rummaged in her bag for a pack of tissues. Catching sight of herself in the rearview mirror, she licked a corner and tried to wipe away a blob of mascara. Her nose was red, her lipstick smudged, and her misery was cut by a measure of gratitude; at least she'd made it to the car before losing it.

"I'm not. Promise. My arrangement with Olivia is similar to yours. I set my own hours. I don't need to bury myself in work anymore. All I want to focus on is you."

"Me. Really. After what you said."

"You, Janie." He paused. "Can we roll down the windows? I'm roasting." Trent did look hot, his wilted shirt sticking to his pecs and biceps. Janelle discovered her skin was damp and patchy red, not only from crying. Amazing how fast cars could turn into ovens in the summer.

"Oh!" Janelle turned the ignition and rolled them down. "It's not much better. We could sit on the bench."

"Or we could go for a drive," he suggested.

"Oh, could we, now. Do you have a destination in mind?" she shot back with all the sarcasm she could muster. "What about your car?"

"I can get it later. If I come up to the front seat, you're not going to try and run me over?"

Janelle shook her head. She moved her bag to the back. The cry had been intense but short, and now that she had it out of her system, she felt better able to listen to whatever Trent had to say.

He changed seats quickly and punched an address she didn't recognize into the GPS. It wasn't far, but it was early afternoon on a Wednesday and traffic was already bogging down. They'd have plenty of time to get it all out there. Though for once, Janelle had nothing to say.

"You can pull into the driveway."

The exterior of the bungalow was painted blue with gleaming white trim. A large porch was painted gray. White wicker patio furniture faced the sidewalk. The small lawn was freshly landscaped. A neatly lettered "For Rent" sign stood in the window.

Months ago, in Las Vegas, he'd teased Janie about her prosaic fantasy of a little house, a yard, and all the trappings of a quiet, comfortable life. Yet her words had spoken to his deepest desire, too.

Coming home to the apartment every day had forced him to acknowledge how much he loved Janie. He'd misunderstood her underlying meaning when she'd claimed to be a good girl. It had less to do with what she was and was not willing to do in bed, and everything to do with what she wanted in a relationship. From life.

Janelle may have been directionless before he'd met her, but she'd found her path and thrived. Mocking her ambition had been so cruel of him. If they hadn't just come from Penny's maybe he wouldn't have reacted so strongly, though it was no excuse. He should've sorted out his shit long ago.

"What's this, Trent?" she asked warily.

"A house." He still wanted the quiet life she'd described with such longing. He needed to know if she did, too.

She made an exasperated noise. "I'm not blind. What are we doing here?"

Her nose was still a little pink, as were the rims of her eyes. Other than smudged makeup, there was no evidence of tears. Trent's skin felt too tight for his body. He'd done that to her. Hurt her. Made her sad. He had every intention of making it up to her, though—if she'd let him.

"Come on, Janie. I'll show you around."

He'd done a lot of talking on the twenty-minute drive over here. A lot of it had had to do with his parents, most of which she'd guessed ages ago. Now it was time to get into the real problem between them: trust.

A flash of worry that Janie would dig in her heels and refuse gripped him. But he'd underestimated her. She still had a stubborn streak a mile wide, but she'd learned to direct it away from reflexive resistance. She grabbed her bag and got out of the car while Trent unlocked the front door.

"What do you think?" he asked. *Say you like it.*

He liked it. The kitchen was small, but renovated, with a window over the sink. The owners had staged the place with stylish furniture, better than anything Trent or Janelle owned. From the moment he'd walked in yesterday, it had felt like something he hadn't had in a long time, even for the seven weeks Janie had taken over the studio apartment next door.

A home.

Janelle wandered the gleaming hardwood floors over to the dining area. She flicked the light switch and played with the dimmer. Then she poked her head into the master bedroom and turned the faucets, checking the water pressure. After a brief tour into the second bedroom, she went to the rear patio and opened the door. The backyard was small and private, with a fence and trees.

Trent followed her.

He stopped a foot away from her, watching her bright eyes scan the grass and the bushes. The lace of her shirt was unwrinkled, but her pants weren't holding up so well in the heat. She'd kicked off one flat. A blister covered the heel of her foot.

"Do you want a Band-Aid?" he offered.

"I don't know. A Band-Aid might not be enough."

Trent's pulse leapt, thinking she meant the house was a Band-Aid and it wasn't enough. But Janie dropped her attention to her foot and examined the raw, pink skin. She meant the wound might soak through the bandage. "If you have one, that would be great."

Trent always carried one in his wallet. It was better than nothing, so he took it out and peeled it open. "Here."

He bent and pulled her foot onto his knee. Janelle steadied herself with a hand on his shoulder. When he stood up, she was watching him intently. "I get what you're after, Trent. You want us to move in here together, right?"

"I was hoping you'd want the same thing."

"How do I know you won't burn me again?"

It was the question he'd been dreading. "For the past six years, everything I've done I did to protect and support Penny. When you said she didn't need me, it was like getting punched in the face, Janie. Caring for Penny was all that kept me moving, when all I wanted to do was give up."

"What's changed?"

"You changed me. You never gave up on me. It took me too long to see it, but I am so happy you didn't take no for an answer. Nobody's ever done that. Whatever you see in me, I want you to keep seeing it. But before I could tell you, you'd moved in with Crystal and it looked as if you'd gotten back together with Ben."

"That was Crystal's doing," Janelle replied darkly. "She thought I'd want to get back together with him, and she could catch you on the rebound. It's just how she thinks."

"I didn't know what was going on with your ex, until I saw you at the networking event. If you'd told me you were seeing someone, I'd never have planned this. I knew I'd hurt you, but I didn't see how badly until you turned my words right back at me."

He brushed a strand of hair away from Janelle's face. She glanced down. "I think I understand, now, what you were telling me in Las Vegas. Remember how you insisted you were a good girl?"

Janelle ducked her head. "I'm embarrassed I ever sorted the world into two neat piles. Worthy and unworthy. I hated being classified as unworthy because of my credit, but I wrote off Crystal's approach to sex as less, as unacceptable. Even while I was trying to imitate her. I'm annoyed with her for trying to take advantage of our situation, but, on the whole, she's been really decent."

"She helped me get through to you, Janie. Not that I deserved to. I've done a lot of thinking since the fight, and I've figured out that the way I'd been thinking about women as if they were cocker spaniels, not human beings."

Janelle's pretty mouth puckered as if she was fighting a smile. "How do you mean, Trent?"

The pressure in Trent's chest eased. Even if she said no today, at least he could give her a meaningful apology. "I spent years developing this vision of an ideal partner who was a negative composite of Penny's worst traits. I had this idea that my next girlfriend would be calm, adoring, faithful, and devoted. Those were all fine traits to look for, but no real person could ever be the perfect selfless love I was after. Women are people. We're all complicated and flawed, and we make mistakes. I'm sorry I made such a huge one with you. Penny and I used to fight like cats and dogs, and I lashed out at you. It'll never happen again."

Janelle swallowed, eyes wide.

Trent kept going. "In Las Vegas, you were trying to tell me how everything you felt for me was real from the start. I didn't hear you. It seemed highly unlikely someone as perfect as you are could drop into my lap. Almost literally."

"Perfect." Janelle snorted.

Trent grinned from sheer relief. He'd said what he wanted to say and she'd listened. He loved her sarcasm. It wasn't always nice, but she was most ruthless when turning it on herself. "Yeah, perfect."

"With my sob story about student loans and crappy job and dumb sugar baby scheme. Anyone with half a brain should've been smart enough to see through me." Janelle sighed.

"I think it was the dress that was see-through."

This time, her snort sounded suspiciously like laughter.

"I don't suppose you still have it?" Trent tried to be casual, but the switch to flirting hung between them. He waited to see if she'd pick it up.

A long pause, followed by a sly smile. "Maybe."

"What's it going to take to find out?" Trent edged closer and slid his arm around her narrow shoulders. Janelle turned him and buried her head in his chest with a sigh. Trent pulled her tight. Her body against his soothed the ache in his chest. He kissed her hair.

"I'd have to know you're not going to cut and run on me again," she whispered.

"However high you want to go, I'm going to help you get there. Stay like this with me." He inhaled her scent and all.

"Trent. I can't...In Las Vegas, I didn't want you to solve my problems for me. I wanted you to solve them *with* me. I didn't know how to say it without sounding ungrateful for everything you did." Janie sniffed.

Oh, shit, not tears. They were supposed to be past the crying stage, now. "Sweetie."

"This house? It feels like you're trying to solve things again." And then she did sob, and the sound was akin to a knife in the belly.

"Like you did, when you moved in across the hall?"

Wrapped in his arms, Trent couldn't tell whether Janie was laughing or crying, or both.

"Technically, it wasn't your space. Even if you were mad at me, I knew I could turn to you if I locked myself out one night. You're... protective that way. It seemed reasonable in my head. I honestly wasn't trying to force you into anything."

Trent had been so blindsided by the boldness of her move, he'd never considered how intimidating it must've been to move to a new city, where she knew no one. He'd only seen manipulation. Entrenched in his comfortable sulk, it'd been easier to believe Janelle was indulging in fantasies than to believe she loved him, or she trusted him to help her if she needed it. After all, he'd already gotten her out of one fix.

Trent kissed her hair again and pulled her tighter against his chest. "I was so scared I'd lost you for good."

"You almost did." Janie's arms were steel ribbons around his waist. "Bringing me here is the first time you've given me a reason to hope that you're looking to the future. But fair warning—if you ever say the words 'clean break' to me again, we're through. I'm not giving you another chance."

"I won't need one."

Then they were kissing, shyly at first, getting to know one another again. It had been too long. Trent's heart hurt, but it was a good ache. The kind that meant healing. Mending. Knitting together. The way their bodies were.

Until the door to the house opened.

"Anyone here?" a stranger's voice rang out.

Janelle didn't move, other than to open her eyes. "I guess we should sign a lease?"

His throat closed. A long beat passed before he could say, "I thought you didn't want me to solve your problems."

"I don't." She bit her lower lip, the way she did when she was thinking hard. "But it's a really cute house."

"There's a community pool two blocks away. For swimming." Trent's heart hammered erratically.

"Off-street parking for two cars," she mused.

"I checked out the house this morning. The agent's going to be ticked I kept the key all day."

"You did what?" Janelle peered up at him, perplexed.

"I figured if I kept the key, and managed to get you here, and convinced you to give me another chance, it might buy us some time." Trent placed his hands on her upper arms, already missing the warmth of her body against his. "This place will rent fast."

"Um," Janelle tucked her hair behind her ear as the intruder appeared, followed by a couple not dissimilar to them. Guy in a dress shirt and jeans. Woman in heels and a skirt. Both had probably taken off work early to come see the bungalow for rent.

Normal. He'd compared himself to ordinary professionals, and for once, it felt real.

"Sorry, the leasing agent must've forgotten to tell you. We're submitting an application to rent the house." Janelle crossed her arms over her chest, friendly but territorial.

Damn, he loved her competitive streak.

"Really," the woman replied, glancing around the kitchen. "The agent told us they hadn't received any applications yet. Some jerk ran off with the key this morning. They had to have a duplicate made."

Trent might've copped to his minor crime, but Janie? Not on your life. "There must've been a mistake. This house is ours."

"Oh?" The intruding woman cocked an eyebrow. Her companion took her by the elbow. Furious whispers ensued.

The real estate agent patted his jacket pocket. "I'll call the leasing office. This was supposed to be an exclusive showing."

"Don't bother. We're on our way to sign the lease." Trent took Janie by the arm and steered her to the front door. He leaned close to speak in a low tone, "If we get there first, we'll be the renters."

"Unless they reject us for stealing the key," Janelle pointed out quietly.

"Noah, let's go." The new woman's eyes narrowed. "I was ready to rent it sight unseen, and now I've seen. Let's get going."

"Amy, *I* haven't seen it. Give me five minutes to look around. They won't be able to leave until we move the car, anyway."

Trent decided Noah needed to be proved wrong. Immediately. He hooked his arm into Janie's elbow and towed her out the front door. Janie's eyes widened. The driveway was a single strip of concrete that barely fit two cars. Hers was parked in.

"We can't get out." A hint of panic flashed in her green eyes.

"Mind if I drive?" he asked.

Janie handed over the keys without comment. In the car, he adjusted the seat all the way back and flicked the mirrors into place. Then he tossed his phone across the seat. "Are you sure you want this?"

"Yes, Trent. If this means we're seeing each other, openly and exclusively, if it means I get to be with you all the time, then yes. Yes!" Janelle clapped.

Trent revved the engine in her little car. He pulled his phone out of his pocket and told her the code to unlock it. "Call the last dialed number. Tell them I'm bringing back the key and we're submitting an application as soon as we get there."

"The agent just came out," Janelle replied as she unlocked the phone and dialed, waiting for someone to pick up.

"Fuck him. Hang on." Trent gunned the engine forward onto the grass, slammed the tiny car into reverse and turned on the lawn, barely avoiding the bungalow. The car tilted at a frightening angle as he maneuvered down the strip, taking out a recently planted flower bed. They bumped over the curb with a jolt.

"Hello?" Janie began spinning the biggest yarn Trent had ever heard. No wonder she was good at pitching new business. The woman was a born salesperson.

Two blocks later she disconnected. "We're good. If we can get to the office by five, we can submit the application today."

"We've got company," Trent replied grimly. "Hold on."

The little car was slow to pick up speed as he jammed the accelerator, but he threaded through traffic with ease. The other couple's SUV faded in the rearview mirror. He skidded into a technically illegal parking spot, and they slammed out of the car in unison.

"How fast can you write?" he asked as he led her into a nondescript midrise.

"Why?" Janie tugged her bag up her shoulder, limping as she hustled.

"I filled out the application this morning." Trent vaulted up the stairway, eyes dim with the sudden change in light.

"Cocky, aren't you?" Janie panted with effort to keep up.

"Only if the statistics are favorable." Trent caught her at the top of the stairs in a long kiss. "I'd gamble on you any day, Janie. I'll always take that bet."

20

"Took you long enough to bring back my key." The leasing agent was thin and balding, with the affable air of someone who'd shiv you if you gave him a reason to. Which Trent had done by absconding with it for most of the day.

"My apologies," Janelle huffed. "I was tied up in meetings that ran over. We really like the house and want to rent it. Right now."

"I've filled out the application form."

Discerning Leasing Agent frowned at the crumpled piece of paper Trent held out. He smoothed it flat with his palm. "I'll need one from the lady as well."

"Sure." Trent picked up a clipboard and held it out to her. Janelle shook her head.

Credit, she mouthed.

"Fill it out, Janie." Trent's low command jolted her into action.

"I have another couple interested in renting the apartment if your application falls through. They're stuck in traffic, but they'll be here in ten minutes."

Trent leaned close. "Write faster, Janie."

"I'll get started running your credit check, Mr. Mason." The leasing agent rose.

"I'm done. You can run mine too while you're at it." Janelle passed the clipboard across the desk. As if sensing she was one good shock away from passing out, Trent took her hand and ran his finger over her knuckles.

"It's okay, sweetie."

"My credit still sucks. Mom said it would take months for any changes to be reported." Janelle tasted panic in her throat.

"I can lease it in my name if necessary." Trent squeezed her hand.

"I have reference letters," she rambled. "I have one from the sublet, and another from Rachel, saying I pay my rent on time. I have a real job, not only consulting fees."

Trent turned in his chair and lifted her chin with his fingertips. "Janie. Breathe. It's gonna be okay."

The leasing agent returned. "All seems in order. I'll need to see your identification, references, and a cashier's check for the deposit and first month's rent."

"That's it?" Janelle gasped.

"I have the money," Trent replied, shifting to pull his wallet out of his back pocket.

"You do?" Janelle scrambled to produce her driver's license.

"Remember the cashier's check you made me sign for?" Trent's mouth quirked up at the corner.

Janelle burst out laughing. "Are you kidding?"

"I can't think of a better way to spend it than on a home for us." He kissed her, sweetly, with the promise of more to come.

The man behind the desk coughed.

"May I see my credit report?" Janelle asked, straightening in her chair.

Leasing Agent passed over a single-page printout. "A little low, but passable. You're young yet. It'll go up with time. Mr. Mason's is fine."

Janelle held the paper in shaking hands. The three-digit score had changed dramatically from several months ago, when she'd leaned on her parents to cosign for the sublet.

Trustworthy.

"I passed," she declared wonderingly. "It worked. Mom was right."

Trent leaned out of his chair and kissed her cheek. "I knew you would."

"I didn't." Janelle pulled out her phone and searched for the letters of reference in her email. "Here," she handed the phone to the agent. "Can I forward these to you?"

"Please. My card." The agent handed her a rectangle, and she punched in the address. She was too busy glowing to notice Leasing Agent's eyebrows pop to his hairline.

"Your boyfriend, on the other hand..." Leasing Agent turned his computer screen to them. "Young lady, are you aware of this?"

The old computer screen flickered with the upfront of Trent's naked body. Beside her, Trent stilled. It was Janelle's turn to squeeze his hand, offering solace and encouragement. She laughed out loud.

"Yes! I'm aware of the video. Trent's led an interesting life. Poker. Penny. Then the military."

"Military?" Leasing Agent perked up. The image on the screen sat frozen.

"Two tours in Afghanistan with military intelligence. Listening in on the Taliban, running counterintelligence, that kind of thing." Janelle spoke for Trent, concocting a tale on the fly.

"I'm not supposed to talk about it." Trent draped his arm over the back of her chair, not paralyzed at all. "Clearance and all."

He squeezed her shoulder. Janelle beamed.

"My sister's in the Air Force," Leasing Agent offered. "My entire family is affiliated with the military."

The door slammed against the wall behind them. All three started.

"That. House. Is. Ours." Amy's face was red, and her blonde hair disheveled. Noah, two steps behind her, was a walking thundercloud. Their agent was an apparition bringing up the rear.

"I'm sorry, we're only taking backup applications at this point. Mr. Mason and Ms. Carlisle are in the process of signing a lease." The leasing agent handed them two neat stacks of papers and pointed to the lines where they needed to initial and sign. Trent bent his head and got to work, so Janelle did the same.

"No. You can't do this to us. They drove over the flower bed!

They'll trash the place! It's zoned for a good school! It. Has. *Parking.*" Amy's voice ratcheted up an octave with each truncated statement.

"Who cares about the schools, Amy? We don't even have kids yet!" Noah pushed her aside. "We're going. I think these two are going to be awful tenants, but if you want to move forward, it's your choice."

"Noaaaaaah." Pleading.

"Amy, let me handle this. If he thinks we're desperate we'll never get the place."

"Done!" Janelle handed over the papers.

"Me too. Here's our cashier's check." Trent collected everything into a neat stack and passed it over.

"Your lease starts Monday. We'll move the staging furniture out by the weekend." The leasing agent signed on his portion of the contract while Amy dissolved into frustrated tears behind them. "I'll make photocopies of the lease agreement. Wait here."

Amy punctuated her words with manicured nails. "Well-priced houses for rent are hard to come by in this town. I've lived for eleven months in the apartment from hell, and I never want to share walls with anyone again. Pot smoking. Loud music. Animals barking. You name it. I need sanity. I *need* this house."

"Amy. There'll be another house." Noah was gentle, though he regarded them reprovingly. Their ashen-faced agent looked on in silent horror.

"This one was *perfect!*" Amy broke down. "I can't take another condo. I just can't."

"I'll find you another house. A better house. One with a bigger yard. A better school." The agent cajoled the disappointed couple out the door.

"Fucking traffic," Amy sniffed. "I hate the D.C. suburbs, and the traffic."

Then they were gone.

"Wow." Janelle collapsed against her chair. "I almost let her have it. Poor Amy."

"Me, too. I kinda feel bad for her." Trent had reclaimed her hand, running his thumb over her knuckles.

"I've been in this business for thirty years. What I see in this office is what I get at midnight on a weekend when the toilet overflows," the leasing agent replied crisply. He tapped paper into place. "You may as well keep the keys. I'll get the other set from their agent and bring it by the house on Monday. Congratulations and welcome home."

It was done. An hour ago, she'd been single, sad, and unsure of her future. Things had moved so fast. She could barely process it.

"Is this real?" she asked Trent as they went in search of her illegally-parked car.

"Is what real?" He draped his arm over her shoulders.

Janelle curled against his body. "This. Us. The house."

"Isn't it what you wanted?" Trent asked. "Because honestly, my head's spinning, too."

"Right? I thought I'd lost you. I thought my whole life was going to be too much work and too little love. I'm so happy this happened. But it doesn't feel real yet."

"Janie. I love you. I'm going to make it real. *We're* going to make it real. I love you. All of you. Always."

EPILOGUE

"Have you thought any more about the trip to Fiji?"

Trent cracked an eyelid. "Hm?"

"Fiji." Janelle poked his defined bicep. "Given it any further thought?"

"It's a long way to go." He rolled over and pulled her close. Janelle's body fit perfectly into the curve of his, her ass snug against his hardening erection.

"That's why they're called destination weddings."

"If we're flying all the way there for Alyssa and Marc's wedding, we should at least stay a week. Maybe a month?" Trent kissed his way down her neck.

"I'd lose so much money." Janelle groaned.

"Nah. Just don't book anything for July. Business slows down then, anyway. When's the last time we took a vacation?" If Trent was trying to convince her to take a holiday, he was using all the right methods.

"Penny's wedding," he murmured from between her breasts.

"That doesn't count."

"Thanksgiving."

"That doesn't count, either. Ooh, keep doing that."

Trent palmed her breast, edging the silky fabric down over the tip to tease it. The man always had stubble in the morning, no matter how often he shaved. Today it was extra rough. They'd gotten stuck in traffic coming home from the airport last night, and hadn't gotten home until nearly midnight. Their suitcases still stood by the door, waiting to be unpacked.

Alyssa and Marc had flown back for a week over Christmas, leaving the boat in South African marina. A few days before, they'd gotten engaged on Table Mountain. They'd wanted to announce it in person to their families before the media got ahold of the story. The plan was to have a small destination wedding when they got to Fiji in a few months. The ad agency managing Alyssa's social media presence was already advertising soliciting sponsors.

"What does count as a vacation?" Janelle asked sleepily.

"A month in Fiji and Australia." Trent kissed his way down her belly. The sun was barely up, but this had become their pattern: wake early, get their fuck on, fall back asleep, then have breakfast and a shower, often together.

After he'd licked and sucked one orgasm out of her, Trent turned her on her side, pushed her left leg high and slid inside. Janelle fisted the sheets and arched against him.

"Next time we go to Florida, we're getting a hotel," she panted.

"That's what you said last time."

Trent was busy making her regret not sticking with that decision. "I mean it. A week is too long to go without you."

"Separate bedrooms are a bit much." Trent grunted a little as she arched her hips and took him all the way.

They'd managed to sneak in a few quickies over the past week, but they'd been starved for touch by the time they stumbled through the door of the bungalow. Tired as they were, they'd stumbled into bed for marathon catch-up sex.

Trent ground slowly into her, aware that she was still sensitive, hitting all the good spots. After, Janelle lay with her head against Trent's chest and traced the outline of his newest tattoo.

Two figures. No wings. One vaguely masculine, the other nominally feminine, the outlines defined like stained glass, entwined together. The shape made a lopsided heart. Intentionally, she suspected. Trent could still be cagey about things that hit deep emotions. He'd gotten better, though. Just as his steady presence evened her out. The past year and half had proven that they were a good match.

"So the answer is yes, if we go for long enough?"

"Mmmm."

Janelle yawned. "I'll book tickets."

"We could make it a double."

"A double wedding? With my sister?" She sat up, halfway, cocking her head.

"In Fiji. Mhmm." Trent curled sleepily around her, kissing her ear.

"Well, that would be one way to knock the Penny video off the top page of your Internet history," Janelle mused, sinking back down to curl against his body. "Ask me again when I'm awake."

"Sure, Janie. Anything you want, love."

The End

AUTHOR'S NOTE

I am grateful to Stoya and Vice for helpful, factual, and entertaining articles about the adult film industry.

Similarly, the professional poker world is sprawling and unfamiliar to me. Thank you to K. for your honesty on the challenges and rewards of being married to a pro poker player.

All mistakes and misrepresentations are my own.

ENJOYED THIS BOOK?

Please leave a review on Goodreads or your eBook retailer of choice.

Get sneak peaks, giveaways and news by signing up for my newsletter. Visit https://carrielomax.com for the link.

ALSO BY CARRIE LOMAX

Say You'll Stay

Book 1: Alyssa & Marc

Being within ten yards of Marc De Luna always made Alyssa feel like she was drowning in lava. Hot didn't begin to describe it. Just seeing him burned away nerve endings. Faded jeans hung low on his narrow hips. The pale blue T-shirt clung to his pectoral muscles and broad shoulders, loose around his body where his waist narrowed. Marc's thick dark hair was just shaggy enough to make her want to run her hands through it.

If he ever looked her way, she'd probably fall into the trash can. She was that suave. And if he spoke to her? She'd swoon and give herself a concussion.

She yanked the lid of her parents' can open, tossed in the bag of paper recycling, and gently closed it. There was no point in trying to attract Marc's attention. For starters, he was the last person she wanted to be around at this exact moment. Ever since her parents had moved to Verona Harbor, Florida, when she was in high school, Alyssa had watched him from afar. He'd been in college then. If he'd gotten as far as declaring a major, it would've been a degree in seducing sorority girls. Despite this, Alyssa still remembered every single syllable he had ever spoken to her.

She glanced up. His intense amber gaze pinned her where she stood.

"Alyssa. I wondered if you were coming home for the holidays." He dropped the lid to the garbage can and shifted his weight onto one foot.

"You did? I mean, of course. I always come back for Christmas." She felt faint. What fresh hell was this speaking words business? If she did fall over she'd blame it on the balmy weather. Marc *never* spoke to her, except to tease.

"You didn't last year."

"I can't believe you noticed," Alyssa blurted. She'd been in Connecticut with Zach's family.

"I've always noticed," he replied with a half-grin that hit her like a tractor-trailer. "I hear we're coming over for dinner later."

"You are? I mean, yes. Right. For dinner." Her voice sounded better, but her words had never sounded so stupid. Her mother hadn't specified which neighbors. Theirs was a social block, and she could've meant anyone ten houses up or down either side of the street. It hadn't occurred to Alyssa to clarify who was coming over.

"See you later," Marc said casually.

Alyssa stumbled into her house, where she caught a glimpse of herself in the hall mirror. Gray smudges lurked beneath her eyes from lack of sleep, her stringy, tangled hair shot from her head in crazy angles, and she still wore the wrinkled, stained black shirt she'd had on since leaving her apartment. Not to mention she hadn't seen a ray of sunlight in about a year.

"Mom! When are the De Lunas coming over for dinner?" *So, what? He talks to you and suddenly you're salivating?*

Also: *Shut up, Inner Critic.*

Catherine stepped out of the kitchen. "Half an hour or so. Why don't you clean up a little before our guests arrive? Janelle, would you help me with the avocado rolls?"

Also by Carrie Lomax

Alyssa squinted at her mother. Could she be…up to something?
Available from your favorite eBook retailer.

ACKNOWLEDGMENTS

I am profoundly grateful to fellow Maryland Romance Writers Association members Mona Shroff and Ingrid Hahn for feedback, insights and general hand-holding. To Christi Barth, thank you for the hand up and cover critiques. (You too, Mona!) You are all amazing writers and friends. Anya Kagan at Touchstone Editing for helping me escape the detail weeds in an earlier draft. To Margaret Bates for final editing—you are a lifesaver. Again. To Liz Durano for continued advice and support, you are an amazing writer and friend. Nichole Giangola, your input on military ranks and relationships was invaluable. All errors are my own.

Last but far from least, to my husband and family for tolerating my side gig despite a messy house, embarrassing PTA conversations and a constant supply of microwave dinners. The next books are for you.

ABOUT THE AUTHOR

Carrie Lomax grew up in the Midwest before moving to New York City for 15 years. She lives in Maryland with two budding readers and her real-life romantic hero.

www.carrielomax.com

CPSIA information can be obtained
at www.ICGtesting.com
Printed in the USA
FFOW02n0926250518
46858726-49083FF